Investing in Vain

Investing in Vain

William Worsley

Distinction Press, Waitsfield, Vermont

Distinction Press
Waitsfield, Vermont 05673
www.distinctionpress.com
www.investinginvain.com

This book is entirely a work of fiction.
There is no representation of any situation,
or anyone living, dead or otherwise, including Al Gore.

Cover photo credit:
By Lesekreis (Own work) [CC0], via Wikimedia Commons

Author photo credit: Aaron Clamage Photography

Cover and book design: RSBPress

ISBN 978-1-937667-19-1 hardcover
ISBN 978-1-937667-17-7 tradepaper
ISBN 978-1-937667-18-4 e-book

Publisher's Cataloging-In-Publication Data
(Prepared by The Donohue Group, Inc.)

Names: Worsley, William, 1951-
Title: Investing in Vain / William Worsley.
Description: Waitsfield, Vermont : Distinction Press, [2017]
Identifiers: ISBN 978-1-937667-17-7 (tradepaper) | ISBN 978-1-937667-19-1
(hardcover) | ISBN 978-1-937667-18-4 (ebook)
Subjects: LCSH: Investment advisors--Fiction. | Financial services indus-
try--Fiction. | Transgender people--Fiction. | Fraud--Fiction. | Social respon-
sibility in banking--Fiction.
Classification: LCC PS3623.O77 I58 2017 (print) | LCC PS3623.O77 (ebook)
| DDC 813/.6--dc23

For my father, who taught me to invest,
and my mother, who taught me to laugh.

1   From Mush-Mush to Hush-Hush

The time appointed for the execution of Beatrice Pillsbury von Vain was at hand. For the red-headed founder of Vain Capital, just having to look at Mush-Mush was punishment enough.

"Beatrice, our investment committee has become increasingly worried about Vain Capital's performance," said the man with hardly any teeth. "That's what I've come to Washington to discuss."

Mush-Mush, a.k.a. Eddie Merrybaker, the balding treasurer of Christians Eschewing Dentistry, was both a hideous sight and Beatrice's unhappy client. His six teeth, a stained and rotted mess, were especially unhappy. They included a couple of incisors on top with a vast gap between them, then the same on the bottom, and the sad ruins of two molars scattered here and there.

Beatrice looked down at her shoes, at the snake plant in the corner, at the coffee pot on the credenza, at anything else in the conference room she could, but against her will, as if by some magnetism of horror, her eyes were drawn right back to Merrybaker's miserable mouth. It was like trying to look away from a car crash.

"I'm afraid the committee has run out of patience," said the toothless treasurer, "as Vain Capital's returns have continued to deteriorate."

Here it comes, Beatrice groaned under her breath: *Another ungrateful client blaming us for humoring them too well.* Beatrice could feel her body tense up as she awaited the blow.

The treasurer looked at his watch. With any luck, he might make it back to Boston in time to catch the Celtics game. He let out an audible sigh and administered the coup de grâce: "The Eschewer Foundation has reluctantly decided to terminate its investment agreement with Vain Capital in thirty days."

Beatrice was officially fired. Or rather, her little investment firm was, which felt just as awful.

Out of the corner of her eye she could see Stanton Butcher III glaring at her, probing with his eyes for her reaction, expecting her to say something this instant to pull the Eschewer account out of the fire. She considered the Butcher even more frightful than Merrybaker in his own way, and far more dangerous. His short, pear-shaped body was topped by a nest of thin blond hair, a round face with a double chin, and beady green eyes that pierced their target like a laser. Lately the veteran manager of private equity funds had developed the irritating habit of exercising his right as her financial partner to drop in uninvited at her client meetings, which he invariably did just as Vain Capital was getting sacked.

Beatrice was determined not to flinch. She would trust her usual maneuver for soothing clients frustrated by Vain Capital's sub-par returns: buy time by turning their focus from recent results toward the long term. "Eddie, I think your committee should reconsider this rash action. Christians Without Dentistry—"

"That's *Eschewing* Dentistry," Merrybaker quickly corrected her.

Eschewing. Avoiding. Shunning. What was the difference? Beatrice wondered why the Eschewers, so oblivious to their appearance, were so hyper-sensitive about their silly name. A century ago they had split off from the Christian Scientists over a bitter doctrinal dispute. Unlike the Scientists, who believed illness to be an illusion and avoided most medical treatment in favor of prayer, the Christians Eschewing Dentistry had realized they were likely to live a lot longer if they limited their medical abstention to their teeth and simply refused to go to the dentist, which they did with great zeal. It was only logical that their investments must be aligned with their abiding faith. The three-billion-dollar Eschewer Foundation, bulging with the Eschewers' savings on dentists over so many decades, was barred from investing in dental products or services of any kind.

"Sorry, Eschewing Dentistry," Beatrice acknowledged. "Anyway, you've been our client for only three years, and we've lagged the benchmark for only two. Such a short period of underperformance is nothing to worry about."

"But you've trailed by five points annualized," Merrybaker said. "That's terrible. Vain Capital doesn't even buy and sell securities itself. All your firm does is hire and fire money managers. How can that be so difficult? Just pick the good managers and eschew the bad ones."

"Oh, it is extraordinarily difficult, Eddie," Beatrice replied. "Finding good money managers is much harder than you might imagine. It's even harder than finding good investments."

But Merrybaker did have a point. Vain Capital, a so-called "manager-of-managers" or MOM, was not a typical investment firm but only an intermediary between clients and their money managers. It hired, fired, and monitored other money management firms that agreed to invest in accordance with a client's moral views. Unencumbered by any particular creed itself, Vain Capital accepted anyone's mission, assembling a roster of moral portfolios upon request. Managers of the Eschewer portfolios had received strict instructions from Vain Capital's investment officers to steer clear of anything even remotely oral.

"Picking money managers looks easy enough to me," said Merrybaker, regarding Beatrice with that pained expression of his. Among the Eschewers an agonized look signaled virtue and ensured social acceptance. A devout Eschewer himself, Merrybaker was always quite properly in pain, piously adhering to the dental strictures of his employer and putting his mouth where the foundation's money was.

His virtuous display was having quite the opposite effect on Beatrice. This is what you get for all your eschewing, Mush Mush, she was thinking. Now you can barely chew at all.

"Consistent outperformers are extremely rare these days, Eddie," she said. "It's true we're a bit behind the benchmark, but we firmly believe that you need to take a longer view of our performance—"

"A bit behind? Five points behind! Is this really the best your managers can do?"

"Well, unfortunately for the Eschewers, dental stocks skyrocketed last year," Beatrice pointed out, "and your moral restrictions barred the money managers we hired for you from owning them, so naturally their returns lagged."

"But when we hired Vain Capital, you assured us that dental stocks are such an insignificant part of the overall market that not owning them couldn't possibly make any difference," Merrybaker said.

"It appears I was mistaken," Beatrice conceded. "The market never

fails to amaze. You never know when one sleepy little group like dental stocks that is normally very well behaved will just explode to the
upside." Then she blurted, "Our investment officer for equities, Alison
Hartswell, points out that denture stocks in particular were red hot."

Beatrice was immediately sorry she had said that, but there again was
the wreckage of Merrybaker's mouth, practically jumping across the table to bite her on the nose. She guessed the poor man would need at
least fifty thousand dollars of dental implants just to stop frightening
small children. When her son Pillsbury was a little boy he would pretend he was a toothless old man like Mush-Mush by pulling his lips over
his teeth and flapping his jaws up and down like he was gumming his
food to pieces instead of chewing it. She was sorely tempted to do that
right now, and she would have if not restrained by her firm policy of not
mocking her clients to their faces.

Red hot, did she say? Merrybaker could not help thinking how Alison
Hartswell was red hot and how badly he was going to miss seeing her
here at Vain Capital. From his first encounter with Beatrice's bosomy
investment officer the old goat had made a point of never missing an
account review meeting. But as much as he enjoyed leering at the in-
toxicating Miss Hartswell, universally acknowledged to be the sexiest
woman in the entire investment industry, even she was not enough bait
to corrupt a committed Eschewer charged with a solemn fiduciary duty.
Miss Hartswell or not, Vain Capital had to go.

"From the moment we first met you, you told us Vain Capital would
outperform despite our restrictions," he said. "Now you say our restrictions are the problem. What a convenient excuse."

Beatrice swallowed hard. She *had* told him that. She routinely assured
all Vain Capital's clients that their restrictions, no matter how absurd,
would have not have the slightest detrimental effect on their portfolios.

"Really, Eddie, five points is not that much of a performance deficit.
We can make it up in a couple of years."

Merrybaker just sat there, unmoved. Beatrice paused, trying to think
of an argument that might appeal specifically to him. She must sympa-
thize with his faith, speak to him in his own moral language.

"You know, in a way, looking at it philosophically," she said, "underperforming the market is very much like dental pain. It aches like the
dickens for a little while, but it's actually an illusion, just a temporary

test of our faith that leads us to God. If you prove your faith by waiting, I'm sure the pain will go away in time. Underperformance will be corrected by faith and prayer! We'll pray for your portfolios—everyone at Vain Capital will! We'll all pray to Jesus for higher returns, every single one of us, even our bond guy! And he's Jewish."

"Only one of your equity firms beat its benchmark, out of ten!" Merrybaker retorted, his brow wrinkling. "I forget its name."

"Quandary Capital," Beatrice answered. "It's a firm in Rocket City that does quantitative investing—a quant firm. The stocks are picked by computer programs, not humans. They are far and away our best money manager. The funny thing is, nobody really has the foggiest idea what they do. But that's how it is with quants. They are the nerdiest fellows, the mad scientists of the investment industry."

"Anyway, except for that one, the money managers you've hired have been very disappointing," Merrybaker said. "We can't just sit by and watch the portfolio lag endlessly. At some point we had to make a decision. It's final—our investment committee has made up its mind."

"Will you be taking your assets back in house?" the Butcher asked.

"No, we've given up trying to manage the foundation's assets ourselves. We're simply moving them to another manager-of-managers firm," Merrybaker replied. "The investment committee doesn't have the staff or expertise to hire, fire, and monitor money managers—too much cost and hassle. Our mission is eschewing dentists, not picking portfolio managers." He paused for a moment and sniffed at Beatrice. "We hoped you could do it."

"I'm sorry we weren't able to meet your expectations, but we understand how investment committees can be," Beatrice said, not actually meaning to imply that the Eschewers were being unreasonable or fickle, which of course they were. "We'll pray for your portfolios anyway."

After showing Merrybaker out, Beatrice and the Butcher returned to the conference room to hold a postmortem, as the Butcher always insisted that they do after a client defection. Beatrice shuffled nervously to the table and sat down.

The Butcher closed the door, waddled over to the credenza, and poured himself a cup of coffee. "Beatrice, this is the third client you've lost this quarter," he began. "This was a big one—three billion dollars! A third of your assets—gone! Poof—just like that!" he said with a sweep of his hand.

At first Beatrice nodded meekly. Then she rallied with an air of optimism and defiant self-confidence. "Yes, but we will make it up, I'm sure! Socially responsible investing is the wave of the future."

The Butcher leaned across the table at her like a tiger ready to lunge. "You lost six million dollars in fees today, Beatrice."

Beatrice struggled to hold her tongue. Vain Capital had never been all about fees to her, although she would never dare tell the Butcher so. As a child she had been taught that money would be morally improved if it were used to save the world, a belief which by adulthood had become so deeply rooted in her that it had even survived her two years at the Harvard Business School. *Money ought to go on a mission*, as her missionary father always used to say, on some sort of high-minded moral crusade. She had built a very profitable business upon that well-meaning premise, founding Vain Capital to assist endowments, foundations, and other institutions in investing their money with a conscience—also known as mission-based or socially responsible investing.

Beatrice's voice grew shrill. "Stanton, look at the students protesting on college campuses! The students are rioting for social responsibility! And we've got it here in spades! We are the only manager-of-managers firm specializing in it! Vain Capital is the moral MOM firm, the MOM on a mission!"

Beatrice felt a volcanic gush of righteous zeal surging up from within her, a sort of moral hot flash. But it came with a secret guilt, a nagging sense that she was somehow demeaning her proud family tradition even as she strove to uphold it, that she had sold her pedigree for mere coin. For she was not just a missionary's daughter, but a Pillsbury, and not of the cookie-mongering Doughboy clan either, but the great-great-great granddaughter of the ardent abolitionist Parker Pillsbury, who had been pretty great himself. A fiery social reformer descended from the most upright Puritans, her illustrious Pillsbury ancestor had thundered from Northern pulpits in the mid-nineteenth century for the emancipation of slaves. Sadly, in Beatrice's own era the noble art of outrage had grown so popular for the cost-free power and gratification it conferred on the aggrieved, and so universally practiced—increasingly on less worthy objects than slavery—that humanity was now compelled to recoil at the horror of dental floss.

The Butcher pressed his point. "Moral MOM or not makes little difference to me. This is business. Mark Weedle and I invested our private equity fund's capital in your firm to get a return, Beatrice. A nice fat return, above twenty-five percent. To hit that target, you would have to grow your assets at least fifteen percent per year."

"And we will, too. Just be patient."

"But you keep losing old clients as fast as you get new ones!" the Butcher snapped.

"Well, a lot of them can't tolerate the underperformance their own restrictions cause. Like the Eschewers not allowing dental stocks and then blaming me."

"But dammit, Beatrice, that's Vain Capital's business model—hiring money managers to run restricted portfolios for conscience-bound clients. Are you saying Vain Capital can't outperform benchmarks because socially responsible restrictions make it impossible? If that's true, your business model doesn't work. There's a fundamental contradiction in it. Your clients would be investing in vain."

"Of course our business model works!" Beatrice insisted. "Well, I think it works. It ought to work. But in any case, we still have six billion left! We don't need old Mush-Mush! Hey, growing an investment firm takes time, and time takes patience. It's just that these days it's so awfully hard to beat the market under any circumstances, even without any restrictions hampering our managers' performance. Meanwhile, we are helping our clients achieve their moral objectives regardless of their returns. And simply being socially responsible, or feeling that they are, ought to make our clients happy while they wait!"

"Apparently, not happy enough to keep their money with Vain Capital. Happy don't pay the bills, Beatrice, not for the Eschewers and not for you. Listen, Weedle and I haven't got time for this." The Butcher poked the tabletop with his fat index finger. "Private equity funds have to deliver good returns or we'll lose our clients too. If we don't see much faster asset growth from you, we'll have to sell the Butcher and Weedle Captivation Fund's fifty-one-percent equity stake in Vain Capital to another MOM."

"How much asset growth?"

"We're giving you until the end of this year to prove to us that Vain Capital can both win and keep new clients. By the end of December, you need to have at least twelve billion. You need a mission? Well, that's your mission. A penny less and we're selling. Now that you've lost the Eschewers, you need to raise at least six billion this year, and it's already March. That's assuming the market doesn't tank in the meantime."

The Butcher paused for a moment, drilling into Beatrice with his laser-like stare. The sale of Vain Capital to a competitor would be devastating. The new MOM would just grab her clients and their hard-won assets and fire her employees. That would be the end of her little monarchy, not to mention her four-million-dollar annual income. She had nobody to fall back on. Gerhard von Vain had deserted her for a flirty twenty-year-old Capitol Hill intern after he had inconsiderately failed to be re-elected to Congress from Boston eight years ago, leaving her divorced and marooned in Washington. Pillsbury had grown up, gone off to college, and moved to the West Coast to run a hedge fund, leaving her to rattle around by herself in her Chevy Chase mansion. Vain Capital was her only remaining child.

"Beatrice, you obviously need some outside help growing Vain Capital's assets, and I have an idea. The Captivation Fund has two clients interested in investing with you."

"Really?" replied Beatrice, perking up.

"I've talked to both of them recently, and it is all arranged. They are planning to attend your spring client conference here in Washington, in two weeks."

"Who are they?"

"The Russky Fund and California Retirement Asset Management."

Beatrice's eyes brightened. Those were two of the biggest pots of gold in the world, with hundreds of billions of dollars each. "The Russky Fund and CRAM? Fantastic! We'll really put on a show!"

"That's fine for CRAM. A state public employee pension fund, especially California's, has to disclose everything it does. But be very careful with the Russky Fund, Beatrice," the Butcher warned. "They are a low-profile client. The Russian government likes its investments kept very hush-hush. Do a private meeting, just you and them, with none of your investment officers there."

"Hush-hush! Understood! I can't wait to meet them!" Beatrice said. Then she paused to think. "But Stanton, about the Russky Fund—don't you think it's peculiar?

"What do you mean?"

"America is practically in another cold war with Russia. Why would the Russians want to invest in the U.S. these days?"

The Butcher shook his head. "International tensions don't affect the Russky Fund. A sovereign wealth fund that big has to be practical and invest its money wherever it finds good opportunities. That's mostly outside Russia."

"Then why are they so secretive about it?"

He gazed at her sternly, as if at the age of fifty-three she was still a spoiled little rich girl from Boston and running an investment firm was all just a game to her. "You always look a gift horse in the mouth, Beatrice. You can't do that. This is an asset-gathering business you're in, not a hobby to pursue your ancestors' outdated notions of social justice. You need the Russians' money. You need everybody's money. And this time, dammit, don't lose it!"

"Yes, I've had quite enough of looking clients in the mouth."

Beatrice wondered what these two huge organizations might want from her little firm, but tossed the thought aside and returned to her celebration. There was certainly never any lack of morality-seeking clients these days, especially in the vicinity of Vain Capital's office at the corner of Seventeenth and K Streets. Just three blocks from the White House, her own building housed several excellent prospects: the Association for Atheist Action, the Baptist Union, Committee for a Progressive America, Conservative Conscience, Environmental Protection League, National Buddhism Board, National Scout Federation, Society of Feminist Educators, and United Black Colleges. Washington was a spider's web of special interest groups, associations, think tanks, lawyers, lobbyists, and retired politicians. It was the ideal milieu for finding mission-driven clients: the morally sensitive neighborhood.

"So, here we go, Stanton! Out with Mush-Mush," she said, raising a glass of sparkling water to toast the Butcher, "and in with Hush-Hush!"

2   Quandary Capital

In Rocket City, Bruce Benson was sitting in his cubicle trying to optimize a multifactor asset pricing model, pondering whether the inverse of the product of two matrices really was the product of their inverses in reverse, when he was summoned from his reverie by the ringing of his telephone. It was the receptionist at the Quandary Capital front desk. His guest for the morning meeting with Vain Capital, Mr. Lee Yong-gi, had arrived.

Bruce got up and strode toward the waiting area. At six four and one hundred and sixty-five pounds, the thirty-year-old analyst was all arms and legs and seemed to walk like a giraffe. He had the look of an honest but homely man, with an angular Lincoln-esque face, straight brown hair combed sideways, and guileless but inquisitive brown eyes.

Lee Yong-gi was nearly a foot shorter and slightly built. Yong, as he preferred to be called, had been his roommate at Stanford, studying for his bachelor's degree while Bruce was getting his third PhD. Bruce was amused by how professional Yong looked now at twenty-four, all dressed up in his little gray two-piece suit, sporting a striped red and gray tie. He recollected him as a Korean kid in jeans and a tee shirt, always either studying with the intensity of a monk or diligently practicing leg kicks in the living room to train for the South Korean Olympic Taekwondo team.

Bruce signed the register at the front desk so Yong could go through the metal detector and past the armed security guards. The two friends walked down a corridor to a conference room.

"How did you wind up at Vain Capital, Yong?" Bruce asked. "Last time we spoke, you had gone into management consulting."

Yong smiled, his narrow brown eyes beaming. "Consulting career not for me, so I leave, two years enough flying around, living all time in hotel," he replied in a staccato Korean accent. "I read about Vain Capital and moral investing with social responsibility. I get most interested to switch to investment management. Big opportunity at Vain Capital—help put capital to highest and best use for good of society. Opportunity not last long. Gotta grab it! Like Confucius say, 'Man who stand on hill with mouth open—"

"Wait long time for roast duck to drop in," Bruce replied with a hoot. He had heard this one a hundred times. The little philosopher, a double major in Chinese religious studies and economics, always kept a ready supply of aphorisms on hand for any occasion. Yong would serve up his Yong-isms, usually a fractured Confucian proverb or macroeconomic principle, at the slightest provocation.

"My new boss at Vain Capital send me here to learn all about Quandary Capital. Alison Hartswell—you know her?" Yong asked.

"Oh, Alison Hartswell!" Bruce exclaimed. "Yes, everyone knows her. She visited us from Vain Capital a few months ago. She's your boss?" He lifted his eyebrows and smiled. "You lucky dog." Pleasant images of Quandary Capital's loveliest client wafted through Bruce's mind.

"Not my type, much too tall for me. I prefer girl I can look in eye without lifting head," Yong replied.

Looking through the glass wall of the conference room, Yong could see a labyrinth of cubicles stretching across the vast open floor, clear to the other side of the building. He estimated that there must be two hundred people inside the fabric-covered boxes.

"So what you doing here at Quandary Capital? You come a long way from South Dakota, cowboy. You give up teaching at MIT for this? Somebody steal PhDs?"

Bruce winced at the tactlessness of Yong's questions, aimed as usual at the sorest possible spot. A look of resignation came over his face. "I needed the money. Eleven years studying mechanical engineering, aerospace engineering, and applied statistics left me broke, with half a million in student loans. One day a headhunter called me up and asked me if I wanted to be a quant and make big money. My starting salary is four times what MIT paid. With the money I earn at Quandary Capital I'll be able to get this debt monkey off my back in just a few years."

"How many people here?" Yong inquired, looking at the cubicles. "What they all doing?"

"We have a thousand people, on seven floors. Some of them, like me, are researching to find investment opportunities. On other floors we have guys programming the code that runs our portfolio management system and trading operation."

"A thousand!"

"Yes, that's a huge staff for a money management firm, but we have fifty billion dollars in assets," Bruce explained. "This isn't a hedge fund—we just run an ordinary portfolio of U.S. stocks with no short selling. But our performance has been fantastic, so we get even better fees than most hedge funds do: three percent of assets and twenty-five percent of excess return over a benchmark. This is an extremely rich firm. In fact, it's closed to new investors. Everybody in the world wants to put their money here.

"Our investment process is entirely quantitative, which means computers pick the stocks in our clients' portfolios. The algorithms we create use hundreds of statistical relationships to identify which stocks are cheap. We have an entire building filled with supercomputers scanning millions of reports and news stories on the Internet for the ones that may affect stock valuations. We have other computer programs looking for patterns in the trading behavior of stocks.

"We have 175 PhDs, two Rhodes scholars, and three Nobel laureates. Half the guys on this floor—all guys, of course, since female quants are so rare—are from India. A bunch more come from China. I'm just about the only American in the whole place. I'll give you a tour on the way to our meeting with Dr. Ozturk."

Bruce stopped in the hallway for a moment. "I'd better warn you about Dr. Ozturk," he said in a hushed voice. "He's one of the two co-founders of Quandary Capital. He has an IQ of 190 and can be a little intimidating. He grew up in Istanbul, graduated from CalTech with a PhD in math, and then spent some years in New York at a hedge fund. Ten years ago, he and Dr. Feiersinger launched Quandary Capital here in Rocket City. They liked Florida's weather and thought they could scoop up some unemployed NASA rocket scientists—the ones who hadn't already left for Silicon Valley to make smart-phone apps and video games."

They strolled down one of the long corridors between the cubicles. A name plate on one of the cubicles was labeled "Sandeep Penkatanarasimharajuvaripeta." A man with a brown face and black mustache looked up from behind his three computer screens and smiled. The next cubicle was labeled "Rajeshmahara Bhamarakatapimbi." Inside it a swarthy man with dark eyes, a full beard, and a turban was typing something.

"South Indians—they all seem to have foot-long names like that. Something to do with honoring their ancestors." Bruce said. "We don't put up with it, though. We have a two-syllable limit here—we call those two Sandy and Raj. That's all the syllables they get. Otherwise we'd never get any work done."

"Hire Koreans!" Yong suggested. "Save many syllables."

They continued past a dozen more Indians, then a handful of Chinese, a Malaysian, three Russians, and a Kazakh. At the end of the long row of cubicles they came to a large glass-lined corner office. A stout man in his mid-forties with a rocket-shaped head and a jowly face looked up and flashed a grin. He motioned for them to enter.

"Dr. Mustafa Ozturk," Bruce said, introducing the client, "this is Lee Yong from Vain Capital in D.C. You remember Alison Hartswell, Vain's head of equities? Yong just started working there as her assistant portfolio analyst."

"Alison Hartswell, ah yes," Dr. Ozturk said with a wry smile. "Beautiful Miss Hartswell."

Yong bowed deeply as he shook hands with Dr. Ozturk. The older man's owlish eyes inspected him up and down. "Are you at all familiar with quant investing?"

Yong hesitated. "A little, from reading," the young man offered. "This my first visit to quant manager. I have much to learn—very much."

Dr. Ozturk recounted the history of Quandary Capital, explaining how he and Dr. Feiersinger worked in tandem to run the firm. He oversaw marketing and client service while his partner, who developed the firm's investment method and systems, supervised the quants, including Bruce.

Ozturk then launched a highly technical presentation describing the firm's complex investment process. Yong grasped only the bare outlines of it.

"Our business is all about finding pricing anomalies in the stock market, using supercomputers to sift through a vast quantity of data," Ozturk said. "We capture this data from innumerable sources: the Internet, purchased data feeds, government documents, company reports, and so forth."

As far as Yong could understand, Quandary Capital was a massive global data gathering and analysis operation, its powerful computers sucking up information like gigantic digital vacuum cleaners. They collected just about every manner and means of electronic emission on earth and beyond, whether made by man, machine, or God, including anything and everything from sunspot radiation down to the ugly burping noise of a frost-free refrigerator de-icing itself.

"Quandary Capital's global data processing operation is state of the art. It would be the envy of the National Security Agency, if they had the brains to understand it," Ozturk said.

"What is anomaly?" Yong asked innocently.

Dr. Ozturk frowned at him. "I see you are unfamiliar with rudimentary investment concepts."

"Yes. Please excuse."

"The stock market is extremely efficient," Ozturk began again. "Do you understand the hypothesis of market efficiency?"

"A little," Yong said.

"It just means that most information about companies is already available to all investors and as a result stocks are usually priced about right, so there isn't much opportunity left for anyone to outperform market benchmarks like the S&P 500 Index. Bargains are scarce because stocks are all picked over. An anomaly is a sort of abnormality, like the last buffalo left after the herd has been hunted to the point of extinction. In a perfectly efficient stock market, an anomaly wouldn't exist. But the stock market isn't quite perfectly efficient in pricing stocks—it's just *almost* perfectly efficient."

"I see. Market not quite perfect."

"That's where we come in. Over the last several decades the stock market has become so ruthlessly efficient that the only way left for anyone to find a stock market anomaly is to develop astonishingly sophisticated tools that no one else can afford. At Quandary Capital we have raised the bar so high that no one can compete with us. We have supercomputers here that can analyze oceans of data in a second, and to work with them we've hired lots of people with multiple highly advanced degrees like Bruce. They develop algorithms based on complex mathematical models to find the few anomalies that still exist by squeezing what profitable information there is out of the data, using statistical relationships between the data and stock prices. We are looking for almost undetectable patterns, so subtle that only our algorithms can find them."

"So say you find pattern, you call that anomaly?"

Ozturk nodded. "Yes, any sort of reliable pattern would be an anomaly. As I said, in a perfectly efficient market, there should be no anomalies. But logically, if you have tools and people available to no one else as we do, only you can find them. That's why we outperform every other U.S. equity money manager. The market is now so hyper-efficient that only we can consistently beat benchmarks. All other money managers who actively pick stocks are faking it, desperately trying to hold onto their clients' assets and their high fees. But they add no value, or what the investment industry calls *alpha*, over and above an unmanaged index's return. Their clients would be better off just giving up and buying low-fee index funds. They are getting no alpha. They are investing in vain."

"Can I see portfolio?" Yong asked.

Ozturk shook his head. "Oh, sorry, we never let anyone outside the firm see the portfolio, not even our clients. We have to protect our anomalies, you understand. The whole investment world would love to know what they are. If we let the information get out, our performance advantage would quickly disappear as our stocks got bid up by our competitors to their true value. That's how market efficiency works. The availability of information eliminates the opportunity to beat the market. It eliminates alpha."

"Without seeing portfolio, how we know you invest according to our client restrictions?"

"We always honor our client's guidelines," Ozturk replied in a superior tone of voice. "We are Quandary Capital."

Yong scanned the maze of cubicles outside Ozturk's office. "Why so few Americans work here?"

"Oh, goodness," Ozturk snickered, shaking his head. "They can't do math at the advanced level we require. Bruce is a rare exception. We need a few Americans to comply with U.S. equal opportunity laws, so we put most of them in marketing, which suits their limited abilities. On the investment staff Bruce is known as our Lone Ranger. We had to have an American cowboy, you know, with all the Indians we have here—*ha!*"

Bruce had wondered why there so few Americans at Quandary Capital. Certainly the pay was good enough. Why wouldn't there be more Americans? Was he an affirmative action hire, a token American in his own country amongst all these foreigners? He had three PhDs in engineering and statistics. He could do math!

"Anomaly very valuable," Yong noted. "So how you keep people from leaving, once they find anomaly, and using it someplace else?"

A forbidding look appeared on Ozturk's face. "We have had a few people leave," he acknowledged, "but the pay is extremely attractive here. We can afford any Einstein on the planet. Everyone has a lifetime non-compete agreement so they can never work anywhere else in the investment business. We own them, in effect. Of course, they are not slaves, technically. In this day and age, that would be illegal."

"What happen to those who leave?"

Ozturk drummed his fingers on the table. "Our secrets are worth many billions of dollars. Naturally, we had to go after the ones who left, to protect our secrets," he disclosed.

"How you go after them?"

Ozturk forced a smile. "No one should want to leave Quandary Capital—we make sure of that with the richest pay packages in the business. And who would prefer to be in New Delhi, Bangalore, or Nishni Novgorod when they can be on the beach in sunny Florida?"

"But I ask how you go after them," Yong repeated. "I read financial newspaper article say you chase quant researcher all the way to Tibet and he wind up in jail." Yong reached into his briefcase and pulled out an *Investments Daily* article on Quandary Capital, entitled "Quant Firm in Hot Pursuit."

Bruce shifted uncomfortably in his chair. He was not surprised Yong had done his homework. Whether the subject was Chinese philosophy, economics, Taekwondo, or Quandary Capital, Yong always did his homework. But why must he always ask such awkward questions?

"There was a Taiwanese fellow who left and tried to set up shop in Tibet," Ozturk conceded. "He's in jail now, in Lhasa. There was also a Ukrainian, but he lost his mind shortly after we had him deported for theft of intellectual property. Dementia, they said it was. A terrible shame."

"Lost his mind?" Yong said, wondering how that could happen to a relatively young man. "Very sad for man so smart, smart enough to work here, to lose mind."

"Yes, we were very sad to hear of it," Ozturk said.

After the meeting Bruce and Yong went out to lunch at a nearby restaurant. Bruce looked around to make sure there were no Quandary Capital employees there and picked a table in a far corner, well out of earshot of anyone.

"You sure made Dr. Ozturk squirm," whispered Bruce, "and me too, with your questions about people leaving. You could have been more discreet."

"Easier for me to be discreet in Korean than English."

"That wouldn't have helped. Ozturk only speaks Turkish and English."

"Quandary Capital is strange place," Yong said. "Very creepy. Like horror movie."

"Yes, it is," Bruce agreed. "And I have seen some strange things already in my short time here."

"Like what?"

"I don't know if you noticed, but there are cameras all over the building," Bruce explained. "They are very small, less than the width of a pencil eraser, embedded in the light fixtures overhead. They seem to be aimed at the desktops and computer screens of all the employees. There are more cameras in the hallways, watching us coming and going. That meeting we just had with Dr. Ozturk was videotaped—all meetings automatically are. And you saw the armed guards at the receptionist's desk. Those were real guns. Loaded guns."

"They want to know what you are doing," Yong said. "More important, what you are not doing."

"And there's something odd about the portfolios too," Bruce declared.

"How they are managed is odd?"

"No, what's in them."

"Portfolios have something besides stocks in them?"

"No, they are all stocks, like they ought to be. I mean they have too many O's."

"Oh's?" Yong repeated.

"The letter O. I noticed this morning that there are too many stocks starting with the letter O for the size of the portfolio. The Quandary

Capital portfolio has only twenty-three stocks, but there are nine stocks whose names start with the letter O. That's thirty-nine percent of the stocks."

"So what? What is wrong with O's?"

"Nothing," Bruce replied. "But stocks starting with O make up only about two percent of the U.S. market. Statistically speaking, it's extremely unlikely that thirty-nine percent of a portfolio's stocks would begin with O when only two percent of the stocks in the market do. The odds of randomly selecting nine stocks starting with O out of just twenty-three stocks are almost nil."

"Ah, you saying stock picking for portfolio probably not random." A look of concern flooded Yong's face. "Somebody *deliberately* picking stocks with O's to put in our portfolio?"

"Yes."

"The crazy bastards!" Yong craned his neck, looking around the restaurant to see if anyone was listening to him, put his finger on his cheek, and asked in a whisper, "Is it illegal in America?"

"No, but it's weird."

"Yes, Quandary Capital very weird," Yong agreed. "But what does it mean?"

"The letter O is a vowel," Bruce said. "That means it occurs more often in words than you would expect it to by random selection. I think they are spelling words with the portfolio."

"The Quandary Capital portfolio spells words!" Yong's eyes grew wide. "But why they want to do that? They playing Scrabble with Vain Capital's money?"

"I don't know why. I need to do more research."

Yong put his hand to his forehead as if he had a splitting headache. "Oh, this not good. I just join Vain Capital last week, and already first money manager I meet playing word games with our stocks! My lady boss send me down here to learn about Vain Capital's money managers, not find spelling scandal! Do more research. Find out why somebody putting too many O's in portfolio."

"I'll try."

"Whatever wrong here, never too late to fix mistake—even job mistake," Yong said. "Man who already made bad mistake but not fix it—he making another bad mistake."

Another Yong-ism. Yet deep in his heart Bruce feared his wise little friend was right, hard as it was to admit. He had wandered a long way from his father's struggling cattle ranch near Lonely Butte, South Dakota, since leaving home for college at sixteen. Giving up his quiet life at MIT to cash in at Quandary Capital was seeming more and more like a grave mistake. But there was no easy road back to either Lonely Butte or Boston. Besides, there was the big paycheck to think about, and the mountain of student debt that hung over him. In this prison of good fortune, could he have become just another one of Quandary Capital's many overeducated and overpaid serfs?

Yong bade Bruce farewell, departed the restaurant, and drove his rental car back from Rocket City toward the Orlando airport. On the way he noticed a sign along the road. It was pointing to the Rocket Garden at Kennedy Space Center. With an hour of spare time to kill before his flight, he decided to take a look. He drove down a long road and parked.

Nearby he saw some of the old rockets that had powered America's space race in the 1960s, standing upright like sentinels guarding an old memory. Yong remembered reading their names in history books: Mercury, Atlas, Saturn. This was an open-air museum commemorating the height of American aspiration, the race to the moon.

To reach the moon, Confucius would say, America must surely have had a mandate from heaven. Even as a small boy in North Korea, in the terrible years after the arrest of his father, before Yong and his mother had managed to escape to Seoul, he had regarded all things American with wonderment, if not always perfect understanding. But what had happened to the proud Americans who used to work here and perform such feats? The launch pads that once challenged the sky were nowhere within view, nor the scientists and engineers, nor the great dreams they pursued. What had happened to the Americans? Why couldn't they do math anymore?

3 The Spring Client Conference

Early that April, Washington's famously unpredictable cherry blossoms—often appearing weeks too early or late for the city's annual Cherry Blossom festival—burst forth right on time for that celebration, Easter, and Vain Capital's spring client conference, shrouding the city in a magnificent cloud of brilliant pink and white and covering the ground like a fog. From the Jefferson Memorial, all along the fringe of the Tidal Basin to the Lincoln Memorial, the river's edge was ablaze, treating visitors riding to the conference from Reagan National Airport to a spectacular show.

Beatrice had prepared her own extravagant show in a sumptuous ballroom of the ritzy St. Regis Hotel, near Vain Capital's offices. In rooms adorned with resplendent chandeliers and carved ceilings, the clients would be regaled for two days with a succession of inspirational presentations promoting the morality of mission-based investing. On an easel outside the ballroom door, a large placard advertised the topics:

> The History of Investing With a Conscience
> Developing Righteous Restrictions
> Shame on Your Portfolio
> Sensitivity and Your Stocks
> Virtue as Your Investment Reward
> ESG for Everyone

ESG, the acronym for environmental, social, and governance investing, was the latest fad among social responsibility activists, who hailed it as a more proactive approach and a surer path to righteousness than simply banning offensive investments. In the spirit of ESG, rather than

merely shunning stocks of coal companies, for example, a money manager might load up on those of solar panel manufacturers. Or, instead
of just excluding a firm that employed children to make sneakers in
Bangladesh, the manager might buy stock in firms whose boards were
dominated by women. Like morality itself, precisely what constituted
good environmental, social, and governance practice was a mystery to
everyone, and its advocates were quietly determined to keep it that way.
All anyone really knew or cared to know was that ESG was hot and new,
and it felt very good to do it. That made it better than sex, as it could be
enjoyed with no consequences.

On a table at the entrance to the ballroom was a stack of Carbon
Footprint registration forms. Clients filled these out to sign up with an
outside firm that would estimate how many tons of carbon their organizations were spewing into the atmosphere each month. On another
table lay a pile of multi-page booklets entitled "Moral Objection Menu."
These checklists enabled clients to screen out whole categories of morally disagreeable securities from their portfolios, such as those involved
in tobacco products, alcoholic beverages, abortion-inducing drugs, oil,
gas, coal, Israeli stocks, firearms, commercial prisons, casinos, child labor, condoms, genetically modified food, pesticides, gluten, slow Internet download speeds, and a hell's worth of other abominations. Multiple
levels of detail within each category allowed the objector to tick a box to
choose between damning, say, all tobacco products or just cigarettes but
not Cuban cigars. The Moral Objection Menu was as comprehensive as
it was flexible, painstakingly kept up to date by Vain Capital's marketing
staff, which stayed abreast of the latest fashions in social umbrage by
regularly perusing the editorial pages of *The New York Times* and *The
Washington Post*.

For the guests' amusement, a talking parrot in a big brass cage had
been placed outside the ballroom. Blue with a red head and streaks of
green and yellow feathers on its back, the bird was a quick study and
would immediately repeat whatever anyone told it to say. It had already
picked up several useful phrases and was squawking prohibitions right
back at the delighted onlookers, screeching "Don't buy coal stocks!",
"No guns in our portfolio!", "No Israeli stocks!", and "ESG's for me!"
The parrot was enjoying the game every bit as much as Vain Capital's
clients, its feathered head bobbing up and down, absorbing their moral

objections with such facility that by the end of the day it would have a repertoire worthy of an investment consultant.

All of Vain Capital's senior staff members were gathered with the clients inside the ballroom, except for one. Stationed at the door was a strikingly beautiful woman with long blond hair, azure blue eyes, extraordinarily large breasts, and a slender but shapely body six feet tall. Investment officer Alison Hartswell looked like a supermodel, and in fact had worked as one part-time during her undergraduate days at the University of Southern California before getting her MBA at UCLA. She was introducing her new assistant Lee Yong to the clients as they entered.

"We need to find the man from CRAM," Alison said to Yong with determination, scanning the room like a lioness searching for her prey.

Yong, just back from Rocket City the night before, looked up at her. "CRAM? What is that?"

"California Retirement Asset Management, the biggest pension fund in the U.S.," Alison explained. "The Queen Bea wants us to take very good care of Morris Morbinders of CRAM. We are meeting with him tomorrow. It's a huge opportunity for us—it could mean billions in new assets."

Just then Beatrice rang a little brass bell and called out to everyone to take their assigned seats. Alison zeroed in on the little man moving toward the nameplate marked "Morris Morbinders—CRAM."

A large U-shaped table with a podium at the end had been set up to enable Beatrice to place key employees next to new clients and important prospects. The equity team of Alison and Yong flanked both sides of Morris Morbinders. Beatrice sat at the head of the table, next to Yegor Yakov, her guest from the Russky Fund. To keep Yakov to herself, Beatrice had installed Henry Bernstein, Vain Capital's tedious investment officer for fixed income, on the Russian's far side. If Yakov breathed so much as a word to him, Henry was instructed to kill the conversation as quickly as possible by holding forth on his favorite subject, commercial mortgage-backed securities.

Beatrice had seated established clients from different backgrounds next to each other to enliven the discussion and "set off some sparks but no explosions," as she liked to say. Sister Lucretia, representing the investment committee of a rich California convent called Little Sisters of

Baby Jesus, was placed next to Clarence Clemson, the chief investment officer of Calhoun University, a Houston school with a big endowment amply funded by its oil-rich alumni. On the nun's other wing was Tony Elfuego, chief investment officer of Yule University in Minneapolis. The Nebraska Jewish Foundation sat between Al Sharpton College and Mormons on the Mount. United Arab Emirates separated Boston Bio-diversity from the National Handgun Association.

This seating arrangement was the product of bitter experience. Beatrice's inattentive secretary had once carelessly placed the National Handgun Association alongside the Little Sisters of Baby Jesus, which strenuously objected to weapons of any kind. The two representatives soon fell into a loud quarrel over the Second Amendment and had to be parted before they could start pulling each other's hair out.

Another time the Nebraska Jewish Foundation had been paired with the United Arab Emirates sovereign wealth fund, which had imposed an absolute ban on Israeli companies in its portfolios. Within minutes, the Jew had nudged his bottled water several inches into the Arab's personal space on the conference table, whereupon the Arab retaliated by pilfering one of the Jew's hors d'oeuvres. The Jew then erected a wall of presentation books, while the Arab began to shake up a bottle of soda water and started unscrewing the cap. The two were quickly reseated just seconds before the bottle would have exploded in the Jew's face.

The Mormons were less troublesome and could usually be located anywhere except next to evangelical Baptists. The college people got along well with each other, as they all thought alike, but they could not bear hearing contrary opinions and so had to be shielded from Vain Capital's conservative clients.

Alison tried valiantly to make small talk with Morris Morbinders. Having been briefed by Beatrice on the vital importance of tomorrow's meeting with CRAM's representative, Alison was supposed to pump the little bald man for advance information so as to be better prepared. But Morbinders was strangely reticent and would not be pumped.

A mid-level functionary within the complex bureaucracy of CRAM, with its assets of three hundred billion dollars and two thousand employees housed in a cluster of thirty-story buildings in Sacramento, Morbinders was in constant dread of being found on the wrong side of any issue. Despite his unimportance inside CRAM, the modestly-salaried civil servant exercised the awesome power of a multi-billionaire over the external money managers CRAM hired. To them he was CRAM incarnate, the gatekeeper of a vast treasure trove that could make them mega-rich. But the power he wielded was not his—it was only borrowed. Morbinders never knew when he would be embarrassingly overruled by his superiors or when an investment program would be hijacked by the whims of the CRAM investment committee, dominated as it always was by Sacramento's highly partisan political hacks. The yawning disparity between Morbinders's internal insignificance and the immense external power he wielded over money managers had utterly warped the little troll's self-image, leading to his schizophrenic behavior and reflexive circumspection. A man both mighty and meek, he would wring his wrists and wiggle his nose like a mouse whenever he was uncertain where he stood, and venture only a non-committal smile.

"So, Morris," said Alison in an effort to break the ice, "how do you like Washington's cherry blossoms? Aren't they lovely?"

"They might be," replied Morbinders, nodding diffidently, reluctant to take a stand on them.

Most of the time it was both easiest and wisest for the man from CRAM just to keep his mouth shut, a skill he had honed to a high art. Since he could never confidently express his own opinions, he avenged his imprisoned ego by withholding not only verbal information but sometimes even body language. He called this cruel game "giving them the Sphinx." When a money manager made a sales pitch to Morbinders, hoping to gauge his reaction, he would simply respond with a blank expression like that of the Great Sphinx guarding the pyramids of Giza. Inscrutable, immovable, and inert, the Sphinx drove money managers crazy, just as Morbinders intended. Today Alison was getting the Sphinx and thinking she must surely be doing something terribly wrong.

Beatrice began her opening statement to kick off the conference. "I want to thank everyone for coming. We have a wonderful program for you today and tomorrow, full of topics I know you will find useful as you consider how you can work with Vain Capital to improve your mission-based investing. Please help yourself to the Moral Objection Menu booklets outside the door, and please don't hesitate to consult with us if you need some help identifying shameful investment categories. We are here to help put your portfolios back on the road to righteousness."

She introduced her key staff members for the benefit of new clients and prospects, and then announced the conference's keynote speaker, who strode into the ballroom on cue.

It was none other than former Vice President Al Gore. Disappointed by his failed bid for the presidency in the year 2000, Gore had salved his wounded pride by parlaying his global connections into deals worth hundreds of millions of dollars, including participation in a successful money management firm specializing in ESG investing. A longtime friend of Beatrice and her ex-husband Gerhard, he was a regular at Vain Capital's quarterly client conferences, flying across the country from his palatial oceanfront villa in Malibu, California, on a twin-engine Gulfstream jet burning four hundred gallons of jet fuel per hour to regale the attendees with lectures on the immorality of using fossil fuels.

Gore charged up to the podium to deliver his sermon. "Ladies and gentlemen, the age of oil is over!" he proclaimed in a soft Tennessee drawl. "As governments ban the use of fossil fuels, investments in oil, natural gas, and coal will soon become stranded assets, locked in the ground by government decree in favor of renewable fuels. The untold billions of dollars that have been invested in these stranded assets have been invested in vain! But we have more than just a fiduciary duty to protect our investors from grievous financial losses. It is our moral obligation to the planet and future generations to rid our portfolios of these climate-killing energy investments. And in that spirit, I want to congratulate Clarence Clemson of Calhoun University for his cooperation with Vain Capital to divest the Calhoun endowment, shamefully funded from oil and gas profits, of its entire portfolio of fossil fuel stocks and bonds. We know that wasn't an easy political step for the Calhoun endowment committee to take. Well done, Clarence!"

Gore began to clap in tribute to Clemson. The entire room joined him, except for the man from the United Arab Emirates, scowling malevolently at Gore from inside his white Bedouin headdress.

Clemson, a middle-aged man with brown hair, a thin jaw, and a pointy nose that curled up like a ski slope, smiled appreciatively back at Gore. Next to him, Sister Lucretia, her severe countenance relaxing some from within the white coif of her nun's habit, put aside the Moral Objection Menu she had been scanning for new ideas and patted his hand approvingly.

"Well, as you can well imagine, our school's deep involvement in the oil and gas business has become a source of growing concern for the investment committee," Clemson said with a proud smile, signaling his virtue. "Our students were demanding radical change, and we cannot oppose them, so we had to do something even if meant upsetting our biggest donors. It's a risky move: they are die-hard oil men and wildcatters, every one of them a knuckle-dragging redneck. They'll be slow to come around."

"Oh, no need to explain, I absolutely agree with what you've done," Sister Lucretia said, drawing herself upright. "I can see you are a man of action." She gazed admiringly at his muscular shoulders and arms. "It takes moral courage to bite the hand that feeds you."

"But it's never enough to bite it just once," Clemson sighed. "Our students are always seething about something, and now are calling for more reforms."

"What kind of reforms?"

"Calhoun University was named after John C. Calhoun, the South Carolina legislator who fought for states' rights. He was a slave owner."

"Oh, my! That must be so hard for you!" Sister Lucretia said, patting and rubbing Clemson's hand again. Then she gave it a longer rub. He smiled back, somewhat surprised, and then shuddered in silent horror. It almost seemed to him that she was...no, he decided, she could not be coming onto him. She was a nun.

"Yes, the students want us to change our name," Clemson continued, withdrawing his hand from her just in case. "They are ashamed to be at a school named after a defender of slavery. And of course, who can argue with them?"

"I understand. We are faced with exactly the same dilemma at Little Sisters of Baby Jesus," Sister Lucretia admitted.

Clemson seemed very surprised. "Really? The same dilemma? But Jesus didn't defend slavery."

"No, but he failed to condemn it, and it was all around him, everywhere he went, so it's just as bad," Sister Lucretia pointed out. "He had every opportunity to condemn slavery. Why didn't he? You can look through the whole New Testament—not a peep from him about it. Why not? If we know better, surely he should have too. Jesus even talked about slaves and masters as if slavery were perfectly normal. Well, it

wasn't normal! We are ashamed to be named after a man in slavehold-
ing times who wouldn't condemn an institution he must have known
was reprehensible!"

"But those were the times he lived in," Clemson said, rushing instinctively to Christ's defense. "There were so many things that were reprehensible back then. How could Jesus know which ones he should go
after? And Jesus wasn't just a man—he was the Son of God. Would you
judge the Son of God?"

"Not if he got things right," Sister Lucretia replied, her eyes glowing
with virtue. "That's what's so awfully disappointing. He had every reason to get it right. What could be his excuse? He didn't know? That
doesn't cut it. Son of God or not, Jesus didn't do his job, so there it
is—we are ashamed of him. In fact, our shame causes us such pain and
embarrassment that we're thinking of dropping Jesus from our name."

"You're going to fire Jesus? Really? But it's practically Easter. It's his
big day."

"Yes, the Mother Superior says it's time for Jesus to go."

Clemson thought about it a minute. Indeed it was a pity to strike Jesus
from the name of one's organization after so many years of creditable
service, but why should the Son of God get off easy and be held to a
lower moral standard than John C. Calhoun?

"Won't that present a problem for you, besides just the name?" Clemson asked. "I mean, with the religious angle and all, like with the Trinity,
for example?"

"Yes, well, the Trinity will need redesigning, won't it? And just think
of all the other logistical details we'll have to take care of—crucifixes,
stained glass, bibles, hymns, just for starters. The Little Sisters will be
very busy. We have two thousand years of history to live down, so it will
take at least a few months to rub him out."

"You can stamp out Jesus in just a few months? I would think it would
take much longer."

Sister Lucretia's face looked strained. "Oh, catching up with modern
times won't be easy, mind you. The cities and universities don't know
how easy they have it. Jesus is more than just a logo. More than just a
statue to be removed from a town square. More than just a nameplate to
be ripped down from a university building."

"He is indeed."

"But what choice do we have?"

"I don't suppose you could just forgive him," Clemson suggested. "Turn the other cheek maybe?"

"No," said Sister Lucretia. "Not for this. We can't just let his name stand. It's offensive. Oh, it's all been so very upsetting for us," said the nun, dabbing her eyes with her handkerchief.

"I can see that. Sorry for your loss," Clemson replied.

During a break in the conference program, Beatrice took Yegor Yakov aside. They slipped into an empty conference room down the hall from the ballroom and closed the door.

Yakov was a heavy-set man with bushy eyebrows and oily hair, about fifty years old, wearing a baggy brown suit. Walking with a slovenly gait, he plopped himself down on a chair across the table from Beatrice and flashed a wide grin.

"*Khorosho!*" Yakov began in a thick Russian accent. "Beatrice, very good of you to meet me at request of Stanton Butcher. Butcher most helpful to us at Russky Fund, give us good advice. We invest in Butcher and Weedle private equity fund five years, no problem."

"Oh, we are always delighted to meet with Stanton's friends and investors, Yegor," Beatrice replied in a cheery voice. "Stanton has quite a wide circle of friends around the world. Over the twenty years I've known him, I have always been impressed with how well connected he is."

Beatrice thought back fondly as to how the Butcher had introduced her to heads of state, legislators, ambassadors, corporate chieftains, and deep-pocketed investors on all continents. He could throw open doors to power and money almost anywhere, from the White House on down. It was entirely because of his global access that she had allowed the Butcher and Weedle Captivation Fund to buy a controlling equity stake in Vain Capital.

"Butcher tell you why I have come?" asked Yakov in a soft voice, looking around at the walls as if wondering whether someone might be looking in, or listening in.

"No, he only told me you wanted to meet privately," Beatrice answered. "I didn't ask Stanton for details."

Yakov leaned forward and lowered his voice some more, almost to a whisper. "We would like to make investment quietly in Russky Fund's name."

Beatrice immediately grew uneasy but tried not to show her concern. The Russky Fund could make investments in its own name without Vain Capital. *Who is "we," who would like to invest in the Russky Fund's name,* she wondered. *And what does this smarmy fellow mean by quietly?*

Yakov understood the uncomfortable look darkening Beatrice's face. "We want money invested in one of your very moral programs, in least likely possible place."

Beatrice hoped she could explain to Yakov without offending him that there were federal anti-money-laundering laws against taking funds without knowing who the actual investor is. "Yegor, you see in this country we generally need to know *who—*"

"He is high-level person who would not like to be named," Yakov interrupted. "Amount is three billion dollars cash, to be wired direct and invested in Russky Fund's name."

Beatrice's mind started to race. *Three billion—enough to replace the Eschewers!* But there were federal laws against taking money without knowing the source. And why was the Russian government so eager to place a large sum of money with an American firm specializing in socially responsible investing, given Russia's hostility toward the United States? She recalled seeing a news story on television just the night before about how Russian President Viktor Bludinov had roundly castigated the new American president, Phyllis Fibby, for reaffirming NATO's commitment to defend the Baltic states from Russian aggression.

The Butcher had taken Russky Fund money as well, perhaps from the same unknown high-level person, and he had sent Yakov to her, after all. Was the Butcher knowingly taking money illegally? Should she call him about Yakov's request, or would it expose him legally in a money-laundering conspiracy? Maybe it would be best to keep all this quiet as the Butcher had asked her to. It was quite possible he didn't know what Yakov would propose to her. But then again, wasn't he the one who had scolded her for looking a gift horse in the mouth?

Three billion! It would help get the Butcher off her back, and perhaps even stop him from selling Vain Capital out from under her.

"I think we can accommodate your request, Yegor," Beatrice declared.

"*Khorosho,*" Yakov replied. "You understand, I have instructions. My mission is to invest money in most unlikely place possible. I leave it to you to choose it."

"I understand. When we have a suitably unlikely investment picked out, I will call to let you know and then you can wire the money and we will invest it in the Russky Fund's name."

They left the conference room and rejoined the others in the hotel ballroom.

Beatrice returned to the conference table as the next presentation, entitled "Shame on Your Portfolio," was about to begin. Thor Nederbrygge, Vain Capital's investment officer for hedge funds, stepped confidently up to the podium to deliver a talk on how to identify and expunge guilty investments to align disgraceful portfolios with an organization's mission statement.

Three billion dollars, Beatrice kept thinking. How could she refuse it? With all the good that money could do, it would be a shame not to take it.

4 The CRAM Mandate

By the end of the following day the client conference had loaded down its participants with as much social responsibility as they could bear. Now it was time to hear what the little man from CRAM had in mind for Vain Capital. Back at the firm's headquarters, Beatrice and her four investment officers—Alison, Henry, Roger, and Thor—were arrayed around a table with Morris Morbinders, who was fiddling with his pen and looking as anxious as a ferret in heat. Alison noticed that he had a little pile of stapled papers under his left hand, and that the papers were upside down so no one could read what was on them.

"Well, Morris," Beatrice began the meeting, looking chipper. "We are so pleased to have had you join us for our spring client conference. I hope you learned something about our capabilities yesterday. What can we do for you?"

Morbinders twisted uneasily in his chair, his eyes darting around the room. He gazed down at his papers, then cleared his throat. "Beatrice, over the years CRAM has become dangerously underfunded and now has only forty-two cents of assets for every dollar of liabilities. The state of California can't afford to close such a huge gap with taxpayer contributions because that would mean massive tax increases. So pension payments to retired state employees are at great risk. If nothing is done, in a few years CRAM's pension checks will be bouncing. Therefore, Governor Patty Pitypander has felt compelled to get directly involved in governance matters at CRAM and has started giving our investment committee some helpful suggestions about how we should invest our assets. Her idea is to make CRAM's roster of money managers more inclusive so that California's money managers reflect the makeup of our diverse population. Like many public pension plans, CRAM has previously asked MOM firms like yours to hire minority money managers for us."

"Ah, you would like us to run a minority manager program," Beatrice said with cheerful assurance. "Vain Capital has done it many times. Al Sharpton College is one of our clients now. You may have noticed their treasurer at the conference. They've asked us to hire only black money managers for them. It can be limiting, since there are only a few dozen black firms in the country versus thousands of white-owned firms, but we would be delighted to do it."

Morbinders stiffened up some more. "That base is already covered. We have more than enough black money managers through our several manager diversity programs. Governor Pitypander wants to take minority investing a step further—"

"We can do it!" Beatrice interrupted. "Asian money managers! Now those are even rarer than the black ones, but we will hunt them down to the last man or woman."

Morbinders shook his head. "No, it's not Asians we're after."

"Of course, Hispanics! Not a problem! Just a tiny handful of them are in this business, but we'll hire every one of them if necessary."

Morbinders shook his head again and drew a deep breath. "No, that's not it. Governor Pitypander asked our consultant to determine whether we could push the boundaries of diversity even further and go beyond race, which has been awfully overdone and has become rather ho-hum. She thought we should break new ground and get into something trendier and more exciting, like sex."

"Sex?" Beatrice responded with a start.

"Um, I mean sexual identity," Morbinders said, quickly correcting himself.

"Sexual identity?"

"The governor wants CRAM to hire gay money managers," Morbinders declared, exhaling. *There it is*, he thought, *it is out in the open, I have said it.*

"Gay money managers!" Beatrice exclaimed, somewhat bewildered. No client had ever asked for gay money managers. Come to think of it, she had never knowingly met one.

"Yes, our consultant's report, which I have here, explains what we— that is, what Governor Pitypander—is thinking." Morbinders turned his little stack of papers over and passed out the consultant's report to the group. It was entitled, *The Next Step in Social Justice: Making CRAM Maximally Diversified and Gay in All Dimensions.*"

"Maximally diversified?" Beatrice was still trying to absorb the idea. "Gay in all dimensions? How many dimensions could there be? Up and down, side to side, front to back, or in and out? I can't think of any other dimensions for sex."

Morbinders reached for his handkerchief to wipe his brow. His hands trembling, he began to quote from the consultant report's executive summary. "The report says 'CRAM could significantly improve its returns by expanding the efficient frontier of investing into the progressive dimension of queer social justice, making the CRAM portfolio maximally diversified, sexually fluid, and gay in all dimensions.' In other words, hire money managers to represent every major kind of gay person there is."

"Goodness, how many different kinds of them are there?" Beatrice had heard of only three. There were men who liked men, women who liked women, and men and women who wanted to be the opposite of what they were and go into the wrong bathrooms. What else could there be?

"The report recommends starting with seven major types of gay person, following the popular acronym LGBTQIA."

"My goodness!" Beatrice exclaimed. "LGBTQIA? What do those letters stand for?"

"Lesbian, gay, bisexual, transgender, queer, intersex, asexual."

"Queer? Aren't they all queer?" Beatrice asked.

"Yes, well, queer is an umbrella term which covers all the bases. Kind of a wild card category. It's sex pointed anywhere but straight."

"And what on earth is intersex? Is that something between the sexes?"

"There's not much of it on earth, actually." Morbinders's face turned red and tensed up again as he stared down at the consultant's report. "It says here it's one whose anatomy is sexually indeterminate—not exclusively male or female. It's someone who has both male and female genitalia—a hermaphrodite. A bit of this and a bit of that. Some ying and some yang."

"And the last one—asexual?"

"Some say the A stands for allies of gay people and some say it's for asexual, so we went with asexual, thinking it's much rarer these days and will provide more of a sporting challenge for you. An asexual, of course, is someone who doesn't have any sexual attraction of any kind. A sexual dud, basically."

"Oh, I disagree, I think that one should be quite easy to find," Beatrice said with a hearty laugh. "Some of my old boyfriends would have fallen into that category."

A concerned look had come over Alison. "So, to be clear, Morris, you want us to find money managers from every single one of those seven types?"

"Yes, and the report recommends equal-weighting the seven, so as to avoid any favoritism, so none of the groups will feel offended," Morbinders explained. "Also, the research is pretty thin on the question of how else you could justify doing it. We don't know, for example, whether more lesbians would be better than fewer vis-à-vis hermaphrodites from a risk and return standpoint, so we just decided to go for equal-weighting to head off the political problem. No need to rile the lesbians unnecessarily."

"Absolutely not," Beatrice agreed. "Stirring up lesbians is never a good idea, on the best of days."

"You will need to find at least one money manager in each gay category. But we don't care which asset classes you pick. We don't want to be too restrictive."

"No, of course not," Beatrice said. "If we're lucky enough to catch a real hermaphrodite, it shouldn't matter whether it prefers to invest in bonds or real estate. In fact, given its versatility on the other front, it might well do both."

"How much should we allocate to each category?" Alison asked.

"We would like to put a billion dollars into each one."

Beatrice's heart rose to her throat. "Oh, seven billion in all?" she squeaked. "That's a nice mandate."

"That's right." Morbinders said with a grin, enjoying her failed attempt at appearing indifferent about the amount.

"Are there any more gay categories? We'll be delighted to do more categories."

"That's where we'd like to start. We want to see how this goes before venturing into additional sexual orientations."

"Do you mind if we create a commingled fund that other clients can invest in alongside CRAM?"

Morbinders shrugged. "Not at all. CRAM would welcome co-investors. The governor's fondest wish is to be a trend-setter and an instigator of social justice."

Beatrice's eyes lit up as she imagined the vast marketing potential of this brave new investment idea. "A multi-manager maximally diversified LGBTQIA portfolio, sexually fluid and gay in all dimensions! That's quite a mouthful. We could call it the MaxiGay Fund for short! That's it, the MaxiGay Fund, there's a catchy name," she proclaimed. "And we could invite our existing clients to co-invest! Kind of like cohabitation— investing sexually, everyone all mingling in the same fund—that should be a big hit at the universities."

Then, out of nowhere, as the wheels of Beatrice's imagination began to spin faster and faster, came another inspiration. Yegor Yakov of the Russky Fund had asked her to invest three billion dollars quietly in the most improbable place possible. What could be a more unlikely investment for the Russian government than a gay fund? Russia was notoriously homophobic. The president of Russia, Viktor Bludinov, had sent thousands of homosexuals to the gulags.

"But there is an important timing issue," Morbinders warned. "CRAM wants the gay managers identified *before* it allocates any money. Governor Pitypander is facing re-election this November. She needs the program to be up and running before Native Peoples' Day, so she can announce it to the gay community in San Francisco at precisely the optimal moment."

"Native Peoples' Day?"

"October 8. It's Columbus Day everywhere else but California. We're ashamed of Columbus and have rubbed him out. If you could get the fund going by Labor Union Day, that would be even better."

Beatrice recalled the news stories about how Patty Pitypander's political problems had deepened as her challenger, arch-conservative state senator Jack Fist, had made California's fiscal mismanagement and the state's deepening pension crisis the central issues of the campaign. Now, with the gubernatorial race tightening by the day, the governor was pulling out all the stops to lock up the gay vote in California. This fund for gay money managers was to be the centerpiece of Pitypander's campaign pitch to a key constituency.

"We can do that! We will get on it immediately," she assured Morbinders, at last noticing the horrified faces of all four of her investment officers.

"Oh, and just one more thing," Morbinders said in passing as the meeting ended. "Will these restrictions hurt your performance? With CRAM already so underfunded we really can't tolerate the slightest underperformance anymore."

"Have no fear, Morris," Beatrice replied, waving off his concern with an air of certainty. "We operate under client restrictions as a regular part of our business. I'm sure we can outperform CRAM's benchmarks."

Beatrice showed Morbinders out of the conference room.

Then she rushed to her office, closed the door, and called Yegor Yakov at the Russky Fund's New York office.

"Yes, Yegor," she said. "We've found a very unlikely investment for you. A commingled fund made up entirely of gay money managers."

"Gay money managers?" Yakov repeated with a quizzical look on his face. He quickly searched for the word "gay" in his worn pocket-sized English/Russian dictionary. Next to the English word "gay" he found the Russian word "*vyesyoli*."

"Yes, the state employee pension fund of the state of California will be the seed investor, with seven billion dollars to start. This fund will be the perfect unlikely investment for your high-level Russian official. We need to find the gay money managers first, but we expect to have the fund open by October at the latest. I will call you when we are ready to receive your three billion."

"*Khorosho*, money will be ready for you," Yakov replied, still puzzled, checking his little dictionary again. There was the word "*vyesyoli*" again. He wondered why it would take months just to find money managers who were merry. There must quite a shortage of them in this humorless country. But the delay would not be a problem. Besides, he felt merry that this matter had been resolved so easily, only a day after his trip down to Washington. Now he could report his success to his Russky Fund superiors in Moscow.

Next, Beatrice called Stanton Butcher III to let him know the wonderful news that she had landed a combined total of ten billion dollars in new assets from CRAM and the Russky Fund. Vain Capital would soon have sixteen billion in all, well above the year-end target of twelve billion which the Butcher had set for her.

"Fantastic, Beatrice," the Butcher responded. "Patty will be very pleased. I will let her know."

He would let her know? Directly? The phone nearly jumped out of Beatrice's hand. The Butcher and Pitypander had already arranged to steer the CRAM mandate to Vain Capital! The Butcher, Beatrice knew, was a Pitypander contributor. Now Pitypander was repaying his investment in her charitable foundation and political campaigns by placing CRAM's money with Vain Capital, majority-owned by the Butcher and Weedle Captivation Fund.

Beatrice pondered the ethics of her situation. The Butcher's insider dealings and conflicts of interest were none of her business. She was not a partner of the Captivation Fund. She had never spoken with the California governor in her life. And CRAM was a natural client for Vain Capital's morality-based investing services. Beatrice quickly determined that her hands were clean. She was not conflicted.

Her mind turned to thoughts of what a master stroke the MaxiGay Fund was. Her novel marketing idea had the potential to solve so many problems.

Soon after the meeting with Morbinders, Beatrice asked her four investment officers to rejoin her in the conference room to discuss their new MaxiGay project.

Her eyes lit up with excitement. "Well there! We've nearly landed a seven-billion-dollar client and a relationship with the biggest pension fund in the country! Now we just need to find seven gay money managers of various types. So who knows anything about gay money managers?" She surveyed the uneasy faces of her investment officers one by one, searching for some spark of enthusiasm. "Henry?"

The head of fixed income, Henry Bernstein, cowered across the table, shrugging his shoulders. At forty-three, he was married with two kids in college. He had eloped in his early twenties, gone to the University of Illinois for his MBA, and then worked for a bond management firm in Denver. He was an expert on mortgage-backed securities and an avid golfer. He could rattle off most of the holdings of Vain Capital's bond managers and the top twenty scores on the leaderboard of the latest major golf tournament. His two interests were bonds on weekdays and birdies on weekends.

"You know, I've never met a gay bond guy, although for the life of me I don't know why," admitted Henry, scratching his bald spot. "I think there's something about bond math that scares them off. I've seen some pretty odd bond derivatives, though. Now if you were looking for perverted investments instead of portfolio managers, I could help you there all day long. Interest rates on European government bonds are negative. Negative! Isn't that queer? The Germans will actually pay you to borrow their money. Yes, the Germans! If that isn't queer I don't know what is."

Beatrice turned next to Roger Ibble, her chubby investment officer for private equity and real estate. Known as Randy Roger in college for his frequent sexual escapades, he had been married three times, having been divorced by his first two wives for infidelity. The first wife caught him *in flagrante delicto* with another woman in a sleazy New Orleans motel, and the second discovered him sexting with a Mexican prostitute on their anniversary. Notwithstanding his colorful past, at forty-four Roger was now a spent volcano who spent his weekends singing in a barbershop quartet.

"Same here. I sure wish I could think of something for you, Bea," Roger said, "but I don't know any gay guys who manage private equity or real estate, or lesbians for that matter. Have you ever heard of a gay venture capitalist? I haven't. I've only run into one of those people in my whole life, an interior decorator my wife hired to redo our living room. I know nothing about such people."

Thor Nederbrygge, Vain Capital's tall Norse god of thunder and hedge funds, was next. The forty-year-old Minnesotan had worked at a large commercial bank in New York after getting his MBA, and then moved to a firm that assembled diversified sets of hedge funds before joining Vain Capital to do similar work. He had been married for ten years and had two young boys. He spent his weekends coaching their sports teams.

"The lesbian we had at the bank in New York wasn't a money manager, just a compliance officer," Thor recalled. "What a horrible woman! If you were a minute late submitting your personal trading form to her, that ugly little carpet-muncher would be after you, screaming like a banshee! And there was my weird uncle Marty, the gay dry cleaner, who all us kids avoided at Christmas. But those were the only perverts I can ever remember meeting. No money managers. Sorry, Bea."

The triumphant smile had vanished from Beatrice's face. "Alison, you're my only hope."

All eyes turned to Vain Capital's sole female investment officer. It was obvious to everyone but her that only she was fit to lead the MaxiGay project. Henry, Roger, and Thor, all of them settled middle-aged family men, would be mauled and appalled in the wilderness of gay diversity. Alison, just twenty-eight, was still open-minded, intrepid, adventurous, and resourceful, possessing such indomitable qualities as could be found only in a high-spirited young woman without the foggiest idea of what she would be getting into. And, as Beatrice realized, the men would not do it. They would sooner eat shards of broken glass.

"Oh my goodness, why me?" Alison replied in a panic-stricken voice as their eyes bore down on her. "I hardly know any of them either, really only my second cousin Bernie, the tort lawyer. But that's all. Really."

"Alison, I'd like you to run the MaxiGay project," Beatrice announced. "You flush out the gay money managers. Roger, Thor, and Henry will evaluate any in their asset classes that you're able to bring back to us."

"But Bea, this isn't a foxhunt! I don't how to find gay money managers. I wouldn't know where to start. Transgendered queens? Hermaphrodites? Are you kidding me?"

"Start with the letter L, for lesbians," Beatrice suggested, thinking it is always best to start at the beginning. "The first letter of LGBTQIA."

"That's not very helpful."

"How about our manager database? Maybe there's somebody gay in there," Beatrice proposed, referring to Vain Capital's computer database of money managers. Using the database, one could set criteria to pinpoint just about any investment firm in the country, such as a large cap growth firm in Boise, Idaho, with between five and fifteen billion dollars in assets and majority-owned by Southeast Asians, if such a company existed in Boise.

"I've never noticed hermaphrodite was a category you could screen on in our database."

"You could call up our existing managers and ask if they are gay," Beatrice offered.

"You want me to just pop a question like that on each of our managers?"

"Maybe not. You might have to tread lightly there. They might not take it well," Beatrice conceded, trying to think through the problem. "I know—you could tap into their network. Go to places where gay people hang out, like bars, and ask if they know someone who qualifies."

"I should just go walking blindly into gay bars asking if they know of any money managers who invest billions of dollars for institutions?"

"Bars might be a start," Beatrice replied. "My dear, you don't need to go alone. You have a brand-new assistant now. Take him along with you. You and Yong can work as a team—the MaxiGay team."

"Yong has met all of two portfolio managers in his three weeks here. Three weeks—that's his entire career in investment management. I don't see how he can help much with this. He's as green and naïve as they come."

"All the better. It will be a wonderful learning experience for him."

"For both of us, I'm sure," Alison said, looking haplessly at Beatrice and her three useless male peers. How could she ever explain this ludicrous project to her young portfolio analyst?

5   The Honey Boo-Boo Anomaly

B ruce Benson stared intently at his computer screen, searching for a pattern in the Quandary Capital portfolio. Was it just an amazing coincidence that nine of the twenty-three stocks had names that started with the letter O? Did the portfolio really spell something, or was it just his imagination?

He had made little progress in solving this intriguing puzzle in the week since his friend Yong had visited. Although he had promised Yong he would get to the bottom of this mystery, he saw just beneath it a far bigger one, a glaring inconsistency that demanded explanation.

Quandary Capital purported to be outperforming every other money management firm in the world because it had an immense data-gathering operation, the most powerful supercomputers, the most sophisticated quantitative investment tools, and the world's greatest assembly of brainiacs writing computer algorithms. The firm marketed itself to clients as having achieved the pinnacle of investment success by raising the bar so high no other firm could compete, using its awesome technology and brainpower to find the last opportunities to beat the market—the last anomalies. But how could its marketing pitch be legitimate if the Quandary Capital portfolio were simply designed to spell something? He examined the list of nine stocks in the portfolio that started with the letter O:

Occidental Petroleum
Office Depot
Offshore Logistic
Old National Bancorp
Olin

Omnicare
Oppenheimer
Orbitz
Owens Illinois

Only two percent of the stocks in the U.S. had names starting with the letter O, so it was statistically unlikely that thirty-nine percent of the stocks in the Quandary portfolio began with O by random chance. And with O being a vowel, someone must be forming words. But Bruce had analyzed the stocks only in this month's portfolio. What about the stocks that had been in the portfolio in earlier years?

He decided to examine the stock names in the firm's previous portfolios, dating from the beginning of Quandary Capital ten years ago, one month at a time.

Bruce quickly noticed that there had always been exactly twenty-three stocks in the portfolio, every single month. Such concentrated portfolios were common enough. It was fixing the number at twenty-three which was odd.

The next thing Bruce observed was that although the stock names changed, the number of O's never did. There had always been exactly nine stocks starting with the letter O every month without fail—for ten years.

Bruce laid out the other fourteen letters: two D's, two B's, two E's, two S's, and one T, G, N, Y, I, and H. Then he looked for those letters in all the old portfolios.

He discovered that the first letters of the other fourteen stocks had never changed—*never*.

If the number of stocks was always twenty-three and all their initial letters were always the same, then the words the portfolio spelled must always be the same. This must be a code, a permanent, unchanging one. What did those letters spell?

It mattered *that* the letters spelled something—which by itself was an extremely peculiar thing for a portfolio to do—but did it matter *what* they spelled? It mattered because this was by far the best-performing stock portfolio in the country, the envy of the investment industry. Yet its stellar returns seemed to be based on spelling a bunch of words—exactly the same words every month—just using different stocks.

For this investment method to actually work would be a flagrant violation of all financial theory. As everyone knew, returns to stocks were based on earnings. Outperforming the market, or "generating alpha" in the parlance of investment management, was supposed to require somehow getting some superior information about a stock's value or earnings growth other investors did not have. To find this information, tens of thousands of stock market analysts around the world were beating their brains out to get the minutest advantage over all the others, which was why the market had become so efficient and alpha was so scarce. This being so, how could a mere string of words, a code made up of twenty-three letters, be the basis of a stock market anomaly?

It mattered to Bruce. Yes, it mattered—most of all because he was obsessively curious. His mind never rested when presented with an intellectual challenge like this one. He simply could not let it go. If only he knew what the magic market-beating words were.

Using Quandary Capital's awesome computing power, he could write a program to form the twenty-three letters into groups of distinct words the computer could recognize, cross-checking the words against a dictionary. But what if the words weren't English? They could be foreign words, or maybe names. And what about word order? A lot of nonsensical word combinations would be found. Even with the limitation that there be nine O's, two D's and so forth, there would be a vast number of word sequences. He needed a better way to reduce the possibilities.

Bruce got up to take a break from his research and stretch his long legs. He ambled down the corridor of cubicles, across the entire floor of the building, striding past the open door of an empty conference room, where he glimpsed his tall, grim Austrian boss, Dr. Otto Feiersinger, who was pouring himself a cup of coffee just as his cell phone rang. Trying not to spill his coffee as he reached for his phone, Feiersinger was too preoccupied to notice Bruce walking by at just that moment.

"Honey Boo-Boo!" exclaimed Feiersinger in his German accent, within earshot of Bruce. "So how was your trip to New York, my darling? Oh, yes, I missed you too, Honey Boo-Boo. Now don't fart again, Honey Boo-Boo! Ha ha!"

Bruce could hear some indistinct conversation about a shopping trip Feiersinger's wife had taken to Manhattan, and then something about her visit to an old friend in Queens. Not wanting to be caught eavesdropping on his boss, he walked to the office kitchen and got a soft drink.

He stopped to think for a moment. *HONEY BOO-BOO. Eleven letters. It has a lot of O's in it—five of them! Besides that, it has the letters H, N, E, Y, and two B's!* All eleven letters would fit neatly within the pattern he had just been analyzing. Dr. Feiersinger was the head quant at the firm and one of the two co-founders. Surely he must know the twenty-three-letter code. As the inventor of the firm's investment process, he must know everything about it. If anyone was spelling something with the Quandary Capital portfolio, it must be the dour Austrian quant himself.

Bruce wondered what the probability was that eleven randomly picked letters would match such a specific pattern of twenty-three letters. He went back to his desk and calculated the odds.

They were infinitesimal! Suddenly Bruce imagined that he might have stumbled onto something big: Hearing Feiersinger say HONEY BOO-BOO was not a coincidence. It meant something. It could be the Rosetta Stone he was looking for.

Perhaps HONEY BOO-BOO was part of the code of twenty-three letters—maybe the first eleven letters. HONEY BOO-BOO was clearly a nickname for a person—Feiersinger's wife. But what did Feiersinger mean by "Don't fart again"? Could it just be a simple request by Feiersinger for her not to cut the cheese? No, his boss was far too deep and complex a man for that. What was the farting really about? There were no F's, A's, or R's among the twenty-three letters, so the word FART was clearly not part of the code. The farting, he deduced, must bear some essential relationship to HONEY BOO-BOO herself.

Bruce conjectured that the farting might explain the words "BOO-BOO." Feiersinger's wife must have farted at some very memorable moment, earning her the endearing sobriquet HONEY BOO-BOO. Evidently, it was Feiersinger's pet nickname for her. Bruce chuckled at the thought.

As hard as it was to imagine, even the nerdiest quant could be foolishly romantic, as Bruce knew from his own awkward experiences with women. Some quants were like a pent-up fissionable atom with a tightly wrapped nucleus held together by powerful inhibitions. If these were ever removed for any reason, the quant could transform like a split atom into the biggest romantic fool in all the world, unleashing a whirlwind of uncontrollable passion. It had happened to Bruce once in high school with Betty Beethauser in the back seat of his father's car, and then again in college with Milly Molinari during spring break in Cancun, so it might even have happened to Feiersinger, as implausible as it seemed. Maybe HONEY BOO-BOO was the seductress who had made it happen.

Bruce knew that if the words HONEY BOO-BOO were truly part of the stock market anomaly behind Quandary Capital's phenomenal success as an investment firm, that fact would have explosive implications. It would turn the investment world on its head. It would overthrow fundamental investment theories such as the Efficient Market Hypothesis and the Capital Asset Pricing Model—the very cornerstones of modern finance. It would mock the highbrow professors of finance in the ivory towers of the University of Chicago, those smug pooh-bahs with their neatly clipped beards and Nobel prizes who had created the theories on which investors around the world staked their fortunes. But there it was right in front of him nonetheless, both impossible and undeniable at the same time, a true quandary. Somehow, buying stocks that fit this unchanging code referring to the flatulent wife of one of Quandary Capital's two genius founders had beaten every other money manager out there. Bruce saw that through a combination of luck and rigorous deductive reasoning he had uncovered the holy grail of investment management, an anomaly—the HONEY BOO-BOO anomaly. It did not make any sense. It did not have to. In the unforgiving world of investing, where every theory must prove itself or die, it worked!

But Bruce also realized that HONEY BOO-BOO was not just a woman, an anomaly, and a revolution in investing—it was a scandal of monumental proportions. The anomaly belied everything Quandary Capital was telling its clients about its technological prowess. The firm's marketing pitch must all be a colossal fraud designed to dupe gullible clients into believing they should pay stratospheric fees for the privilege of investing in what they were told was a high-powered investment process. The firm's much-vaunted supercomputers, 175 PhDs, two Rhodes scholars, three Nobel laureates, and their incomprehensible computer algorithms were mere window dressing concealing the biggest financial scam since Bernie Madoff's split-strike conversion strategy. Quandary

Capital's real secret sauce was the HONEY BOO-BOO anomaly, perhaps the last surviving trick for beating the stock market—for generating alpha. Rarer than the most precious diamond, the HONEY BOO-BOO anomaly was a gem of incalculable value.

But even with this earthshaking insight, Bruce knew he had only part of the anomaly. There were still twelve letters left to decipher. What words did they spell? HONEY BOO-BOO *what*? Those letters must describe something critically important about Feiersinger's gaseous wife. The stocks themselves changed monthly, so he could not predict which twenty-three would be in the portfolio the next month, only what their first letters would be. Perhaps, if he could decipher the remaining words, he would also learn how the stocks themselves were picked to spell those words.

Bruce decided to write a computer program to crack the rest of the HONEY BOO-BOO code, the twelve remaining letters, using the firm's supercomputers. To this effort he resolved to commit the bulk of his spare time. When he had more information, he would report his findings to his friend Yong at Vain Capital.

As Bruce examined the twenty-three letters of the code, a tiny camera embedded in the wall outside his cubicle was capturing and transmitting the image on his computer screen. In a windowless room on the floor above, Dr. Ozturk and Dr. Feiersinger stood gazing at one of dozens of monitors aimed at their captive army of quant researchers.

Ozturk frowned, the furrows in his elongated forehead folding like an accordion as his dark eyes began to simmer with anger. "It appears Mr. Bruce Benson has been studying our old portfolios with an interest in discovering our secret."

Feiersinger stroked his grey beard. "*Ach*, look there, he has noticed that the first letters of our stocks never change. You can see on the screen he has isolated the twenty-three letters. A very bad sign, indeed. His mind is probing for answers. We must watch this one much more carefully."

"He might try using our supercomputers to find the anomaly, like the last one did," Dr. Ozturk speculated. "Americans! Nothing but trouble. They simply won't obey rules. I told you we shouldn't hire any more of them. We learned that lesson with the NASA scientists, remember?

Quants from wretched places are much less likely to poke around in our business, knowing we'll ship them back where they came from."

"But we must have a few Americans around, Mustafa," Feiersinger said. "A staff of only foreigners holding green cards might raise suspicions at the SEC. There are some Americans who can still do math. And even a few of our foreign quants have gone bad."

"Yes, I suppose you're right," Ozturk conceded. "That reminds me, have you heard from Disposo about the status of our Chinese runaway?"

"No," Feiersinger said, "but we are hot on his trail. Last we heard he is hiding out in Shanghai. Disposo is closing in on him fast."

"And then the Mind Melter will be administered."

"Yes," confirmed Feiersinger, "and that will be the end of the nosy Mr. Bao."

6 Bludinov's Message

A convoy of eighty green trucks started rolling slowly through Ivangorod toward the Estonian border at four o'clock on Sunday morning. Pavel Demyonovich, wearing a black face mask, rode near the back of the convoy in a canvas-covered troop transport truck. He searched for some sign of consciousness among his fellow Russian soldiers, but most of them were fast asleep, their masked heads resting on each other's shoulders as they slumped against the sides of the truck. He noticed that Sergei Petrovsky was still awake, and he was near enough the small window in the back to see out.

"Sergei, can you see anything? Where we are going?" Demyonovich asked.

Petrovsky peeked out the window. "I think we must be in Ivangorod by now, but I can see only a little of where we have just been," he answered. He saw a manned gatehouse and a line of razor wire receding behind them. A sign along the highway warned they were in a prohibited zone and any intruders would be shot. The truck exited the highway, made a few turns, and squealed to a stop.

A sergeant barked an order at the men to get out.

Demyonovich scrambled toward the back of the truck and jumped down to the ground. He looked around in the darkness. Surrounding them on all sides were crenelated stone walls more than forty feet high, interrupted over their long expanse by towers with conical spires. A couple of small white churches with domed roofs huddled in the middle of the vast interior of the walls. They were inside a castle.

"Ivangorod Fortress, built by Ivan the Great in 1492 on the Narva River to secure Russia's right of access to the sea," he said, reading a sign in the moonlight.

The trucks arriving behind them were parking in long rows. Dozens of masked soldiers were unloading boxes from supply trucks that had backed up to temporary storage buildings. Demyonovich's squad was directed toward one of the supply trucks.

"Unload that one," a sergeant yelled out to them, pointing to it.

Demyonovich scrambled into the truck, lugging boxes to the rear and stacking them up so the soldiers behind him could place them on a forklift. The truck was piled to the ceiling with boxes. Markings indicated that they contained AK-47s, rocket launchers, and ammunition.

"There must be enough weapons on this one truck to supply dozens of men for a good while," he said to Petrovsky, who was handing him a box of AK-47 rounds. He looked around at all the trucks that had rolled into the fortress. "I wonder what Estonia has done wrong. They must have been very bad," he said with a laugh.

Petrovsky shrugged. "It's Bludinov plotting again, of course. He's a terribly crafty fellow, our president. A few thousand little green men in masks showing up on the Estonian border can do wonders for an unhelpful attitude. The Estonians will remember what happened in eastern Ukraine when the little green men appeared. So will the Americans."

"Do you think he will actually have us attack Narva? Estonia is a NATO country."

Petrovsky passed Demyonovich a box of rocket launchers. "All the better. Bludinov wants to cripple NATO. The Estonians should not have joined it. We warned them not to. And the Americans need to be taught a lesson about encroaching on the Russian border and provoking us."

"But why do you suppose the generals picked this old fortress for storing supplies? It's just a big open area with stone walls around it. The Americans can easily see it with their satellites. In no time they will detect these storage buildings and all this military hardware rolling in."

"You are so naïve, Pavel!" Petrovsky snickered. "Think! Why would Viktor Bludinov, a master strategist and schemer and the nastiest bastard alive, place military supplies for thousands of soldiers in a medieval fortress easily visible by satellite right smack on the Russian border with Estonia?"

"I have no idea," said Demyonovich, pausing for a moment before laying a box of AK-47 rounds onto the pile. "Ah, I know, to be seen?"

"Yes, of course, you idiot. This old castle is not defensible. It's a symbol from our history, from a time when we projected the power of Great Russia, secured our frontiers, and demanded respect from the world. Bludinov wants the Americans to see us. He is sending them a message."

"What is Bludinov's message?"

"Get lost, I think. Get out of our neighborhood. Or up yours. Something appropriately rude like that."

"Well, if Bludinov wants so damn badly for everything to be seen, he might have been thoughtful enough to let us unload these trucks at midday instead of at this ungodly hour. I would have been only too happy to look up and smile for the American satellites in broad daylight," Demyonovich said with a yawn. "He is a strange fellow, that Bludinov. I hope the Americans do get his message before we have to do this all over again tomorrow night. All I want to get is some sleep."

7   Nattering in Baltimore

As Alison drove her blue BMW convertible up the interstate high-way from Washington to Baltimore, Yong was struggling to understand the logic of the CRAM mandate.

"No joke? We gonna invest with managers just because they're queer?" he asked.

"That's the idea," Alison said. "The governor of California wants to reach out to the gay community. This is her way of being socially responsible. She wants to spread money around to strengthen her political base and win the election."

"Whose money is it?"

"Taxpayer money, technically. Dedicated to paying California's retired employees their pensions."

"Taxpayer money, but not invested for taxpayers? Is it proper?"

"It's legal, if that's what you mean," Alison said, not sure what Yong was getting at. "I wouldn't say it's proper. In fact, I'm pretty sure it's not. Lots of things are legal that aren't proper. Most things, I think."

"Principle of economics say for property to be invested for highest value it must be invested for highest and best use."

Alison chuckled at Yong's childlike sincerity. "Economics? Where did you get that idea?"

"College textbook. Economics 101."

"I think you may be confusing economics with philosophy. The two have nothing to do with each other," Alison said. "In America taxpayer money is misspent by politicians and bureaucrats for some misguided social benefit, or their own careers. That's our principle. How do things work in Korea?"

"The same. Except in North Korea after they take your money they kill you anyway."

"There you go. There's your universal principle: don't give money to politicians."

"Universal, yes. But is it rational?" Yong asked.

"Rational? Why do you expect things to be rational?"

"Theory of rational man is foundation of economics," Yong explained, reciting his freshman economics textbook from memory. "Man is rational economic animal called *homo economicus*—economic man. Theory say economic man make rational decisions for maximum benefit to himself. In great country like America man is free to be rational."

"Or irrational," Alison said. "Your knowledge of economics is impressive, Yong, but I'm not sure your theory applies in this case. Besides, economic homos aren't the kind we're after. We are looking for money manager homos. And I'm very afraid they won't be rational at all."

"We will find these homo managers in Baltimore?"

"Probably not, but we have to start someplace. I have to come up here once a year to visit Nattering Asset Management anyway as part of our ongoing monitoring. Maybe they will have some ideas about where to look. I sure don't."

Yong leafed through Nattering's most recent client report. "Returns seem poor last year. These guys any good?"

"I wish I could say so. Their performance has been treading water just about forever. I've been on the fence about what to do with them. One year they will get ahead of their benchmark and the next they fall behind. It's so hard to beat the market these days that a lot of money managers are becoming closet indexers, barely daring to stray from their benchmark with their stock picks for fear of underperforming and getting fired by their clients. I worry that Nattering is having such a tough time they may soon turn into a closet indexer too."

"So why not fire them now, before they go hiding into closet?"

"Because if I do I'll have to find another firm that's better, which is a very hard thing to be sure of. Nattering is the devil I know."

"Why not just invest in index?"

"We have to try to beat indexes, no matter how hard it is. No clients would pay Vain Capital's fees just to have us invest passively for them. Our clients can do that for themselves. They want more than that. They want to believe they can do better than benchmarks. Everyone wants to be above average."

"Many questions produce many answers. Leave it to me. I find out what Nattering's problem is."

"Go for it," she said. "Pummel them with questions, Yong. There's no better way for you to learn this business."

Yong gazed out the window as they entered the city. He had never been to Baltimore or seen so many slums anywhere else in America. Along the interstate, down nearly every street they passed, he glimpsed dozens of red brick rowhouses standing shoulder to shoulder, each with four or five little white steps rising from the sidewalk to the front door. Many rowhouses were boarded up. Others were crumbling, had been defaced with graffiti, or had tree limbs growing through their windows.

His eyes caught sight of an abandoned church. A white plastic sign in front proclaimed in black letters "Unless the Lord builds the house, the builders labor in vain—Psalm 127." But the builders of this neighborhood had been gone for a century, and Ebenezer Baptist Church, the last thing standing on its block, was just now being demolished by a couple of yellow backhoes. The machines had already stripped off its old slate roof. As the backhoes tore into the stubborn stone walls, the stained glass windows first shivered and then shattered to pieces. Then the whole edifice collapsed into a pile of debris. Yong wondered what higher and better use the city would make of a church.

They arrived at a gleaming new fifty-story tower in downtown Baltimore. In the penthouse Alison and Yong were greeted by Archibald Shambeau, a distinguished-looking man with a square jaw and salt-and-pepper hair who managed Nattering's large cap growth strategy for Vain Capital's clients.

He led them to a mahogany-paneled conference room with a panoramic view of Baltimore harbor. In the distance they could see dozens of sailboats cruising to and from the Chesapeake Bay.

"I admit we had a tough year, three percentage points below benchmark," Shambeau began his presentation in a confident tone of voice. "Our shortfall was due to a combination of factors. One was that we owned the wrong healthcare stocks. But our biggest problem came in the consumer staples sector when the Goody Cookie merger fell through and all the other cookie stocks dropped sharply in sympathy, including our big position in Cuckoo Cookie."

"Your cookie stocks felt sad about other cookie stocks?" Yong asked, cocking his head in sympathy.

"No, that's not what I meant by sympathy," replied Shambeau, peering skeptically over his reading glasses at the rookie portfolio analyst. "I meant the investors in those other cookie stocks were sad when the Goody Cookie merger didn't go through because that reduced the chance that their cookie stocks would also be bid up in a merger."

"Ah, I see!" Yong said. "Cuckoo Cookie investors go cuckoo when Goody Cookie merger go bad?"

"Yes, I suppose you could say that," Shambeau replied, wondering what the young Korean was up to. "It was baddy, I mean bad, for the Cuckoo Cookie investors when the Goody Cookie merger went bad, so they went cuckoo."

"I see," Yong said. "You still own Cuckoo Cookie, even after Goody go bad? You think Cuckoo's good?"

"Yes, we still favor Cuckoo Cookie for its strong earnings growth. We think it would be cuckoo, I mean inadvisable, to sell now."

"If you say it is cuckoo to sell Cuckoo, why is it not cuckoo not to buy more?"

Shambeau directed a glance at Alison, signaling it was time for her to curb her inexperienced protégé, but she just sat back with a smile and let him go. "We have all the Cuckoo Cookie we want right now given our preferred risk-return profile," the portfolio manager said flatly. "Owning more Cuckoo would be too risky, and that would be cuckoo."

"Because it is risky to have too much in cookies?"

"Yes," said Shambeau, "you could say that."

"Ah, maybe buy some milk stocks too?"

"I beg your pardon?"

"Milk and cookies. Diversify portfolio to cut risk?"

"We don't see any opportunities in dairy stocks at the moment."

"Ah, I see."

Yong had no further cookie questions.

Alison inquired about Nattering's poor results from healthcare stocks. Shambeau reacted with his usual irritating pretense of unconcern. "Oh, some of our biotech stocks disappointed last year when clinical trials for their experimental drugs showed the drugs were ineffective," he said with a shrug. "Nothing to be worried about."

"So now you saying you don't know what you doing because you pick wrong healthcare stocks?" Yong asked.

"Well, goodness no! That's not at all what I'm saying," Shambeau said, looking very startled. "I would say our holdings in healthcare were un-rewarded last year. You know, sometimes stock selection just takes a while to work."

"You mean it take long time because you slow and stupid?" Yong asked.

"No! Absolutely not! That's not what I mean," Shambeau responded at once.

"Because everybody else is slow and stupid?"

"No, I wouldn't say that either. It's very hard to beat the market. Nobody has to be slow and stupid. It just takes stock selection some time to work."

"Your stocks not performing. Somebody must be slow and stupid."

"Our stocks just need more time for their value to be realized by the market."

"How long then?" Yong asked. "You have five years so far, not good record. How we know you able to beat market? Maybe you don't know what you doing, maybe turning into closet indexer. You going into closet to be gay? Why we not just invest money in cheap index fund and save fees? What are your fees for Nattering?"

"Sixty basis points," Shambeau replied curtly.

"Wow, sound like bad deal! We can get passive index fund of large growth stocks for five basis points, save fifty-five basis points for clients and not worry any more about crummy returns or going into closet."

Shambeau glared at the young upstart. "Yes, but then Vain Capital itself would have no chance to outperform, and then how could you pretend to add any value to justify your fees to your clients? That is what Vain Capital offers, customized portfolios for mission-based clients, right? You can't beat benchmarks yourselves without having some active managers like us in your clients' portfolios. You have to add value yourselves somehow, don't you?"

"Yes," Yong admitted. "We must add value too."

"Oh, really, there's no need to worry about our performance," Shambeau said. "It always comes back. I have been in this business for twenty years and have been through many battles with the market, many ups and downs. I am like a general—a battle-hardened general with many, many medals on my chest!"

Yong pictured Shambeau as a North Korean generalissimo with golden epaulets on his shoulders, the breast of his uniform covered with dozens of colorful medals. When he was little Yong had seen such fancy generals reviewing a military parade in the great square in Pyongyang. Instantly, the memory triggered a contemptuous look on his face. "Ah, I see, now you are great big general?"

Alison, surprised by the fiery look in Yong's eyes, finally decided to intervene. "Could we meet with your healthcare analyst to ask him about his stocks?"

Flustered, Shambeau disappeared for five minutes and returned with Dr. John Bones, a slender man with curly brown hair and horn-rimmed glasses. The Nattering presentation book noted that Dr. Bones was the former assistant head of pediatrics at Johns Hopkins University Medical School.

"Why you leave top medical school to work as Nattering healthcare analyst?" Yong asked the doctor at point-blank range.

"It was a tough decision, at first," Dr. Bones replied calmly. "I had three kids in college and no chance at the top job in the pediatrics department. Nattering needed a pharmaceutical specialist. Here I have no insurance hassles, no government bureaucracy, and no sick kids to deal with. I just follow drug companies and recommend stocks to put in Archibald's portfolio. And the pay is four times what I used to make. It's worked out very well for me. Nattering beats doctoring hands down."

"So what was the problem with your stock recommendations last year?" Alison asked.

"Oh, last year was a disaster. I'm very frustrated about my stocks," Dr. Bones admitted. "In the case of Geneton Labs, their genetic anti-baldness drug HairGain seemed very promising until a new study revealed that it causes permanent impotence, which may limit its appeal for men."

"Impotence?" Yong interrupted. "What is that?"

"You know," Bones replied with a smile, holding his index finger out straight and letting it go limp.

"Ah, old man disease," Yong said. "We have that in Korea too. You are right—much better to let all hair fall out. Nobody gonna buy that drug."

"We also had a problem with Maximum Pharma and their breast enlargement drug, Bubivir. Its value proposition seems challenged, since it only increases breast size by a quarter inch on average, makes women poop uncontrollably, and costs a thousand dollars a month."

"That is an awful lot for a laxative," Alison said.

"And then another one of my clunkers was Healfast, a maker of splints for bone fractures, which have slumped sharply with kids no longer being allowed to risk having their feelings hurt by playing sports. Fortunately we were somewhat hedged. With the fat kid population exploding we made back most of our Healfast losses on Kidflab, a mail-order dieting and diabetic products service." Dr. Bones sighed. "It's such a tough market out there. My fourteen-year old son has a better track record than I do. He just buys the latest Internet stocks."

"We hear that a lot from our managers. They can't outperform their kids," Alison said. "Do you know of any other firms that have done well lately?"

Dr. Bones looked to Shambeau, who shook his head. "Only Quandary Capital, the super quants in Rocket City. They seem to beat everybody somehow."

"Vain Capital has money with Quandary," Alison said. "We know all about them."

No, not all about them, Yong was thinking, not about the suspiciously excessive use of O's in Quandary's portfolio.

"By the way," Alison said, "before we go, I have a question to ask you. It's nothing to do with you guys. It's a manager research question. Nothing at all to do with you. Really, I mean that."

"By all means. What's your question?"

"We have a client who wants us to find them some gay money managers. Do you know of any?"

There was a brief, awkward silence as Shambeau and Dr. Bones looked blankly at each other. Shambeau thought of Lizzie the Lezzie in the mailroom, but the only thing she managed was a postage meter. "Can't say I do, Alison. Nobody here would qualify."

"Any ideas where we should look?"

"You got me with that one," Shambeau said. "I think you'll have to find someone obvious, a real screaming queen, I would imagine. Investment managers don't normally market that they are light in the loafers. Being fruity doesn't fit our moneyed image. How many of them do you need?"

"Seven, at least."

"A tall order, I'd say. Good luck finding them."

8   A School Named Yule

In an ivy-covered brick building overlooking the leafy Yule Universi-ty quadrangle, Tony Elfuego, a sixty-year old man with a ruddy face and a mane of white hair, showed Alison and Yong to their seats and brought the meeting of the endowment committee to order.

The conference room looked like a nineteenth century gentleman's club. On one wood-paneled wall hung the imposing portraits of the institution's founder, Oscar Erickson Yule, a Swedish immigrant to the upper Midwest who had made his fortune in railroads during the Gild-ed Age and dedicated it to educating the nation's spoiled youth in a new temple of learning. Another wall displayed the framed photographs of the university's storied athletic teams. In the far corner stood Yule University's famed mascot, a life-size illuminated plastic Santa Claus, his rosy face laughing merrily as he held a football in one hand and a banner flashing the words "Yule Rules!" in the other.

Alison felt a lump in her throat as Elfuego introduced her to the twelve committee members. At the spring client conference Beatrice had excitedly told Yule's chief investment officer about Vain Capital's plans for a new fund and promised to dispatch Alison to Minneapolis in her stead to sell the idea to the entire Yule investment committee, as Elfuego wanted to hear all about it as soon as possible.

"It is intended to be a fund of gay money managers, at least one man-ager for each of the seven letters LGBTQIA," Alison explained. She wrenched her lips into a dignified smile. "It will be maximally diver-sified, sexually fluid, and gay in all dimensions, so we are calling it the MaxiGay Fund."

"Will this be a hedge fund?" asked a professor in the sociology de-partment, a thin man in his thirties, with long, straight brown hair tied up in a ponytail.

"No, it is a fund of several gay money managers from various asset classes," answered Alison. "But there may be hedge funds within the fund, depending on who we find."

The professor frowned. "Well, our students just absolutely hate hedge funds and the financial pirates who run them, and so do I," he declared flatly. "Hedge fund fees are shameful. Charging two percent of a client's assets and twenty percent of any positive return every year is a scandal. But the Yule endowment just can't seem to get enough hedge funds, for some reason I can never fathom."

Elfuego bristled at this slap in the face. Fixated like many endowment chiefs on keeping up with Yale University's top-performing endowment, he had first tried copying its investment method wholesale, adopting the so-called "Yale model" of investing. That essentially meant stuffing the endowment with hedge funds and other illiquid investments in hopes of goosing returns. The Yale model worked wonders for Yale but bombed at Yule, as Elfuego invariably picked the wrong hedge funds. When mimicking Yale's overall method failed, Elfuego planted a spy at Yale to feed him intelligence about its specific funds, hoping to ride them to victory. Time after time he found himself arriving too late in whatever innovative investment Yale had pioneered, as the first investors usually enjoyed the best returns, leaving Yule to eat the crumbs from Yale's table.

"Nonsense," said a man sitting across from the professor, "Yule does not have too many hedge funds. I would remind you, professor, that the fees I earn from my hedge fund paid for the new arts and sciences building. Did you find hedge funds so deplorable when you were moving into your fancy new office? I don't see any sociologists here buying new buildings for dear old Yule."

Immaculately dressed in a five-thousand-dollar herringbone wool suit with a white shirt and solid gold cufflinks, the man was the endowment's biggest contributor, a billionaire hedge fund manager. The sociology professor shot an angry stare back at him.

A female professor of gender studies with grayish brown hair tied up in a bun gazed dreamily at Alison through big brown glasses. "Are there going to be women money managers in the MaxiGay Fund?" she asked. "I'm happy to see there are women in charge at Vain Capital at least, if not in the senior administrative positions at this university," she said, pursing her lips.

"There will have to be at least one, a lesbian," Alison assured her.

"Well, I suppose we should be grateful for that one," the professor of gender studies grudgingly acknowledged. "More lesbians would be better, of course."

"They will have at least seven different kinds of gays in the fund," Elfuego intervened. "It's designed to be gender-fluid and diversified across the various gay species, following the letters LGBTQIA."

"Species!" repeated the black Yule vice president of student affairs. The professors drew back in horror at the slur. A hush filled the room at its utterance.

"Sorry, I meant sexual orientations," Elfuego quickly corrected himself. "Anyway, there will be whatever anybody can dream up."

"Oh, then I think you will end up with quite a lot," the sociology professor said. "We have a very active imagination for sexual orientations at Yule, especially in my department. Does the "A" stand for animalism?"

"No, I think you are thinking of bestiality," the professor of gender studies replied. "They didn't include that one. The "A" stands for asexual."

Alison breathed a sigh of relief, not fully appreciating until now that the CRAM mandate was not nearly as dreadful as it might have been. At least she would not have to find money managers who molest sheep.

"Is the "I" for incest?"

"No, that's for intersex. You know, hermaphrodites and such," Alison said.

"How about polyamorous?" suggested the sociology professor. "Got that one?"

"No," answered Alison, not at all sure what polyamorous meant, but suddenly concerned she soon might need to. "We're doing a starter set of gay categories. We might roll out some more later, depending on how all this goes."

"So it's not so inclusive, really," sneered the sociology professor. "Not so MaxiGay, after all—more of a MiniGay Fund, I'd say. Rather disappointing."

"Hold on there—be fair to them," Elfuego said in defense of his two guests. "It's the first gay money manager fund in the world. This is a major innovation, a bold first step in sexual investing. Vain Capital is in the vanguard of morality-minded investing in the whole country—you know, the moral MOM as Beatrice von Vain likes to call them. They have to walk before they can run. The best part is, Yale doesn't know about this gay fund yet, so we'd be the first endowment to have it. I think our students will love this idea."

"Well, I don't love it. I think it's a waste of time. Frankly, I'd rather see a women-only fund," the professor of gender studies complained.

"Or a black-only fund," said the vice president of student affairs.

"Not with my money!" the billionaire hedge fund manager objected. "I don't like any of these nutty ideas. Look, Elfuego, why don't you just invest for the highest return you can get and forget all this politically correct nonsense? Isn't it hard enough to beat benchmarks without all this? Lord, why do I invest in this goddamned school? I must have better uses for my money than giving it to you freaks."

At that, the conversation froze. The prospect of losing a multi-billionaire donor seized the professors and administrators as if by the throat. Their mouths puckered up as if they had been sucking lemons.

"Well, that's what I'm *trying* to do—get the best returns for Yule," Elfuego retorted.

"Not very successfully, judging by the most recent endowment performance rankings," the hedge fund manager said. "You're seventeen places behind Yale this year. I for one am convinced Yule needs more hedge funds. The fees be damned, it's higher returns we need, wherever we can get them. Where's the alpha these days? Hedge funds. With your sorry performance, I wouldn't take my job so much for granted if I were you. You're investing our endowment in vain!"

Elfuego could feel his stomach churn as he absorbed the outrage of being threatened with the loss of his job. His compensation of two million dollars was already an open wound. He ought to be worth at least half as much as Coach Bubba, the six-million-dollar Georgia cracker who crowed before television cameras about sending Yule's young men into battle on the gridiron one day a week. Elfuego was risking Yule's ten billion dollars in battle *five* days a week on global markets— without shoulder pads or helmets—and with the same even odds of victory or defeat. But whereas Coach Bubba's fifty bone-headed combatants survived every game, usually with only bruises and sprains, defeat for Yule's endowment was frequently catastrophic. In any given year, millions of Elfuego's ten billion soldiers would return horribly maimed, with half their value blown off, and others would be lost entirely. Elfuego's pay was every bit as precarious as Coach Bubba's, depending upon the cruel whims of markets, manager performance, and the financially illiterate members of this surly committee of intellectual poseurs whose evil delight it was to turn each of his most cherished investment proposals into a political food fight. At least he made a million dollars more than Yule's embattled president, and fourteen times more than the pony-tailed sociology professor. He could draw some modest satisfaction from that.

"So why can't Yule keep up with Yale?" the billionaire goaded him.

"I'll beat Yale someday. But first I need to get the damned students off my back," Elfuego insisted. "This fund is perfect for Yule, don't you see? It would take some political heat off us. A fund for gay money managers would give us visibility as a savvy, leading-edge university endowment committed to progressive values. For once we can get in before Yale."

At that moment the committee heard the approaching sound of a raucous crowd outside the building, drowning out the room's conversation. Everyone stood up to get a view of what was causing the commotion. Yong and Alison looked out the windows at the quadrangle below to view a hundred angry students shouting and carrying signs, marching toward the president's office in the building next door. Yong noticed that there were bars installed on the president's windows.

"Uh-oh," said Elfuego, "it's the crybullies. They are coming after the new president. And look, the protesters have brought the football players along with them for muscle. Quick! Lock the door!"

Elfuego's secretary rushed to the door, closed it, and turned the deadbolt.

"What's their issue?" asked Alison.

Elfuego sighed. "It looks like it's the school name this time. Yule evokes thoughts of Christmas. Surely you must have heard of the war against Christmas. As you can imagine, the war on Christmas is a very big deal here at Yule."

"Why fight Christmas?" Yong asked, looking mystified. "I like Christmas."

"They say it's not inclusive enough, offensive to non-Christians, and part of the nation's legacy of racism. They disapprove of the idea of a white, all-knowing Santa who keeps secret lists of who's naughty or nice, with no due process for appeal. They want to change the school name to something secular and non-judgmental."

The students were now milling around outside on the quadrangle, carrying signs reading "Death to Rudolph" and "Santa is a White Supremacist." One of them, a young blond man, tossed a rope over a tree branch and tied a noose around a red and white effigy of Santa Claus stuffed with straw. Another student struck a match and touched it to one of Santa's boots. The jolly old elf lit up like a torch, the orange flames consuming him from the toes up, licking at his round little belly, then setting it ablaze like a bowlful of jelly. This charred all his fur, from his head to his foot, and all his clothes were turned into ashes and soot.

Elfuego shook his head with a mix of disgust and terror. "There goes Santa Claus," he said sadly, as the burning remnants of the effigy fell to the ground with a thud. "Is nothing sacred anymore?"

"Does this happen often here?" Alison asked, surprised at how much things had changed in the few years since she had been a university student.

"Yes, on average we get a protest about every week, usually on Fridays as a warm-up for the pot and keg parties," Elfuego said, taking her and Yong aside so as not to be overheard. "The students have taken over the asylum," he whispered. "No one in the administration can stand up to them—it's much safer for our careers to give in. The slightest offense will set off a protest. I just hope we don't lose another president this year."

"What happen to last one?" Yong asked.

Elfuego sighed. "President Tweedy was booted out by Coach Bubba and his boys when the team refused to play in any bowl games unless their demands were met. Do you have any idea how much money the university makes on a bowl game? A lot more than it makes on a president, I can tell you! The television broadcast rights alone are worth ten presidents. We don't dare challenge the football team—they can bring the alumni down on our heads. And of course that's where contributions to the endowment come from."

The presentation to the committee was over. Alison and Yong left the conference room and walked next door to the president's office to witness the growing uproar.

They saw a young white woman with brown hair flowing over her shoulders screaming profanities at a black man with a mustache. She began to shake her fist at him menacingly. The man backed away from her, raising both hands in surrender.

"You're the Dean of Humanities, do something! Yule is oppressive to atheists!" she shrieked at him, gesticulating wildly. "What about us non-Christians? Every year we have to put up with endless months of Christmas this and Santa that. Why can't you people understand the alienation we feel when sleigh bells and reindeer and tinsel and candy canes and fruitcakes and HO-HO-HO are constantly thrust in our faces? Do you ever consider how these micro-aggressions make an atheist feel deep down? At Yule there's no safe space from Santa, no refuge from Rudolph! The very name of this school is an act of violence against non-believers, an emotional trigger, a year-round reminder of our oppression by insensitive capitalist greed-heads and tyrannical holiday-makers. The name's gotta go!"

A chorus of students began to chant in unison, over and over: "YULE'S NOT COOL! RENAME OUR SCHOOL!"

The students began to surround the dean in a circle. One of them, the blond football player who had strung up the Santa effigy, tied the dean's arms with a rope. Then he gagged the dean with a Yule tee shirt with a smiling Frosty the Snowman emblazoned on it and bound him fast to a tree trunk.

"Hang him!" shouted one of the students. The football player formed another rope into a noose and threw one end over a tree branch.

As the noose dangled before the dean's face, the young woman brandished her fist at him again, this time just inches away. "WHERE'S MY SAFE SPACE?" she bellowed, her voice reverberating across the campus. "A university is supposed to be a safe, nurturing environment for everyone!" She paced back and forth in front of the gagged man, his eyes wide open with terror as he tried to grunt an apology. "We demand that Yule provide a safe space for atheists!"

"And anarchists!" a masked student added.

Yong turned to Alison in great alarm. "I do not understand. American students have such great freedom. Why use it for this? These students were tricked to come to a school named Yule?"

"No, that's not it. These are crybullies. They are testing their freedom by forcing adults to submit to their demands. Submission of the adults is their goal—the grievance itself is unimportant and could change tomorrow. The students assume a real adult will stop them eventually, like they would a screaming baby."

"They want to be treated like babies? But then they will lose their freedom."

"Sort of. The game is to see how far they can bully the adults into accommodating them."

"But nobody is stopping them."

"No, that's the problem. On a college campus there are no adults anymore. College is a refuge from adulthood. You ought to understand. You were a refugee."

"Yes, I was refugee, but only to gain freedom. Losing freedom, it is not small thing to play with, believe me," Yong said. "They do not know what losing freedom means. They must respect their freedom."

Suddenly, for the millionth time in his life, he recalled a man's image. It was his father in handcuffs, as always being led away by soldiers to a North Korean slave labor camp, looking back at his wife and six-year-old son for the last time. Yong could feel a suppressed rage straining to break its bonds within him.

"I will stop them. I will save their freedom for them," he said, clenching his teeth.

Before Alison could say a word, Yong walked out of the crowd and approached the bound dean of humanities. He removed the gag and proceeded to untie him from the tree.

"Hey, what are you doing? Get that kid!" yelled the young woman.

The blond football player immediately rushed over. He shoved Yong to the ground with a flick of his huge arm.

Yong leapt to his feet, dusted off his suit, wheeled around on one leg and with the other delivered an explosive Taekwondo kick, striking the football player squarely in the chest and hurling his two hundred and eighty pounds violently backward several feet, where he landed on the grass, sprawling on his backside. He began to whimper in pain from the deep bruise on his chest.

Astonished at the power of the little Asian, the crowd of students took a step back. Alison, suddenly remembering the item on Yong's resume about his winning an Olympic gold medal in Taekwondo, was in shock. Her little assistant was a master of martial arts, with a murderous look on his face.

Yong glowered at the mob as he continued to untie the dean. "All of you, go! Crazy bastards, get out of here!" he yelled at them with a wave of his hand. "You get no freedom by taking it from others!"

The young woman who had been screaming at the dean simply stood there, seemingly at a loss as to how to respond. The leaderless mob began to disperse.

"This not American! Not American!" Yong shouted at them, the tears streaming down his cheeks.

9   The Flight From Rocket City

One morning, upon arriving at his cubicle, Bruce Benson took a thumb drive out of his pocket and plugged it into his office computer.

Twelve letters of the HONEY BOO-BOO anomaly were still undeciphered: OOOOIESSDDGT. To make sense of them, he had spent two weeks of his spare time writing a decoding program on his home computer.

Bruce had a hunch the letters spelled English words. They might be foreign words or just random gibberish, of course. But since the letters HONEY BOO-BOO referred to Dr. Feiersinger's wife, it seemed the remaining twelve letters must also have something to do with her.

There were more than a million words in the English language. Isolating all the ones that could be made out of the letters OOOOIESSDDGT and fit grammatically in a sentence would take enormous computer processing power. But there, at his fingertips, Bruce had access to the mightiest supercomputers in the world.

He would start by searching for verbs. Bruce uploaded his program from the thumb drive into the Quandary Capital computer system. It leapt into action, extracting English verbs from OOOOIESSDDGT and displaying them on his screen: IS, GOT, GET, GETS, GOES, DIE, DIES, DOES, DIED, TIED, TIES, SAG, SAGS, SIDE, SIDES, SIT, SITS, SITE, SITES, ….

Any of these verbs could be part of the HONEY BOO-BOO code. The supercomputers would have to match each one with all the possible words formed from the remaining letters. But each wrong verb opened up whole avenues of false leads. To focus on the most likely ones, Bruce had written his program to analyze word combinations which not only formed sentences but made sense. For example, he knew that HONEY BOO-BOO was alive, so the program would eliminate DIE, DIES, and DIED. As the words spilled onto the screen before him, Bruce considered how they might fit into a sentence: HONEY BOO-BOO IS...., HONEY BOO-BOO GETS....., HONEY BOO-BOO GOES....., HONEY BOO-BOO DOES...., HONEY BOO-BOO SITS...."

Watching the word permutations form, Bruce wondered whether HONEY BOO-BOO might be the object of the verb instead of the subject. That possibility alone doubled the number of potential answers. Even with Quandary Capital's supercomputers, this would take time.

But there was no time left, for at that very moment a new e-mail arrived in Dr. Feiersinger's inbox. It had been sent by the Quandary Capital security system. The subject line shouted in red capital letters "ALERT: SECURITY VIOLATION TYPE 12 DETECTED IN CUBICLE 671."

Feiersinger reached for his telephone and called Dr. Ozturk. "Mustafa, we have a security violation. It is Bruce Benson. I will see you in the security office in five minutes."

Quandary Capital's two co-founders gathered before the television screens in the windowless room on the seventh floor. A camera trained on cubicle 671 showed the list of letter combinations forming on Bruce's screen.

"See his program there? He is using our system to match words against the first letters of the names of our stocks," Feiersinger snarled. "I will take a look inside his program."

Feiersinger pressed a button on a computer keyboard. The coding of Bruce's program suddenly appeared. Feiersinger studied the screen, scrolling down hundreds of lines of code, finally reaching a subroutine rearranging letters into words. "There it is!" he said. "He is only working on the letters OOOOIESSDDGT. Then he must have the rest of the letters already. Which ones? Let's see... *Ach*, HONEY BOO-BOO!"

Ozturk looked perplexed, his dark eyes squinting at the screen. "How could this happen again? How could he possibly know that silly nickname you gave Minnie?"

"Silly nickname?" Feiersinger said. "You think it is silly, do you? How silly can it be? Has it not made us filthy stinking rich?"

He was right, of course. Ozturk's mind drifted to the fateful day more than a decade ago when both he and Feiersinger were working at the Harbison hedge fund in New York. Feiersinger, a designer of esoteric quant models, came to him in a flurry of excitement, breathless with the news that he had discovered a most unusual stock market anomaly. The Austrian PhD in physics explained how he had fallen madly in love with an irresistible young woman named Minnie. The day after a night of torrid sex during which Minnie had farted, Feiersinger was so enraptured by the experience that he commemorated the occasion by playfully designing a portfolio of twenty-three stocks using the first letters of words he had cried out in the heat of passion. The mock portfolio, to Feiersinger's utter amazement, generated returns far in excess of those of any strategy he had ever been able to devise before using standard quant models. He attributed this irrational effect to the transforming power of love. To exploit Feiersinger's discovery, the two men immediately quit their hedge fund jobs and set up Quandary Capital. To this day Ozturk remained astonished that the anomaly—an affront to the very logic of investing—worked at all, and even more so that it had made them both billionaires. But on the heels of their phenomenal success came a quandary: how to keep their secret out of the hands of the young quant geniuses whom Quandary Capital needed as a cover to fool their clients into believing they were running a highly sophisticated quant process for which they should be paid exorbitant fees.

"Who knows how Benson found out?" Feiersinger said. "Maybe he has tapped our phones. What difference does it make? We cannot let anyone know that our portfolio's success comes from a simple string of twenty-three letters! It will ruin us! We will be the laughingstock of the investment world."

Ozturk nodded. "Worse than that, we will go to jail for fraud for the rest of our lives. We have to stop him now, before he finds out any more. Benson must go! Out with him!"

Two minutes later, Bruce turned and saw three beefy security guards appear at cubicle 671.

"Mr. Benson," announced one of the guards, "Dr. Ozturk has asked us to escort you to his office."

Bruce, realizing he had been caught, was seized by fear. To this point he had lived an almost unblemished life, except for the cowtipping incident. That was the time when as a bored teenager he and his buddies had been caught upending his father's heifers just to prove that cow-tipping was not just an urban legend and that with sufficient leverage four thin boys could overcome fifteen hundred pounds of bovine inertia after all. It had taken months to live down that scandal.

This offense was unquestionably worse. The three jug-headed guards marched Bruce to Feiersinger's office, where both founders were waiting. The heavy door slammed behind him, as the guards stood outside to bar entry to anyone.

Feiersinger scowled at the lanky American. Bruce stood before him, hanging his head in shame.

"Mr. Benson, you have violated the terms of your employment agreement! You agreed in writing not to steal our company secrets. We have recorded every keystroke you have made on your computer, we have video of you entering your code into our computer systems and the code itself. We know exactly what you are up to. What do you have to say for yourself?"

Bruce could think of nothing. In trying to decipher the HONEY BOO-BOO code, he had committed a flagrant act of industrial espionage, and Feiersinger had the proof. He stood in silence for a moment. "Sorry, I didn't mean any harm. I wasn't going to steal anything. Really, I was just curious to know how it all worked. My curiosity got the better of me."

"Curiosity! Thievery is more like it! You are terminated—as of this minute," Ozturk said, his eyes smoldering with anger. "You will be escorted out of the building at once. Your possessions will be mailed to your home address. Quandary Capital will pursue you for any further violations of your employment agreement. Don't think for a moment you can abscond with our proprietary secrets and get away with it. We will track you down to the ends of the earth. You know we have the will and means to do it. We have done it before."

Ozturk motioned to the security guards through the glass window of his office. They opened the door and stripped Bruce of his security badge, then walked him to the elevator, rode down with him to the first floor, and saw him past the security desk.

Bruce looked around the first floor lobby, bewildered. One minute he had been working away in his cubicle and the next he was in oblivion, cast out into the cruel world of unemployment, bereft of income, deeply indebted, disgraced, and alone. *What a miserable fool I am*, he rebuked himself. *For this I left MIT.*

With no other idea of what to do, Bruce decided to return to his apartment.

Driving there in his car, he suddenly focused his attention on a black van with tinted glass. It had appeared in his rear view mirror several blocks back and seemed to be following him. He could just make out the face of the driver, a man with slicked-back hair like Elvis Presley. Bruce took a right turn to see whether the black van would turn with him. It did. He took a few more turns, ending up on the same highway he had been on. The black van turned with him each time.

Bruce noticed a Florida state police cruiser parked along the highway and pulled over in front of it, daring his pursuer to follow him to the police. The van sped away and disappeared into the traffic. Bruce continued on to his apartment.

He rushed inside and locked both the doorknob and the dead-bolt. Then he called Vain Capital.

"They fired me, Yong!" Bruce yelled into the telephone. "I figured out some of what they're doing, and now they're after me. Their secret is worth billions. They'll do anything to silence me!"

Yong remembered his conversation with Dr. Ozturk about the former Quandary Capital employee pursued all the way to Tibet, and the suspiciously unfortunate Ukrainian employee who had lost his mind. The former refugee did not hesitate to offer his aid, knowing only too well what it was like to be hunted. "Not safe to hang around Rocket City," Yong said. Come here now—I hide you."

Bruce hurriedly packed a suitcase and drove to Orlando, where he managed to get on the very next flight to Washington.

A couple of hours later, Alison and Yong were summoned to a meeting with Beatrice. Almost a month had passed since the man from CRAM had brought the MaxiGay mandate to Vain Capital. The Queen Bea wanted a progress report.

"There's been no progress, Bea," Alison said with a nervous groan. "I've run into dead-ends everywhere. I've contacted all of our current managers—none of them has the slightest idea where to look. We've searched our manager database from end to end. It doesn't identify firms by sexual orientation, so it's useless. Yong says there's nothing about any gay money managers in any of the trade journals. We have no idea what to do next."

She glared at Henry, Roger, and Thor, sitting there so smugly and avoiding the MaxiGay project with all their might. "Hey, isn't there something these guys could do to help out?" she demanded.

"You and Yong must have done a bang-up job in Minneapolis, dear," Beatrice replied excitedly. "I got a call yesterday from Tony Elfuego at Yule University, asking when we will be opening the MaxiGay Fund. He made me promise not to breathe a word about it to Yale. He's positive the MaxiGay Fund will be all the rage at the universities—says he's 'hot to invest with the homos.' I knew this fund would be a big hit on campus!"

"Bea, listen to me, we can't deliver on your promises. We can't even find garden variety gay money managers, your basic limp-wristed hairdresser types," Alison insisted. "How will we ever find the more advanced varieties like transgenders and hermaphrodites? I don't have the slightest idea where to go."

"Have you visited any bars?" asked Beatrice. "That is where they hang out, isn't it? It was, in my day. All the nelly boys went there. Of course, we never went anywhere near those places, but we vaguely knew they existed somewhere in the seedy parts of town."

"No, I haven't resorted to that yet," Alison admitted, leery of Beatrice's insane idea of wandering into gay bars to ask total strangers if they knew of any gay money managers. How could that possibly work? Was this in her job description?

"Well, if as you say there's no other information about where they might be, we have to go where we know they actually are, don't we, dear?" Beatrice said in a sweet voice.

She finally perceived the resistance in Alison's face. "Without this fund," she said, looking at her investment officers one by one, "Butcher and Weedle are likely to sell us out. What a tragedy that would be when we have clients like Yule practically beating down our door to go gay! If the managers are not conveniently listed somewhere, we just need to do some original research and make our own list. We have to go to them, wherever that is. I don't care if that's Fairyland. Just get on a plane and go there, and quickly for God's sake. We haven't got much time."

"We're going to gay bars then, Yong," Alison said with a sigh.

"To Fairyland?" Yong asked, looking confused. The only Fairyland he had heard of was in Disneyland, where he had once seen Tinker Bell herself, wearing an emerald green dress with a pair of lace wings sprouting from her back, waving her wand and smiling irrepressibly at the tourists. She seemed perfectly harmless.

"No, San Francisco. Where better to find them?"

10 The Curious Guide

Bruce showed up at Yong's door lugging two suitcases crammed with all his clothes. The little apartment building on Lee Street in Alexandria, Virginia, was nestled inconspicuously in an enclave of exclusive townhouses built in the old city's colonial era. The sidewalks were paved with mossy old bricks and smelled of history.

"This is an interesting neighborhood. How did you find this place?" Bruce asked.

"I see Lee on street sign—in Korea it is good luck to live on street with one's name on it," Yong replied. "Landlord in big hurry to rent, give me good deal."

"The Lee family of Virginia lived around here," Bruce said. "A sign on the way into town said Alexandria was the boyhood home of Robert E. Lee, the great Confederate general."

"Then it is a great street! Now it is home for Lee Yong."

Yong offered Bruce the pull-out sofa in the apartment's den. Bruce began to unpack, recounting how his investigation into the peculiar investing practices of Quandary Capital had gone so awry that he had to flee for his life.

Yong scratched his head. "So Quandary Capital just fooling everybody?"

"That's right," Bruce confirmed. "I didn't have time to get all of the code before they caught me, but I know their operation is a total sham, except their HONEY BOO-BOO anomaly, which is worth a vast fortune. That's why they're after me—I'm a big security risk to them now. To protect their secret, they need to eliminate me."

"How long can you hide? They chased that other guy to Tibet."

"I don't know," Bruce said. "They already sent a goon after me in Rocket

City. They're sure to find me sooner or later. And that will be the end."

"You need disguise," Yong said. "Make you look like somebody they never look for, somebody your own mother never know."

"What could that be?"

Yong's face suddenly lit up like a match. "Ah, yes! I have crazy idea! Crazy idea!"

"What?"

Yong explained the MaxiGay project to him. "My lady boss, she gotta find queer money managers fast!"

"So you need to hire seven gay money managers?" Bruce asked. "Okay, but what does that have to do with me?"

"Your mother! We make you look like her! You become queer money manager," Yong said, his eyes gleaming with excitement. "Quandary Capital never find you looking like woman. Then you get job at firm somewhere as queer money manager and Vain Capital hire you."

Bruce looked at Yong like he had two heads. "Are you nuts? I couldn't dress up as a woman. I don't know anything about gay or transgendered people. Look at me. I'm as tall and ugly as a moose. Nobody would ever believe I'm a woman."

"Ah, for this, ugly is best. No need to be pretty woman—just man trying to look like woman. Nobody expect you to look real."

Bruce rolled his eyes and began to turn away. "Oh, be serious. No way. Maybe I can hide in Canada or Mexico or South America. That should buy me a few months at least."

"You too easy to find like you are. Soon the crazy bastards will hunt you down," Yong insisted. "Better to live as woman than die as man."

"Did Confucius really say that?"

"No, I say that. Obvious common sense. Better to stand up in dress for while than lie down in coffin forever."

"Oh, that's not fair—now you are just making up your own sayings," Bruce said. "How would I find a job as a transgendered money manager? What firm would hire me?"

"Maybe you get job as quant at Quandary Capital. Maybe they need to fill transgender quant quota."

"There's no such thing. And I can't go back to Quandary Capital. They wouldn't hire a transgender. Also, if I went back there and they recognized me, then I'd be done for."

"Okay, then maybe Vain Capital hire you. My lady bosses sound pretty damn desperate. Maybe they willing to put you in business and hire you to solve their problem."

"Would they help me set up my own firm?"

"Why not? They need transgender to run billion-dollar portfolio. Any kind of strategy is okay. You start firm. Vain Capital hire your firm. You live. Vain Capital live. Bosses happy. I keep job. You get job, pay off student loans. Many problems solved. Everybody happy."

There was a long pause as Bruce mulled the issues.

"Alison Hartswell run MaxiGay project. You get to work with her," Yong pointed out.

Bruce began to see the mad genius in Yong's suggestion. At this early stage in his investment management career he had not considered launching his own firm, thinking it might be something he would do after gaining several years of experience, if the entrepreneurial urge struck him. But the urge to stay alive had just now struck him first, followed by another urge.

"Alison Hartswell?"

"Yes. Every day."

"I think it's nutty as hell," Bruce said. "How do we do it?

"We get clothes and shoes and dress you up. Then I take you to work and show you to my lady bosses."

Bruce looked in the mirror. "I'm six foot four. Where can we get women's clothes to fit me?"

"Internet, where else? No need to take risk of being seen outside apartment now. We buy disguise online. Then we take you outside as woman. Neighbors will think I have tall ugly girlfriend."

Yong started his computer, opened the search engine, and typed in the words, "transgender woman clothes." A list of websites appeared. Yong clicked on one listed as "Fabqueen.com."

Crossdressing accessories spilled across the screen: dresses, skirts, blouses, wigs, high-heeled shoes in men's sizes, pumps, foam rubber breast forms with nipples, corsets, drag queen jewelry, makeup kits, stockings, and pantyhose for men. Yong noticed a link to something called "Butt and Hip Builder."

"You got no hips. You gonna need woman hips." Yong clicked on the link. Up popped pictures of men's underwear with silicone pads attached to the sides and back. The accompanying advertising copy promised to deliver instant feminine curves: "Our silicone-filled pads are designed just for men to turn themselves into a curvy gal. Our patented Butt and Hip Builder will add several sexy inches to your butt and hips to create the perfect female figure."

Peering over Yong's shoulder, Bruce saw a link to The World's Finest Genital-Hiding Gaff. "What the hell is a gaff?" Bruce asked.

Yong clicked on the link. A dozen photos of thong-like underwear appeared. The advertisement explained that a gaff was a kind of extremely tight jock strap worn by the serious drag queen to hide his member underneath his crotch. Gaffs were available in pink, raspberry, black, purple, and zebra stripes, and in waist sizes from twenty-eight to fifty inches.

"Yikes!" Bruce cried out. "And I thought briefs were confining. Let's pass on the gaff. No need to become a eunuch for this gig. Can't we just cover it all up? They must have a starter costume."

Yong ordered only what seemed to constitute a single outfit: a blond wig, a Butt and Hip Builder, breast forms, a pair of pantyhose, a long loosely fitting blue dress with a high neck, a pair of black high heel shoes, and a makeup kit. "We see if this works first," said Yong. "Then we take you to Vain Capital. If they buy idea, we buy more stuff."

"My God, that's four hundred dollars!" Bruce exclaimed, seeing the total on the screen. "Does it really cost this much to become a woman?"

"Sex never come cheap," Yong replied. "Sex change even more expensive. Only need one set of butt and breast each—one-time investment. Not a lot for you to lose."

"Only my dignity."

"Better to lose dignity for short time than life forever."

"I'll bet Confucius never went around in drag," Bruce groused.

"Confucius live in more normal time."

"Of course. All times before now were more normal."

Two days later, a package arrived on Yong's doorstep from Fabqueen. com. It was time to do a dry run.

Bruce spent two hours shaving himself everywhere, inside out and from head to toe, in places he did not know he had hair. Then he tried to don his costume, but was baffled as to what to put on first.

"Doesn't this stuff come with instructions?" Finding none, he tried on the pantyhose. Fortunately, it was so stretchy and forgiving he was able to wriggle his long legs all the way into them and pull the top up over his rear end to his waist. The breasts were a DDD cup, the largest size, which Yong had guessed would best match Bruce's great height. Strapped to his body, the breasts sprang from his chest like swollen missiles ready for launch. Bruce yanked the patented Butt and Hip Builder up over the pantyhose, unsure whether the device should be on top or underneath. He tugged the loose blue dress over his head like a tee shirt and let it drop down onto his shoulders. It hung over the front edge of his bosoms like a table cloth.

Bruce looked in the mirror and frowned. The colossal tits, dwarfing his hips despite the bulky Butt and Hip Builder, were threatening to pitch him forward onto his knees. He yanked his shoulders back to counterbalance, but knew from his advanced training in mechanical engineering that the quantity of energy needed to continuously resist the inertial gravity of the breast forms would soon exhaust him.

"Big breasts feed many children," Yong said encouragingly.

"Real ones do, maybe. We'll have to return these plastic hooters for something more modest. I don't have the build for these boobs. I'll bet I'm a B cup."

Bruce took a stab at applying eyeliner and eye shadow, and after a few misses almost managed to hit his mark. Yong doused Bruce's face with talcum powder to hide his five o'clock shadow. The wig slipped onto his head without a fuss, and Bruce's size 13E feet slid comfortably into the black high heels.

"There! Do I look queer enough?" Bruce asked.

"Yes," Yong confirmed. "You look like serious pervert. Everyone will run from you."

"Too much perfection and they won't recognize I'm not a real woman."

"More such perfection and maybe they not recognize you are human."

"Nobody said I have to be Caitlyn Jenner," Bruce said in his own defense, beholding his ghastly visage in the mirror. "Speaking of which, what will we call me?"

"What is girl's name for Bruce?" asked Yong.

"Brucilla. But it's very rare."

"Yeah, then it fits. And now you a woman because you too curious to mind own business. Brucilla the Curious."

"Brucilla Curious—a scary name for a scary gal," Bruce said to the mirror with satisfaction, rolling on his ruby red lipstick and smacking his lips. "You've come a long way from Lonely Butte, baby. Now you're a transgendered quant. You got your own Rocket City right here," he said, pinching his enormous nipples. "Nobody will mess with you now."

"No, unless you mess with Quandary Capital again."

The replacement breasts arrived within a couple of days. The B cup fit as well as could be hoped. It was time to put Brucilla Curious to work.

Yong requested a meeting with Beatrice and Alison, explaining that he had discovered a transgendered quant who would like to come in to discuss his vision for a new investment firm. Thrilled by this news, the two women cleared their calendars for a meeting the following day. The next morning Brucilla rode with Yong to work.

Awaiting Beatrice and Alison in the conference room, Brucilla struggled mightily to keep his breast forms from riding down and slipping off to one side. To square the things up, he wriggled his chest inside his dress as well as he could without actually touching himself with his hands. *The damn straps*, he fretted, *I didn't tighten them enough.* "My boobs are falling off," he whispered to Yong.

Just then Beatrice and Alison strolled in.

"So wonderful to meet you, Brucilla," Beatrice said, approaching him gingerly. She offered a handshake. Brucilla pumped Beatrice's hand hard three times. "Yong has told us about your interest in starting a firm," she said. "Oh, thank God you're here."

As they sat at the conference table, Brucilla start to shift his shoulders alternately up and down to level his breast forms. He tried folding his arms to prop them up from below. That seemed to stabilize them for the moment.

Brucilla cleared his throat, then raised his voice into a falsetto, where it fluctuated several octaves before settling down into a husky croak. "Yong told me all about your MaxiGay mandate from CRAM. A maximally diversified gay portfolio, gay in all dimensions! As soon as I heard about it, I thought that's it, maybe I could be one of your gay dimensions. I could set up an investment firm specifically for the MaxiGay Fund, to operate here at Vain Capital with your backing."

Brucilla described the proposed investment strategy as a passively managed account designed to imitate the S&P 500 Fossil Fuel Free Index, used by CRAM as a benchmark for several of its U.S. equity portfolios. It would be a core account within the MaxiGay fund, run with low costs and virtually no risk of significant underperformance, its goal being only to match the benchmark's returns. "It's so simple, I can have it up and running by myself in a few weeks. All I need is a couple of computers, some benchmark data, and an office."

"A very intriguing concept," Beatrice responded. "When Yong told me about your idea yesterday, I wondered how CRAM might react to it, so I called Morris Morbinders to check. He said CRAM's chief investment officer positively loves the idea! He's sure Governor Pitypander would agree that creating a gay firm is an even better way to support the gay community than hiring an existing one. CRAM is delighted by Vain Capital's willingness to sponsor a…a…a"

"Transgendered person," Brucilla suggested, smiling at Yong. He remained immobilized, his forearms still cradling the breast forms from below.

"Are you cold?" Alison asked. "It does get a little nippy in this room."

"Oh, no," Brucilla replied, relieved as he watched Alison's eyes shifting from his unstable breasts to his powdered face. "I'm just fine, thanks."

Meanwhile, it was all he could do to take his eyes off her breasts. *How round and perky they are*, he thought, *like ripe cantaloupes*. His gaze lingered on her lustrous blond hair, her radiant face, her soft blue eyes…

"What would you call your new firm?" Beatrice asked.

"Well, if it's okay with you, I'd like to name it after myself: Curious Capital," Brucilla suggested.

"A perfectly wonderful name! Curious Capital it is!" Beatrice declared. "Very creative, Brucilla. I love this whole idea. Let's go ahead with it at once. I'll have our lawyers draft a partnership agreement this afternoon."

"Brucilla, since your strategy is so simple and will be pretty much run by computers, it won't keep you very busy, will it?" Alison asked.

"No," Brucilla replied. "Not busy at all until there is actual money for me to manage."

"So maybe you'll have time to help us in another way too," she said.

Brucilla's eyes locked onto hers, his heart melting. He was sure he would gladly die for Alison Hartswell. "Oh, just name it," he said.

"Come with us to find other gay money managers for the MaxiGay Fund," Alison proposed. "Yong and I are flying out to San Francisco next week to search for them, but the two of us have no clue what we're doing. With you along, we might have a better shot. You can be our guide."

Brucilla marveled at the sudden turnaround in his fortunes. How quickly some women's clothes, proper padding, and a good helping of makeup had transformed him from a desperate fugitive into a colleague of the exquisite Alison Hartswell! He forgot himself and unfolded his arms. His breasts suddenly slipped from their moorings, sinking slowly below the edge of the table.

"I'll be happy to join you," he said in great earnest, catching them with his forearm.

11 The Diesel Dykes

On a cool Thursday evening in San Francisco's Mission District when nothing out of the ordinary should have been happening, Polly Hancock, a fat tattooed woman wearing cargo shorts and a tee shirt, sipped her beer just inside the door of Norma's Bar and Grill. She was looking aimlessly at the street outside as she chatted with her friend Meg, a woman in a bomber jacket and combat boots who was chomping on buffalo wings. Outside, above the dark green canvas awning, fluttered a rainbow flag.

Suddenly, into the bar glided a blonde goddess wearing a lavender knit dress, followed by a transgender in full regalia and then a small Asian man. The two women turned from the table to stare at the three invaders.

"Look at that. There's a hot femme for you, Meg," Polly remarked upon seeing Alison. "Pretty and tall too. A regular lipstick lesbian. Just your type."

"Polly, what's that standing next to her?" Meg said, gawking at Brucilla. "Is it anatomically correct?"

"Hard to tell," Polly replied. "What gender is that, do you know? Get a load of her makeup. Does the law allow that much eye shadow? And how about the pink pumps? What do you suppose the little Asian kid is doing here with them?"

"Maybe they are tourists from Mars who didn't notice the flag out front," Meg said. "Let's see how long it takes them to figure out where they are."

Alison ordered three margaritas at the counter as she glanced at the other women in the bar. Some of the lesbians were watching a women's mud wrestling event on a big television screen. In a corner booth there was a thin young woman with a boyish haircut who was wearing bib overalls. Her chunky companion sported a brown mullet that spilled down the back of her neck. A black woman with spikes of orange hair and huge brass earrings trotted over with drinks and sat down with them.

"These are your people, Brucilla," Alison said. "Do any of these lesbians look like money managers to you?"

"No, not at all," Brucilla said with revulsion, patting his wig to make sure it was still sitting properly on his head. "More like truck drivers."

Yong noticed a tough-looking bull dyke in a leather vest who was leaning against the wall and guzzling a liter of beer. She almost seemed to be growling at him. "Are they angry? Man who approaches angry woman must guard manhood with both hands."

"Yes, better watch out. They might get aggressive," Brucilla agreed. "It's best we don't upset them."

"Maybe we can get some leads from them, though," Alison said.

"We might try engaging them in conversation," Brucilla suggested, eyeing the pool table at the end of the room. "If we start playing pool, maybe one of them will come over and join us."

Brucilla clopped over to the pool table in his pumps and proceeded to set up a game of eight-ball. "Have you ever played pool before?"

Alison nodded with a smile and grabbed a cue off the wall rack. She shot the white cue ball into the mass of colored balls. The number four ball rolled into a corner pocket.

"Okay, you're solid, I'm stripes," Brucilla said helpfully.

Within two minutes, Meg and Polly had swaggered over toward them. Meg slapped down a quarter on the table's edge to challenge the winner of the game. "You guys just take your time," she said.

"Are you three from here?" Polly asked. "Never seen you in Norma's before."

"No, we're from an investment firm in D.C.," Alison answered. "We're just in town for a few days, doing some research."

Brucilla knocked the cue ball into the twelve ball. Both balls went flinging off into the middle of the table.

Polly took a swig of her beer and burped. "What kind of research?"

"We're looking for lesbian money managers," Alison said. "Do you know any?"

"Money managers?"

"Yes, you know, people who manage portfolios of stocks, bonds, hedge funds, that sort of thing."

Meg and Polly traded vacant glances with each other.

"Are you straight?" Meg asked.

"Yes," Alison admitted.

"It figures. We don't see many straight girls in here," Meg said. "Polly here is a firefighter with Daly City. I'm a paralegal downtown. Don't know much about managing money. Never had any to spare."

"Your shot, Alison," Brucilla said.

Alison swung around the table and took aim at the six ball. She smacked it straight into a side pocket. "Do you have any friends who work in the financial district?"

The one ball was resting just outside a corner pocket. Alison tapped it in gently. Then she sank the five ball with a glancing bank shot off the side. Next, she hit the seven ball at the far end of the table a little too hard and it bounced off a corner.

"No, I don't," Meg said. "Do you, Polly?"

"I know a gay guy who's a bank loan administrator," Polly offered.

Brucilla leaned over the table to take aim at the twelve ball. He felt his breast forms hanging down from his chest into his dress, swinging like pendulums with every move of his arms and throwing him off balance. He misfired, driving the cue ball into the corner pocket.

"No, a banker won't do. That's not quite what we're looking for." Alison slapped the seven ball into the corner pocket with a straight shot down the side, and then clipped the two ball to drop it neatly into the side pocket. The three ball was blocked, so Alison stroked the cue ball hard off the far end of the table and hit the three from the back, sending it spinning into the corner pocket near her.

"Holy crap," Meg said. "Where did you learn to shoot pool like that?"

Alison chalked her pool cue and grinned. "I had three older brothers growing up in Santa Monica who taught me. I've been playing since I was five. Eight ball in the corner pocket," she announced, pointing her cue stick at the pocket farthest away and driving her last ball into it. Game over.

Brucilla slunk away from the table with a mix of humiliation and awe. Alison racked up the next game with Meg.

Polly sidled up to Brucilla and gulped some beer. "Your friend's a regular pool shark, isn't she?"

"She's awfully good," Brucilla replied. "Better than any girl I ever saw."

"Say, honey, speaking of girls, I can't help noticing you look a little new at this transgender thing. I can see you're trying real hard but you don't seem the girly-girl type."

"No?" said Brucilla, feeling more relieved than insulted.

"I can tell a newbie a mile away. Don't get me wrong. I don't mean to be critical, I just thought you if you're going down this road anyway you might want some pointers, that's all," Polly said. "For instance, you might want to lighten up on the eye shadow. Less is better than more with that stuff. It's eye shadow, not war paint. And purple's probably not your best color. It looks better on the black girls. Stick with blue."

"Thanks, I'll remember that."

"And go easy on the face powder too. Too much makes you look like the bride of Frankenstein."

"Yes, I'll do that."

"If you don't mind me asking, are you pre-op or post-op?"

Brucilla looked down at his crotch for a second. "Oh, pre-op," he said.

"Had to think about it?"

"No, that's what I am. I'm pre-op," Brucilla said. "Definitely pre-op. No question about it."

"Good idea, keep your options open. Whacking it off is serious business, you know. Don't want to have buyer's remorse with that decision. Cause this transgender thing isn't everybody's cup of tea. A lot of people don't understand that when they first get started and get all carried away by the glitter and glamor of cross-dressing. They think they're suddenly at the Oscars in Hollywood. Not everyone can be Caitlyn Jenner, you know."

"No, I suppose not," Brucilla said, wondering how anyone could get carried away, given how much his Butt and Hip Builder was chafing against his pelvis. He was beginning to worry about getting a serious rash down there.

"Still got any interest in straight girls?" Polly asked.

Alison stretched her sinuous torso over the pool table to take a shot at the four ball, raising her pretty rear end high into the air and the edge of her skirt well up her thigh. He felt his heart begin to throb. "Oh, yes."

"Best to stay pre-op then. No regrets that way. If you change your mind, you can always go under the knife later."

"Good tip, thanks. I'll be sure to consider it," he said.

Alison proceeded to sink four balls in a row.

Meg munched on a buffalo wing as she continued to admire Alison's skill at pool. "Hmm, did your big brothers happen to teach you how to play slow-pitch softball too by any chance?"

"No, but I've played lots of softball."

"Ever play third base?"

"Yes, I was on an intramural slow-pitch softball team at USC. They always put me on first or third because of my height," Alison said.

"I'll bet," Meg said, looking up at her. "You must be six foot. You'd be perfect. We could sure use somebody like you at third base on my softball team. Most of my players are shrimps."

"Really? What team is that?"

"The Daly City Diesel Dykes. It's a C division dyke softball team in Daly City. I'm the coach. My name is Meg Johnson."

"Nice to meet you. I'm Alison Hartswell."

"Say, there's a big regional tournament in town this weekend, starting tomorrow, with teams from all over," Meg said. "We're missing some of our players for the first game in the morning and we need a pickup player bad. Would you be interested in joining us? It's just for one game until our regulars show up. We'll have an extra uniform and glove we can lend you."

"Will there will be a lot of lesbians there?" Alison asked, thinking a softball tournament might be just the place to widen her net for lesbian money managers.

"Tons of them. Four or five hundred at least," Meg said.

Alison promised to be there.

The softball park had four fields arranged like a four-leaf clover, with tournament games running on all of them all day long. Hundreds of women wearing shorts and softball jerseys were watching the game behind the chain-link backstops, sitting in the bleachers, and buying burgers at the concession stand. Alison spotted the Daly City Diesel Dykes, nine short women in green jerseys who were practicing in a grassy area between two fields and tossing softballs back and forth to loosen up.

Meg came running over to greet Alison. "We're on at ten, playing on field three over there against the Pottstown Pussies," she said. "Gotta warn you, sister, they're pretty damn good. Oh, and better watch out— their coach is a real asshole. We got a kind of running feud going on between us. The Dykes and Pussies are like oil and water. They ain't got no class."

Yong and Brucilla took a seat in the bleachers. "Why you not playing?" Yong asked.

Brucilla's eyes feasted upon Alison as she limbered up at third base, twisting her lithe body from side to side and doing leg bends with the grace of a ballerina. "They're more interested in Alison than me. And I don't blame them."

The Pussies drew first blood. In the first inning, a very large woman with a crew cut and massive arms smashed a fly ball to the fence and lumbered around the bases. Soon the Pussies had jumped out to a three-run lead. Then a hard line drive was hit chest-high at Alison, who caught it cleanly and fired it to second base to double up a runner, ending the inning. Alison led off the next one with a double smashed past the right fielder, sparking a celebration in the Diesel Dykes's dugout. "Way to lick it, Lipstick!" they yelled.

Just then, the coach of the Pussies, a dumpy little woman with a blond Mohawk, called time out and walked up to the home plate umpire. She pointed at Alison. "Excuse me, ump. Who is that player?"

Meg hustled out of the dugout over to home plate. "She's a friend from D.C. who's in town for a few days, that's who. She's a pickup player. We're allowed to fill out our squad with pickup players."

"Is she a lesbian? She don't look like a lesbian. She don't walk like a lesbian," said the other coach.

The umpire turned to Alison. "Are you a lesbian, honey?"

Alison shook her head. "No, sorry, I'm straight," she admitted. "I even have a steady boyfriend. Is that a problem?"

"She's not qualified to play in this tournament, ump!" the coach of the Pussies declared. "No straights. Those are the league rules."

"But she's a girl, ain't she?" Meg countered. "We're all girls here, ain't we? Ain't it good enough for you that she's a girl?"

"No, that's not good enough. She has to be queer. This is a tournament for queers."

"Without her, we got only nine players," Meg shot back. "You know we can't win a competitive softball tournament with a player missing. You'll do anything to get a damn trophy, you bitch!"

"You're the one who showed up here with only nine eligible players. That's your problem, not mine," the coach of the Pussies sneered. "Rules are rules. Your Barbie doll has gotta go. She's ineligible."

Meg turned, looked up into the stands, and caught sight of Brucilla sitting with Yong. "Ump, how about transgenders? Are they allowed?"

"Yes," the umpire said. "Transgenders are allowed to play in either men's or women's games."

Meg motioned to Brucilla to come down to the field. Brucilla stepped gingerly down from the bleachers and came around the backstop in her pumps.

"But that don't make any sense!" protested the coach of the Pussies. "This is a woman's tournament! You can't replace a straight girl with a huge man in a dress! He's even taller than the straight girl. A foot taller than we are!"

"Ump says I can. He identifies as a girl, and that's all that matters. And you started it, bitch! A real girl wasn't good enough for you." Meg looked up at Brucilla. "Wanna play softball, sweetie?"

"Sure."

"Ever played before?"

"Yes, lots of times," Brucilla replied.

"Ump, can we have a few minutes to fix her?" Meg requested.

The umpire consented to a short break. Meg yelled to the dugout for her Diesel Dykes to scrounge up some elastic shorts, an XXXL jersey, and some cleats, pronto. Minutes later, Brucilla emerged from the ladies room in softball garb. But the cleats did not fit. None of the Diesel Dykes wore anything close to men's size 13E shoes, so they found some tube socks to protect the transgender's huge feet.

Brucilla took Alison's place as the runner on second base. The next Diesel Dyke at bat drove him in with a single over the middle. Later, playing third base, he fielded a few easy grounders cleanly. In his first time at bat he swatted a triple to the fence. Next he hit a double, and then another triple. But it was no use. The Diesel Dykes were pudgy and short, and no match for the heftier big-bottomed Pussies. By the sixth inning, there was only a minute left in the game and the Diesel Dykes were down by three runs, with the bases loaded.

"You're up, Brucilla," Meg said. "Smack it to hell, honey."

Brucilla strode to the plate. He pointed to the centerfield fence with his bat. He wiggled his shoulders to adjust his breast forms and ground his feet into the soft dirt in the batter's box. He looked over at Alison, sitting in the stands.

"Do it for the Diesel Dykes, Brucilla! Go Dykes!" Alison yelled out.

Brucilla let a couple of pitches go by, one of them a ball and the other a strike. The next pitch came floating into the strike zone. He drew the bat back, swung with all his might, and crushed the ball. It went flying high into center field and sailed over the fence.

The Diesel Dykes ran jumping and screaming out of their dugout to greet Brucilla at home plate, making a sound like the blast of a diesel truck's horn: "Braaaaaaah, braaaaaaaah!"

The dejected Pussies began to file out of their dugout, led by their snarling coach.

"You did it, Brucilla!" Alison said. "I'm so proud of you!"

"You saved us," Meg said, throwing her arms around Brucilla and Alison. "We can take it from here. Our regular players will be here for our next game. Anything we can do for you girls?"

"Do any of you on the team know of any money managers?" Alison inquired.

None of them did, but they would ask their friends. Alison got the same answer from the women in the other bleachers and dugouts. Not one lesbian in the entire softball park had ever heard of a lesbian money manager, and most doubted such a person even existed. Someone suggested that if there were any gay money managers in San Francisco they were most likely men. And the biggest men's bar in town was a leather place called Davey's Dungeon.

12 The Mind Melter

Freddie Disposo, a stocky man with black slicked-back hair and a rumpled suit, sat across the table from Dr. Ozturk and Dr. Feiersinger, occasionally glancing out the window at the neat rows of white yachts moored at the Rocket City docks below. He was thinking he might be able to afford one of those fine boats himself someday if he could pull off a few more million-dollar hits for his high-end clientele.

"Well, boys, I've taken care of your Bao Yi Chen," he said with a self-satisfied smirk. "I finally found him. He had been staying with Chinese relatives in Sydney until January, when he realized I was on his trail and made a run for it. I tracked him from there to Shanghai, where I caught him working in a factory making American stick flags. He runs the stapling machine. Here are some pictures."

"A stapling machine? For stapling the flag to the stick?" Feiersinger asked, looking at the photographs of a man standing at a table covered with little American flags.

"Yes."

"That is an unusual job for a man with a doctorate in particle physics. Were you able to trace his computer? Was he trading any stocks?"

"No trading, but he would go online at night after work and do stock research. My computer guys hacked into his computer regularly to see what he was doing. It seems he was trying to run some kind of deciphering program, but we couldn't figure out what he was trying to decipher."

"How could you tell it was a deciphering program?" Ozturk asked.

"The program was analyzing letter and word combinations as if it was trying to make sense of them. Some kind of decoder."

"In what language?"

"Three languages: English, German, and strangely enough, Turkish," said Disposo, eyeing the two quants suspiciously.

"Did he find any word combinations?" Ozturk asked.

"We don't know."

"So what did you do with him? Did you administer the Mind Melter?" Feiersinger asked.

"I followed him home from the flag factory one evening and shot him in the leg with the drug dart myself. The stuff worked within minutes. All he can do now is repeat meaningless words over and over again, nothing but gibberish."

Feiersinger sat up straight. "Meaningless words? What meaningless words?"

"HONEY BOO-BOO."

Feiersinger bit his lip as he looked at Ozturk.

"Oh, that's all?" Ozturk laughed loudly. "Ha ha, that is gibberish, isn't it? Nothing for us to worry about then."

"Yes, that's it," Disposo said. "That's all he can say. The Mind Melter has turned his brain into oatmeal. It causes instant dementia by scrambling the neural synapses, creating a kind of short circuit so almost all higher-order intellectual memories become inaccessible. The FSB, the Russian spy agency, uses it to silence turncoat agents. They forget everything of importance, or almost everything, permanently. There is no antidote. And the best part is no one can be accused of murder, and the drug doesn't leave the slightest trace. It's the most effective way to get rid of people who know too much without actually killing them."

Ozturk leaned forward and stared hard at Disposo. "You're absolutely sure he says nothing more than that gibberish you mentioned? Nothing at all?"

"Nothing. He still works at the factory, smiling and mumbling HONEY BOO-BOO like a simpleton all day long to his Chinese co-workers. HONEY BOO-BOO, HONEY BOO-BOO, just like that, over and over. They think he's lost his marbles, and he has. The drug has seen to that. But the Mind Melter did not affect his great work habits or his upbeat personality. He can run the stapling machine just fine, so they have kept him on the job, happily pumping out American stick flags by the thousands. The factory even elected him worker of the month."

"Turning a top-notch quant into a babbling cretin—such a shame," Ozturk observed with sincere regret. "He had so much potential. Such a waste of a PhD in physics, and a Rhodes scholar too. But it couldn't be helped. It was more humane than killing him, and he really left us no choice. We warned him, as we do all our employees. It's right there in the employment agreement: Don't run off with our secrets or we'll get you. At least now he is adding value by making a useful product that's worth what people pay for it. That's more than a lot of money managers can say."

"And Bruce Benson, what happened to him?" Feiersinger asked.

"He left Rocket City. He's given me the slip, for the moment."

"How did he manage that?"

"He got to the Orlando airport before I did. I know he flew to Washington, D.C., the same day you fired him. But I don't know why he went there, of all places."

"He's not from D.C., is he? I thought he was from out West, somewhere in cowboy country," Ozturk said. "I would have expected him to head home."

"Home for Bruce Benson is Lonely Butte, South Dakota," Disposo said. "I went out there. It's in the middle of nowhere—just prairie and cattle ranches. The town has a population of two hundred. The biggest building there is Annie's Gas 'N Go. We know Benson's not living with his parents at their cattle ranch. And I couldn't find him around MIT or anywhere else in Boston. He does have one connection to the Washington area, but it didn't pan out."

"What was that?"

"He had a roommate at Stanford by the name of Lee Yong-gi, a Korean who's now working at Vain Capital in Washington. He's an assistant portfolio analyst who recently joined the firm."

"Oh, I remember that little fellow!" Ozturk exclaimed. "He visited Bruce Benson here from Vain Capital just two months ago. A very annoying, impertinent young man—with too many questions."

"Yes, well, I checked him out. No sign of Benson anywhere near him." Disposo opened his dossier on Yong and flipped the pages. There was the photo of Yong leaving Vain Capital with a tall awkward woman with a blond bouffant hairdo. "I must say he sure has an ugly girlfriend. A real bow-wow. She's a foot taller than he is."

"So what will you do now?"

"Continue to snoop around Washington until I pick up Benson's scent again. An unusual fellow like him can't escape this private eye for long."

13 Danger in the Dungeon

It was so dark in Davy's Dungeon in San Francisco's Castro District that the MaxiGay trio could hardly see where they were going, although to Yong it seemed they might be descending into the pits of hell. He stumbled toward the flickering lights, with Alison and Brucilla following tentatively in his footsteps.

As they drew closer, they could see that the lights were wall sconces made to resemble flaming torches, mounted alongside iron manacles, chains, whips, and thumbscrews. The walls themselves were painted as black and white murals depicting the inside of a castle's prison chamber.

Standing against the walls of the Dungeon were phalanxes of pot-bellied men ranging from thirty to sixty years old, many wearing jeans and black leather vests, others with harnesses of riveted leather straps stretched across their bare torsos. One fellow with a neatly trimmed goatee sported a pair of black leather chaps. Yong wondered why it was open in both front and back.

Some of the men were chatting, others drinking alone, their eyes searching, stealing glimpses of each other. Mammoth television screens overhead displayed the flashing images of a rock video as loudspeakers pounded out beats of raucous music. Yong noticed that some eyes had turned to follow him. He timidly ordered three beers at the bar.

He caught sight of a room beyond the bar and realized that the Dungeon was much bigger than it first seemed. There were rooms and corridors connected to the front bar room where God only knew what might be happening. On the walls of one adjacent room were screens where a film was being projected, showing a pair of naked men with beards cavorting with each other, one of them kneeling with his head bowed in front of the other, performing oral sex amid loud grunts and groans. A dozen men gawked at the images, looking up at them as if held in a trance.

"Oh Lord, where are we?" Brucilla asked, his eyes widening. "We've come to Sodom and Gomorrah. These people look like they might have AIDS or something. What kind of investment person would we find here? Don't you think this place is a mite downscale for an institutional portfolio manager to hang out in?"

"Yes, even for portfolio assistant," Yong agreed.

"Oh, I'm not afraid," Alison said. "These guys won't bother us—they're perfectly harmless. Let's keep a professional attitude about this. We'll just ask them whether they know of any gay money managers."

"Do they look like they would?" Brucilla asked.

"Relax, these guys aren't axe murderers, they're just sissies with a leather fetish. We have nothing to fear from them. And don't be a snob. Congressmen have been found in worse places than this." Then she paused and smiled at him. "Sorry, no offense to sissies. I just meant that—"

"None taken," replied Brucilla, attempting to nudge his drooping breasts upwards with the rim of his beer glass as discreetly as one could. "You're right, there's nothing to fear here. Nothing at all."

"Nothing," Yong echoed.

Brucilla looked admiringly at Alison, awed by her steely demeanor. What a trooper she was to come here. For his part, he was comforted only by the thought that his disguise made him immune to this crowd.

Yong gulped his beer and fidgeted, trying his best not to return the glance of a burly middle-aged white man in a black leather jacket who was staring arrows of lust at him from across the room.

"Hmm, I wonder what Confucius would say about this place," Brucilla whispered to him.

For a moment Yong tried to picture the Chinese sage in a leather bar, but the image was far too disturbing. "Confucius preach virtue and moderation," he said.

"He'd sure have his work cut out for him here."

"Yes," Yong said. "So why these queers like leather so much? Why they all trying to look the same?"

"It's part of gay culture," Brucilla said. "Leather is a kind of cultural uniform for the leather queens, like we saw with the lesbians. Anthropologically speaking, it imbues them with a sense of communal protection from the majority culture, a sense of belonging to a special tribe, a self-reinforcing identity similar to that adopted by urban gangs and other marginalized social groups."

"They are afraid of us?" Yong asked.

"Yes, but they are afraid outside the bar, not in here. This is their safe space."

"In here, we are afraid of them."

"I'm terrified," Brucilla whispered.

Alison noticed a man standing against the wall wearing a black leather captain's hat. She stepped forward to strike up a conversation. "Excuse me, sir."

"Yes?" said the man.

"Is that a captain's hat?" Alison said, pointing at his hat.

"Yes, it is."

"Oh, a man in authority. Just what we're looking for," she said. "Do you have a local gay leader you could point me to, someone of higher rank, a gay general or commissioner maybe? I have some important questions for him."

"Sorry, lady, there is no gay leader," the captain replied.

"Oh, then what's with your captain's hat?"

"It's just a hat. I bought it in the gay clothing store in the back of the bar for forty-nine bucks," the captain said. "There's all sorts of cool stuff back there—harnesses, chaps, thongs, hats, cock rings, dildos, lube, you name it. Captain is the highest rank for gay leather hats. Actually, it's the only one. All leather queens are captains. Except in my day job—I'm actually a restaurant manager in Burlingame."

"Oh, I see. Then I might as well ask you. We need some advice about the gay scene. Do you happen to know any gay money managers?"

"You looking for stock tips? In a leather bar in the Castro district?"

"No, I'm with a firm searching for some gay money managers to hire."

"Wow, what kind of crazy firm is that?"

"We specialize in morality-based investing. We're from Washington."

"Washington, D.C.? And you thought you'd find something to do with morality here? In the Castro?"

"No, we're just looking for gay money managers. It's complicated."

The man in the captain's hat thought for a moment. "I tricked with a stockbroker once. He gave good head. Will that do?"

"No, not really."

"Just as well. I wouldn't know how to tell you to find him anyway. It's been a few years and I've lost his number."

Yong began to guzzle his beer, drinking more with every new stare that fell upon him. The most intense one was coming from the burly middle-aged man. Yong tried to avert his eyes, but the harder he concentrated on looking at no one the more aware he became of everyone.

A few beers later he was heading urgently to the men's room.

Yong was soon standing at a urinal. Out of the corner of his eye he saw he had company at the next urinal. It was the burly middle-aged man. Yong said nothing and kept his eyes fixed on the wall in front of him. He quickly finished his business, escaped the bathroom, and scampered back to Alison and Brucilla.

"That big hairy guy over there is after me," Yong said to Brucilla.

Brucilla craned his neck to look. The burly middle-aged man disappeared in the crowd for a moment. "I don't see him," he said. "But there are enough big hairy guys here to fill a gorilla convention. Actually, they're called bears, daddy bears in your case. According to my research, the official term for someone like you is a twink. You're a hot commodity in a place like this."

Just then two men passed in front of them, one a shirtless man with a studded leather collar around his neck, followed closely behind by a bald bearded man firmly holding a chain hooked to the collar.

"What is that?" Yong asked with astonishment.

"A slave and his master," Brucilla said.

Yong looked horrified. "But that is illegal now, yes?" He recalled reading about Abraham Lincoln and the freeing of the American slaves in the nineteenth century.

"Oh, don't worry, he's not a real slave," Brucilla explained. "He's a sex slave. It's make believe. One guy is dominant and the other is submissive. They are having a little mutual fantasy. The slave is starved for attention, and the master craves ego gratification and power. It's a sort of psychological relationship, satisfying both parties. You see, in this country there's a buyer and a seller for everything, including freedom and attention. Modern slavery is volitional. That's the distinction between the bad old slavery and this perfectly acceptable version."

"So it's still okay in America to be a slave?" Yong asked uncomprehendingly.

"Yes, here you are free to be a slave if you want to be. There are lots of things people will happily give up all their freedom to get—money, sex, love, drugs—as long as they think they can get their freedom back when they want it."

Yong had never heard of anyone who wanted to be a slave, even in North Korea, where people knew a lot about being in bondage. "If it is okay to be a slave, is okay to have one?"

"Yes," Brucilla said. "That's only logical. It's a two-way street, isn't it? Somebody has to take the other side of the transaction. It's okay as long as you don't enslave people against their will. Think of all the people who willingly sign contracts to give up their freedom or money in exchange for something else. Don't people give up their freedom when they marry or have children or take on debt? They wouldn't like it if you took away their freedom to give up their freedom. The Bible says every borrower is a slave to his lender. By that definition, most people are slaves, including me with my huge student loans. People work half the year for the government to pay their taxes, but nobody calls them tax slaves. These two guys here are just pretending for the night. Tomorrow that guy with the chain on his neck will be freer than I am."

Before long Yong took off for the men's room again. Brucilla noticed a burly middle-aged man following him there.

Back at the urinal, Yong heard a voice to his right. "Hello, there," said the burly middle-aged man. "My name's Bob. What brings you here?"

"Beer. Drink way too much. Gotta pee bad."

"I mean what brings you to the Dungeon."

"Looking for queer money managers."

"Money managers? Here?" said Bob. "Okay, I manage some money."

"You do?" Yong said, with a look of surprise. "What kind of money you manage?"

"Stocks," Bob replied.

"Wait for me outside."

He found Bob waiting patiently outside the door. "Follow me," Yong said, leading Bob toward the spot where Alison and Brucilla had been.

On the way Yong ran into Brucilla, who had come looking for him. "Look, I find queer money manager right in bathroom. Name is Bob. Very queer guy."

"Oh, really?" Brucilla said. "What kind of portfolio do you run, Bob?"

Bob began to drape his hairy arm around Yong's neck. "It's not a portfolio, really," he said. "Just Amazon and Apple, the two stocks my grandfather left me from his trust fund."

"You don't manage portfolios for institutions, like pension funds and endowments?" Brucilla asked.

"No, I'm a librarian from Sausalito. Who said anything about portfolios and institutions?"

Yong rolled his eyes and cringed.

Brucilla grabbed Yong by the hand. "Oh, that's too bad. We were hoping to find professional money managers here. Yong, sweetheart, can you show me to the men's room? Please excuse us, Bob, my husband needs to take me to the men's room."

"Your husband? Oh, sorry, " Bob said, quickly removing his arm from Yong.

Brucilla patted Bob on the shoulder. "No problem." Pulling Yong by the hand, he clopped away toward the men's room.

"But he told me he was money manager," Yong said.

"He was lying," Brucilla said as they went into the men's room. "These leather guys are like piranhas. You better be more careful."

A security guard suddenly burst through the door after Brucilla. "Sorry, missy, you can't be in here," he barked. "Transgenders have to go to the bathroom of the gender they identify with. It's a San Francisco city ordinance. The ladies room is on the opposite side of the bar."

"But I don't want to go to the ladies' room," Brucilla protested. "I've never been in one."

"Never been to a ladies' room? Why the hell did you become a woman then, sister?" the guard asked. "Well, it doesn't matter. There's a city ordinance about this in San Francisco, and it's strictly enforced. Transgenders fought for your right to go the ladies' room, so that's where you have to go."

"But you don't understand. I'm not a woman," Brucilla said indignantly. "This is just a dress. I really identify as a man—because I am one. I demand to be treated like a man."

"Really? I think you're trying to look more like a woman," the guard said. "The bar will be in violation of the transgender rights ordinance if you stay here. We'll lose our liquor license if we don't get you to a ladies room. Besides, we don't want you making our other patrons feel uncomfortable in here."

"But they shouldn't feel uncomfortable. I'm pre-op, dammit, and I have the junk to prove it." Brucilla stretched himself to his full height and crossed his arms in defiance. "Wanna see my junk?"

"Hell no, keep it to yourself," the guard said. "Listen, pal, I'll admit you make an awful sorry-looking woman, but you can't have it both ways. The city of San Francisco says we have to send you to the restroom of the gender you identify with, and that's ladies as near as I can tell, so that's the one you're gonna use. Don't make me call the cops, cause I'll do it."

Brucilla strutted out of the men's room in a huff. "This isn't worth a scene with the police," he said to Yong. "There won't be any women in the ladies' room anyway." He set off for it by himself.

Yong's head began to swim. He leaned against the wall outside the men's room for a couple of minutes to steady himself. He staggered down a hallway, then realized he had turned the wrong way. Walking farther down, he clutched the wall to keep his balance, and then stumbled into a darkened room he had not noticed before. Inside it he could make out the shadows of several men formed in a circle around a shirtless man in jeans who was kneeling in front of them. In the blackness Yong could not tell what was happening.

"Hey, kid, you want some of this?" one of the men said to Yong, pulling him by the arm into the circle.

Yong's eyes began to adjust to the dark. Suddenly he could see what the man in the middle of the circle was doing.

Yong shook his head in disgust. He started to walk away, toward the light in the doorway, and then suddenly felt dizzy. The light first swayed from side to side, and then it started to spin. He reached his arms out, feeling for the floor or the wall as his legs crumpled under him. Then he felt hands groping him.

Some time passed. The next thing he knew, he was hearing the sound of someone's voice.

"Yong, wake up, wake up," said the voice.

Yong opened his eyes slowly and looked up at a blurry figure. Feeling a chill, he realized he was lying on the floor, completely naked except for his socks. He turned his head and saw his clothes and shoes in a pile on the floor about five feet away.

"Yong, it's me," Brucilla said. Yong blinked his eyes and began to make out the face as it came into focus. Brucilla was kneeling over him.

"Oh, my God! What happened to you?" Brucilla asked. "I've been looking all over for you. We thought you might have left."

"No, I pass out, too much to drink," Yong said. "My clothes, why they over there?"

"Why are you naked? What the hell did they do to you? Did somebody put a mickey in your drink?"

"Don't know, don't remember. Fell down. Last thing before I pass out, I was trying to get away. They were grabbing me. All of them."

Yong put his clothes back on.

"Do not tell Alison, please!" Yong begged.

"No, absolutely not."

With Brucilla steadying him, Yong stumbled out of the room, still feeling very woozy. They headed back into the crowd toward the main part of the bar. As he worked his way through the crush of bodies, he began to feel someone pinching his buttocks. He turned and looked behind him. A little bald man with an earring and arm tattoos grabbed him around the waist. Yong slipped away and pressed forward.

Finally they made it around to the other side of the bar. They caught sight of Alison and squeezed through the crowd to her.

"Where have you been?" she asked frantically.

"Gotta go outside, now! Feel sick." Yong made it just through the front door of the Dungeon before falling to his knees and puking onto the sidewalk outside.

"They wouldn't be here," Brucilla said, holding Yong up by his arm as the MaxiGay trio staggered back to the hotel. "I could tell the minute we set foot in the place. Too downscale."

14 Calling Bludinov's Bluff

President Phyllis Fibby, a sixty-year old woman with artificially blond hair and a florid complexion, looked skeptically at the Chairman of the Joint Chiefs of Staff. She had been in office only four months, and already he was presenting her with a major international crisis of just the sort she had pledged to avoid.

She squinted at the black and white photograph the general had spread out before her on the table in the Oval Office. "Are you absolutely sure that's what those dark clumps are?" she asked.

The snapshot showed a big rectangle next to a river separating two towns, one marked "Ivangorod, Russia" and the other "Narva, Estonia." Red arrows pointed to military equipment along the Russian side of the river.

"Yes, Madam President," General Barker replied in a low baritone. "Those dark clumps are trucks unloading guns and ammo into temporary warehouses. Our satellite surveillance started picking up activity in that area a few weeks ago. At first we thought it might be a military exercise, the kind the Russians routinely conduct on their borders from time to time. But when we saw them erecting barracks for three thousand men we realized it must be a preparation for something much more serious."

"Like what?"

"Like a small invasion."

"Of what?"

"We're not sure, ma'am. But it sure looks like it would be the country there, across the river from Russia. That's Estonia."

"Estonia! But Estonia is a NATO country."

"Yes, ma'am. I think the Russians know that."

"What's that place they're putting the supplies in? It looks enormous."

"It's an old castle, the fortress of Ivangorod."

"Why would they pick an old castle? Does it have any military significance?"

"No, the castle of Ivangorod was built more than five centuries ago. It just happens to be right on the border, directly across the bridge connecting Russia to the Estonian town of Narva."

"What do you think the Russians are up to, General?"

"Saber rattling, Madam President. They know we have satellites that can read a license plate from space. They want us to see them getting ready to invade Estonia. It's a show of power. If they wanted to launch a surprise attack on the country they could easily do it from hundreds of miles away from many places in Russia, without all this overt activity right on the border."

"Why would they want us to see them?"

"Because they don't actually want to invade Estonia. That would be messy, and then they would have to run the place, which would be even more of a bother. They just want to control Estonia from the outside, to get it out of NATO," General Barker said. "But they might be willing to invade it if they have to."

"Do you think they're bluffing? They wouldn't dare attack a NATO country, would they? They know we and our NATO allies are obligated by treaty to defend it."

"I don't know, Madam President. Viktor Bludinov likes to play head games with his adversaries, and maybe this is just a tactic," General Barker said. "But those are real weapons and those are real soldiers unloading them. We estimate hundreds of troops are already involved. Since they are building so many barracks, a lot more troops must be coming."

"Viktor Bludinov! He's testing me, that horrid little man," Fibby declared. "He thinks I'm weak just because I'm a woman. The sexist pig."

"We've been expecting Bludinov to retaliate at some point for the sanctions we slapped on him after he invaded the Ukraine," General Barker said. "What better time to strike back than at the beginning of your administration, to test the resolve of America's first woman president?"

Fibby got up, walked over toward the window, and gazed out over the lush grounds of the White House toward the Washington Monument. Confrontation was not the way she had intended to conduct foreign relations. She had run on a feminist platform promoting peace through greater international cooperation, diplomacy, and bridge building to America's foes, as promised by her campaign theme, "The Woman's Way to Peace."

"Well, he's a bad, bad man. Push me around, will he? I won't let him have the satisfaction." She turned to her Secretary of State, Javonda Hernandez, the former mayor of Detroit and a close confidante. She could always count on Hernandez to tell her exactly what she wanted to hear. "What do you think, Javonda?"

Hernandez shrugged her shoulders. "Leave them alone. Maybe if we don't say or do anything, they'll get bored and just leave the border on their own. The Russians are still in Russia. That's where they belong, isn't it? Can't we mind our own business for once? Why do we need to bother them in their own country?"

"Do you think that's a possibility, General? Do you think they'll just pull back from the border and go away?" Fibby asked.

"No, Madam President, I don't," General Barker said without hesitation. "This is a power play. The Russians want a response from you. If you don't do anything, that will show weakness, which will encourage Bludinov to become more aggressive. He'll keep pushing harder and harder until he meets serious resistance."

"We can't let that awful man have his way," she said with a determined look on her face. "Bludinov thinks he's very clever, but he expects us react the way a man would. Well then, that's how we'll fool the little so-and-so. I wasn't elected to run the country the way a man would. We've had more than two centuries of that, and what has it gotten us? Nothing but one war after another. I was elected to run the country the way a woman would. For once we'll push back the way a woman does it."

"How's that, ma'am?"

"We won't cooperate. We'll ignore him, that's what. Bludinov's expecting me to play by his man-rules, just like my ex-husband Arnold did. Well, I have my own rules. Nothing drove Arnie crazier than being ignored when he threw a tantrum. The man is strutting his stuff like a cock of the walk and demanding attention, is he? Well, he won't get it from me. We won't do or say anything for now. Our policy will be to respond with no response. We'll pretend we don't know about his troop buildup, that we don't see it. Let his troops sit there shivering in that old castle until next Christmas for all I care. I don't believe Arnie, I mean Bludinov, will cross the river and attack Estonia. It's too dangerous for him. He doesn't have the balls."

"That's right," Hernandez seconded. "Arnie's got no balls, just bluff."

"But Arnie, I mean Bludinov, did attack Ukraine, Madam President," General Barker pointed out. "He sent in his masked soldiers in their un-marked uniforms, the little green men, pretending they were Ukrainian separatists. First he took over the Crimea, and the West did nothing. Then he rolled into eastern Ukraine, and again the West did nothing. Why wouldn't he take over Estonia the same way?"

"Because Estonia is a NATO country," Fibby insisted, more convinced of the rightness of her position than ever. "Other than that, it's not worth fighting for, not even for the Russians, and certainly not for us. Bludinov is a bully and a coward, but not a fool or a suicidal maniac. Besides, I've slashed our defense budget in half. This country doesn't have the money to play these global power games anymore. Let's try ignoring Bludinov first. We'll see what he does when his bluff is called."

15 The Gospel Hour

It wasn't easy getting reservations at Gurlz," Alison said to Brucilla and Yong as they entered the drag palace in San Francisco's Tenderloin district. "Only one table was left for the Sunday dinner. They said it's the Gospel Hour and the Gospel Gurlz are here to do their weekly show. Some sort of gay church service. Who knew they were religious?"

A slightly built young man in a tuxedo escorted them inside the palace, which looked like it had once been some kind of dance hall. The walls were decked with flocked red wallpaper and mirrors. At one end of the palace, framed by long golden curtains, was a stage. Alongside it two marble statues of naked Greek goddesses stood on pedestals, gazing at the audience with an expressionless indifference as if they could no longer be shocked by anything they saw. Twelve large glass chandeliers and four rotating mirrored disco balls hung down from the twenty-foot ceiling as whirling spotlights sent a thousand flecks of white light splashing off them onto the walls and floor below.

"Kinda garish for a dinner theater, isn't it? It's more like an old western whorehouse, minus the straight guys," Brucilla remarked, looking around at the other tables. Half the crowd seemed to be made up of older gay men and the other half boisterous twenty-something bachelorettes getting smashed on margaritas. Slender young male waiters flitted back and forth from the kitchen and bar bearing trays heaped with food and alcohol.

Suddenly out of the speakers overhead issued a flourish of music announcing the start of the Gospel Hour.

"What is that?" Yong asked, his eyes growing big like he was seeing a monster. "Is it a man?"

"It's the diva," Brucilla replied.

Two hundred and fifty pounds of feminine fabulousness in the form of Deena D'Amour had strutted onto the stage in a cloud of glitter, her black sequined gown sparkling under the lights amid the shrieking and howling of the single women at the tables.

"You better work, bitch!" one of the gay men called out.

A spotlight followed the diva around the stage as she flounced back and forth across it, wiggling her rear end while lip-synching the words to Beyoncé's song "Put a Ring on It."

Deena D'Amour flashed a huge smile as she descended the steps from the stage to mingle with the seated crowd below, wading between the tables to harvest tips from her admirers. Three inebriated young women jumped up from their seats laughing. She floated into their midst, pausing to allow them to press dollar bills into her breasts. A line quickly formed for making deposits into the diva. She kissed each of her fans lovingly on the cheek as they made their contributions.

"This isn't at all like the Lutherans in Lonely Butte do their gospel hour," Brucilla said to Yong.

"What did you say?" Alison asked, raising her voice over the din.

"Something tells me this isn't a religious service," Brucilla said. "By the way, the girls in this crowd look straight."

"True, but the guys look gay. Maybe they will know a money manager."

Brucilla glanced skeptically at a man seated nearby, a boozy fifty-year-old with a buzz cut and a pot belly. How charming it was that Alison was still willing to believe that there might be a money manager here among these lost souls. She was so pure of heart. *And blessed are the pure of heart*, Brucilla recalled from Sunday school, *for they shall see God. Or if not God, at least the diva.*

Deena D'Amour finished her drag number and returned to the stage, the crowd roaring its approval.

"Thank you, thank you, everyone, for coming to our blessed Gospel Hour on Sunday night, when we raise our voices and our champagne glasses to make a joyful noise unto the Lord! We have a wonderful program for you tonight with the three Sainted Sisters of Sequins. But first we have our birthday blessing. All you ladies who were born in May, line up right over here for your blessing!"

As the line formed, waiters dashed over to give the birthday girls slices of birthday cake topped with little burning candles.

"I should go up there," Alison declared. "I was born in May."

"Could be embarrassing," Brucilla warned. "You don't know what that drag queen has in mind."

"I can handle her," Alison said, leaving the table to join the birthday queue.

"Oh, come hither, doll," Deena said upon spotting Alison. "My, what a lovely blond thing we have here! My, my, my! Oh, look at your tits! They're as big as mine, and I believe yours might be real! Where are you from?"

Alison stepped up to the stage. "Washington, D.C."

"Oooh, a political pussy!" Deena said with a sexy growl. "Do you do Democrats or Republicans?"

"Um, I'm really not into politics."

Batting her big black eyelashes, Deena leaned over to Alison and asked in a gravelly voice, "So what are you into, honey? Do you do sixty-nine year old men in drag by any chance? We could make an arrangement after the show. I'm always available for an *assignation*."

"No," Alison said with a laugh. "I'm here on business."

"Oh, we're all here on business, sweetheart, aren't we, girls?" Deena said, shaking her hips and blowing a kiss to the audience. "What is *your* business?"

"I oversee money managers for a firm that specializes in morality-based and socially responsible investing."

"Socially responsible investing?" Deena repeated with a laugh. "Oh, darlin', you come to the wrong place." She turned toward the crowd of bachelorettes and gay men. "Do you see any signs of morality in this place? I don't think so!"

"Not here, bitch!" a man in the audience yelled.

"My colleagues and I are in town looking for gay money managers," said Alison, pointing across the room to the table where Brucilla and Yong were sitting. "Do you know of any?"

"Your colleagues?" Deena caught sight of them. "Oh, my heart, what is that?" she said, aiming her finger at Brucilla. "Come up here, honey. Mama wants to take a better look at you!"

Brucilla hesitated.

"Yes, I mean you, honey, get yo' ass up here, girl," said Deena.

Brucilla rose from his chair and clopped up to the stage.

"My, my, what have we here? One of her colleagues! Now that's what I call a colleague! Get a load of her, folks!" Deena walked slowly all the way around Brucilla's sequined pink dress to do a closer inspection, turning her face back to the audience and forming her lips into a circle. "Oooh, child! And what's your name, darlin'?"

"Brucilla."

"Brucilla, as in Godzilla? Oh my, how tall are you?"

"Six four."

"Goodness gracious! Without the pink heels?"

"Yes."

Deena looked him up and down from head to toe. "My, my! You must be the tallest queen in captivity, honey! And what do you do?"

"I'm a transgendered quantitative investment manager."

"I have no earthly idea what that is," Deena said, looking stupefied.

"That's okay. No one else does either," Brucilla replied. "But the state of California says it needs one very badly, so here I am."

Deena stared at Brucilla in awe. "I love the dress, but who does your makeup, honey? Laying it kind of thick on the cheeks, aren't you? You gotta lighten up on the powder and eye shadow. Mama should show you how to do drag right."

"I am very new at this," Brucilla admitted. "But I'm not a drag queen. I'm a transgender."

"Every girl has to look her best, honey, no matter what kind of girl she is," Deena declared. "Good taste is all that separates any of us from the tramps."

"Yes, I suppose."

"Are you pre-op or post-op?"

Brucilla looked down. "Pre-op."

"Not quite sure? Mama could help you figure it out," Deena said, pretending to grasp at Brucilla's crotch.

"No, that's it," Brucilla said, jumping away. "I'm definitely pre-op."

"Then it's not too late for you to become a drag queen. Can you sing and dance?"

"I don't know," Brucilla said, thinking she had barely learned how to walk in heels. "I've never tried."

"Then this might be the career opportunity of a lifetime for you. We drag queens get tips. Do they give you tips where you work?"

"No. In my line of work, some of us get performance fees, if we out-perform."

"Performance fees, tips, it's all the same, honey. In any line of work, a girl gets paid for shaking it with a smile. Hey, it's time for my next drag number. It's our anthem here at the Gospel Hour," Deena said to Brucilla and Alison. "Would you two like to do a drag number with me?"

Alison, by now feeling the effects of her champagne, was nodding with a big goofy grin. "Sure, why not?" she said.

"It's time to go looking for a city!" Deena called out to the disc jockey. "Let's make a joyful noise unto the Lord! Hit it, Randy."

Deena grabbed Brucilla and Alison and led them down arm-in-arm from the stage, the loudspeakers pouring out Vestal Goodman and Johnny Cook's rousing rendition of the gospel song "Looking for a City" as everyone in the place, even the waiters, began waving white napkins back and forth in time to the music.

As the song continued, a line of tippers formed to stash one dollar bills into Deena's bosoms. Then they came for Brucilla and Alison. A man with a black mustache pressed a greenback into Brucilla's breast forms and kissed him on the cheek. Then other diners did the same. By the time the song ended, Brucilla had been stuffed with twenty-three dollars and Alison with eighteen.

"Thank you so much, ladies," Deena said to Brucilla and Alison. "So you said you are looking for money managers?" She turned to the crowd. "Anybody know of any gay money managers?"

Silence filled the drag palace.

"Didn't think so. Lordy, you won't find any money managers in a place like this, doll. Money is like sex. Queens don't manage either one," Deena declared. "We spend it all like water, or give it away." She turned toward the crowd again. "Isn't that right, you bitches?"

"Hell, yeah, you gotta give it away, Deena!" one of the plastered patrons answered. "We sure as hell ain't paying for what you got!"

"Well, best of luck to you," Deena said. And then in a flash she was back up on the stage again, introducing the first of the three Sainted Sisters of Sequins, Amber Alert, a black drag queen with a two-foot high platinum blond wig who skittered across the floor in her vagabond shoes, lip-synching to Liza Minnelli's "New York, New York." Juana Bang and Doona Train then followed with their numbers.

It was almost ten o'clock when Alison, Brucilla, and Yong left Gurlz to head back to their hotel.

"How long do you think it takes those guys to dress for that show?" Alison asked Brucilla as they walked out of the drag palace and down the street.

"Hours and hours, I'll bet," Brucilla said. "They probably have a lot of help backstage. I could use some help."

"Yes, man in dress need help," Yong said with a laugh. "Go back to school, get PhD in eye shadow." Just then to his left he noticed someone moving in the alley as they were passing by it.

Three men jumped out of the darkness at them.

They went first for Alison. She could feel one of the assailants seize her by the waist and pull her into the alley. Brucilla was knocked off his pumps onto his knees by the second man. Yong felt one pulling him down by the shoulders.

"Get these queers!" one of them yelled. "Take the girl!"

Yong quickly got himself free of his attacker by punching him in the gut with his elbow. Then he wheeled around with a high flying kick and drove his shoe into the man's ear, sending him reeling backwards. Brucilla got on top of his man and started pounding his face when he saw one assailant kneeling over Alison and groping at her dress. Brucilla jumped up and lifted the man, turned him around and smashed his nose with a right hook. Then someone hit Brucilla from behind and knocked him face down onto Alison.

And then there was silence. The three thugs had slithered away down the alley into the darkness.

"Crazy bastards!" Yong yelled after them.

"Alison," Brucilla said, still lying on top of her, looking down into her beautiful blue eyes glinting in the moonlight. He gasped for air, his heaving plastic breast forms pressing down on her chest. He could feel her hot sweet breath on his face as he gazed longingly at her. "Alison, are you alright?"

"Yes, thanks to you. You were so brave. Are you okay?"

"Yes."

"Brucilla?"

"Yes?"

"You can get off me now."

"Oh yes," he said, jumping up and helping her to her feet. He found his pumps and adjusted his breasts and wig, knocked askew during the fracas.

"That's it, now we've been assaulted. We could have been killed," Alison said, her eyes boiling with rage. "I'm done with San Francisco. Some gay mecca. We'll never find them here, not this way. Let's go home."

16 The Global Tit Test

Yong noticed something different about Percival Quigley the minute he met him at the Vain Capital reception desk. Quigley, a portfolio manager, had arrived from London to pitch the global equity strategy of Brixbury Asset Management. It was more than just Quigley's supercilious English accent that struck Yong as odd. Quigley's associate, Nigel Farnsworth, had one too.

It was something about the way Farnsworth, a tall man about forty who was going bald, looked at Alison and Brucilla, as opposed to the way Quigley did, or rather, did not. Alison had worn a thin white blouse that showed off the shapeliness of her magnificent breasts and even hinted at the outlines of her brassiere. As they walked to the conference room, Yong caught Farnsworth's eyes sweeping up and around Alison's figure, lingering for a while around her hips, but always returning to her breasts. When Farnsworth encountered Brucilla and his polyurethane foam breasts, the Englishman's eyes seemed to be repelled by an invisible force field of distaste. He turned away at once, instinctively.

Yong perceived nothing of the kind with Quigley. The thirty-year-old with thinning blond hair took little notice of Alison. The magnetic fields emanating from Alison and Brucilla did not seem to affect him at all. As Quigley laid out his detailed explanation of the Brixbury investment process for picking global small capitalization stocks, he looked at Alison and Brucilla with perfect equanimity and indifference.

To top it off, Brucilla was an even more alarming sight than usual that morning. He had dressed in a big hurry, donning a tight chartreuse gown that made his plastic bosoms press out from his chest like tumescent eggplants. He had smeared his rugged face with an extra layer of rouge to mask his hastily shaved beard. His elongated eyelashes flapped like flyswatters as if he were trying to deter winged insects from laying their eggs on his purple-green eye shadow. Even his blond wig was out of kilter, making his head seem to lean to one side as if it might tip over at any moment and come crashing down on his shoulder. But none of these irregularities drew the slightest notice from Quigley.

Yong, who watched Masterpiece Theatre regularly and had been to London once, was reasonably sure most English women did not look like Brucilla.

"How do you find portfolio managers for your firm?" Alison asked her guests.

"Oh, we have a small staff and are most particular in our hiring," Quigley answered her, rubbing his left hand with his right as if he were applying lotion to it. "Like our peers, we draw most of our staff from firms in the City of London, investment banks, and Oxford and Cambridge. Last year we took on a chap from a bank up in Edinburgh. But our prime objective in hiring for Brixbury, I'm proud to say, is to ensure that everyone who works with us is amusing. Wouldn't you agree, Nigel?"

"Oh, yes, quite so," Farnsworth concurred. "With all the hours we spend in the office, everyone must be amusing. It is an absolute prerequisite." He smiled, his eyes hovering over Alison's breasts once again. "But we are easily amused."

"Our clients must be up to standard as well," Quigley insisted. "You see, we have only so much capacity in our global small cap equity product, only a billion or so pounds really, and we rather like to reserve it for our preferred clients. Stable money of the right sort, you know. It's frightfully expensive to buy and sell small cap stocks. Transaction costs for small caps can eat one alive, if one isn't careful."

"Yes, up to standard," Farnsworth agreed, his eyes resting peacefully on Alison's plentiful bosoms. "Bloody well over the mark, both of them. Er, I mean, every one—of our clients."

After forty minutes Quigley concluded his presentation, and the guests were shown out.

"Aha, that one is gay!" Yong said to Alison and Brucilla.

"What do you mean?" Alison responded.

"Quigley is queer. I watch his eyes. Farnsworth staring at you but looking away from Brucilla. Quigley, different story I think."

"How can you be sure he's gay? He's English. They can be very re-served. You have to make allowance for that," Alison pointed out.

"Where was Farnsworth staring?" Brucilla asked.

"Down there," Yong said, pointing at Alison's chest. "And not there," he said, indicating Brucilla's.

"What are you suggesting?" Brucilla asked.

"Do tit test—separate straight managers from gay," Yong said. "We put both of you in room together with manager, watch eyes for straight or queer. We flash tits at manager, then boom—find out who queer. Sex work, no matter which asset class—bonds, stocks, private equity, real estate, hedge funds, no matter. Any manager, any country, sex work. Even on Englishmen."

"That's it—a global breast reaction signal," Brucilla said. "Why didn't we think of this before? A binary response to sexual stimuli, indicating sexual preference. I'll bet the signal will be highly predictive. And with our findings we could create a database to test the signal's efficacy."

"I suppose it might work, and we have to try something," Alison agreed. "We could drop in on every manager meeting that any of the other three investment officers are having at Vain Capital and record the reactions."

Roger Ibble, as it happened, was being visited by a Chicago manager promoting an infrastructure fund that very afternoon. He welcomed them to attend his meeting.

Yong planned how to set up the conference room. Alison and Brucilla would be placed next to each other, with Yong at the end taking notes. A small video camera was placed inconspicuously among potted plants on a window sill to record the movement of the money manager's eyes.

Roger brought portfolio manager Martin Howitzer and market-er Benny Lombardo of Occidental Oxidation Partners into the room and positioned them as instructed. Lombardo passed out presentation books for the OOPS Fund and began his sales presentation.

"Occidental Oxidation Partners invests in America's rusting infra-structure," Lombardo explained. "Thanks to short-sighted politicians and taxpayers, this country's infrastructure has been run into the ground for sixty years. The U.S. desperately needs four trillion dollars in new airports, sanitation systems, highways, subways, and bridges or our infrastructure will sink to the level of Zimbabwe's. The OOPS Fund, run by Martin here, makes targeted infrastructure investments in the form of loans at fabulously high interest rates to strapped municipalities and states."

While Lombardo spoke, Yong monitored Howitzer's eyes as they bounced off Brucilla and drifted toward Alison's plump breasts, where they settled in for a long, lazy stare.

Lombardo continued his pitch. "It's a vast investment opportunity. Hundreds of cities, towns, and counties all across America with abysmal bond ratings will gladly pay Occidental Oxidation hundreds of basis points over junk bond rates to keep their sewage from backing up into the streets, their bridges from dropping into the river, and their subway cars from derailing and catching fire."

"Is this strictly a fixed income investment?" Brucilla asked Howitzer, trying to draw the portfolio manager's attention.

"Not just fixed income," said Howitzer, wresting his eyes from Alison to respond to Brucilla. "Essentially OOPS is a vulture fund. But instead of focusing on bankrupt companies, we target the most distressed local and state governments suffering from decades of neglect, incompetence, and corruption."

"How do you pick your investments?" Brucilla asked.

As he looked at Brucilla, Howitzer's eyebrows seemed to twist into knots. His gaze quickly returned to Alison.

"I have developed a proprietary metric—the OOPS ratio, which we maximize," Howitzer said. "It measures three key factors that make an infrastructure investment attractive: the criticality of the infrastructure item, the desperation and stupidity of the government, and the length of time we can milk the situation. In every deal we insist on a guaranteed piece of the government's revenue stream. For example, if it's a hydroelectric dam about to burst, in exchange for the funds we provide to save the town below from destruction we contract for a slice of the electricity revenues. We also will hold a mortgage on the asset."

"So you can repossess the dam if they don't pay, I assume," Brucilla suggested, forcing Howitzer to look at him again.

"Yes, and the town too. We did that in one case. Mintonville, Ohio."

"Wow, you repossessed a whole town?" Alison asked.

"Not exactly all," Howitzer said, turning back to her and smiling. "Only the public parts: city hall, police stations, fire stations, water authority, schools, municipal hospital, senior care center, and the parks. We can't get a mortgage on what the town doesn't own, such as the businesses and residences. Of course, once we shut off the water and sewer, the privately owned part of town clears out fast. Then we move in and buy up those properties for pennies."

"What good is town without people? How is this highest and best use of capital?" Yong asked.

"Oh, it's the very best use of capital," said Howitzer. "When we own the whole town we can rebuild and repopulate it with residents who are willing to pay for infrastructure. Or we can auction off the parts of the town to the highest bidder, or sell it for scrap, or convert the town to some other income-generating use, like a theme park or sanitary land-fill. At that point we have control. Actually, as the portfolio manager of the OOPS Fund, I personally have control. I become mayor, police chief, and czar. But getting so directly involved in running a town is a lot of work. I very much prefer not to repossess. Nonetheless, we have to ensure that our clients are paid fairly for the great risks they take with these bankrupt governments. We can't have our clients investing in vain."

"Who are your clients?" Alison asked.

"Mostly government pensions looking for steady income. And man-ager-of-managers firms too, although as of yet no MOMs as socially responsible as you guys."

"You mean you have government clients who are investing in a vul-ture fund designed to exploit the incompetence of other governments?" she asked.

"Yes. Or they can even invest in their own incompetence, which is often a surer bet. One of the OOPS Fund's investors is an underfund-ed city pension, while the same city's government has borrowed heav-ily from OOPS to fix its collapsing sewers. In effect, the city is hedged against its own poop."

"I thought hedging was supposed to reduce risk, but that sounds aw-fully risky for the city. I hope they don't default on their loan to OOPS," Alison said.

"If they did, we could take control of their sewers and shut them down. We've found that sewage is the best incentive to pay ever devised. Voters don't like effluent oozing up out of their floor."

After the meeting, the MaxiGay team gathered in the hallway to assess the results of the tit test.

"Straight," came the verdict from Yong.

At the manager meetings that followed that week, Alison wore her most seductive dresses, revealing inches of cleavage and baring her breasts scandalously close to the nipples. As before, Yong videotaped the results and fastidiously noted the portfolio managers' every eye movement.

The portfolio managers were straight in all cases but that of a short-haired female portfolio manager of a high yield bond fund who could not keep her eyes off Alison. Yong scored her as a lesbian.

"We have two positives. Now what can we do with this information?" Brucilla asked. "Do we go back to the two we found and confront them with their sexuality?"

"Yes, how do we confirm our findings?" Alison asked. "Even if we suspect one of them is gay, how can we force a money manager to come out of the closet?"

The issue was still unresolved when word arrived that within an hour the man from CRAM would be dropping in for a surprise visit.

Morbinders fidgeted with his pen at the conference table, looking like he was in a hurry. On his way to New York he had stopped in Washington late that day to get an update from Beatrice on Vain Capital's progress with the MaxiGay search. The Butcher also happened to be there.

"Over the past two months since we last saw you, Morris, we have formed a little task force for the MaxiGay search," Beatrice explained. "Alison, Yong, and Brucilla have just been out beating the bushes for gay money managers, even visiting gay bars in San Francisco."

Morbinders began to wring his wrists and wiggle his nose. Something had to be amiss. "And how many gay managers has this task force found?"

"Er, well, as of yet, none," Beatrice admitted. "Except, of course, for Brucilla."

"No one else at all?"

"No, but they certainly have met a number of fascinating gay people and have learned a lot about the homosexual culture," Beatrice said. "A rather interesting story, to hear Alison tell it. It's a wonderful world full of tattooed lesbians with the strangest sorts of clothing, hairstyles, and odd habits, and leather queens with very queer predilections and sordid behaviors, and lip-synching drag queens with the most outrageous and flamboyant costumes. All very nice, harmless people, however, according to Alison, once you get past the initial horror of meeting them."

"But no gay money managers?"

"Well, Morris, you know there's always a steep learning curve with these sorts of things. After all, it's a new concept. I'm sure we will soon have a breakthrough. We will discover some queer ones, and voilà!— we'll be maximally diversified, sexually fluid, and gay in all dimensions!" Beatrice promised with a wave of her hand.

Morbinders rubbed his bald head anxiously. "Let's see, it's June. Governor Pitypander wants this MaxiGay Fund to be up and running by Native Peoples' Day. That leaves you—"

"Two and a half months," the Butcher answered, boring into Beatrice with his little green eyes. "Not much time to find and sign up six more money managers in addition to Brucilla."

"Oh, but we are just on the verge of finding more. We'll make it," Beatrice assured them.

"What else have you tried?" Morbinders asked.

"Well, that's about it," Beatrice replied, unaware of the breast tests the MaxiGay trio had just been performing. "But we'll come through all right."

Morbinders frowned. "I certainly hope so. We are counting on it. I would not want to report otherwise to CRAM headquarters."

Beatrice and the Butcher both felt a shudder of terror running down their backs.

After Morbinders had left, the Butcher confronted Beatrice in the conference room. "Everything depends on this gay fund of yours, Beatrice," he warned. "The re-election of Patty Pitypander is on a knife edge. Jack Fist has been bashing her daily for mismanaging CRAM and the state's finances, and now he has pulled even with her in the polls. Without a big gay turnout, Pitypander might lose. God help you if that happens. You'll lose your CRAM account. And then you know what Weedle will do."

"We've pulled out all the stops for Pitypander, Stanton," Beatrice insisted. "Alison was almost raped in San Francisco trying to find these people. What more can I ask of her?"

"Ask of her? Haven't you gone to any of these gay dives yourself?"

"No, I should say not," Beatrice said flatly. "Never. Goodness no."

"Get directly involved, Beatrice," the Butcher advised. "Consider what's at stake here. You can't just delegate a project of this importance to an investment officer and walk away. It's your firm that's at risk."

Beatrice promised to accompany the MaxiGay team on its next expedition, starting tomorrow night.

17   Finding Deep Throat

Oh, look, they still have disco balls!" Beatrice exclaimed upon seeing the three mirrored globes spinning from the ceiling. "Get down tonight!" As the MaxiGay team entered the Far Side disco she began to shake her booty like it was 1977.

Alison regarded Beatrice with the mortification of a high school girl whose mother has decided to tag along at the senior prom. Next, she imagined, they would be searching for John Travolta in his white dancing suit. Maybe they would find him here and he would turn the beat around.

The big room encircling the bar was full of casually dressed men, mostly small groups of preppies in their twenties and thirties chatting with each other. A disc jockey was perched in an elevated glass enclosure encased in the wall above the dance floor. Several dozen men boogied to the music booming out of the speakers.

Brucilla, wearing a light blue dress and pink pumps, went to the bar with Yong to get drinks.

Beatrice inspected the men standing around them. "Aren't they cute? So many pretty boys. If I were twenty-five years younger, this place would be full of possibilities. That is, if they weren't all queer."

"Did you like disco music much when you were young?" Alison asked.

Beatrice was mildly annoyed at the suggestion that she looked old enough to be part of the disco generation. "Disco music was already passé by the time I was your age, dear, but I do remember going to some fun dance places that played a lot of Madonna's music, before Gerhard and I were married and Pillsbury was born."

"How is Pillsbury?" Alison asked, changing the subject. The topic of Pillsbury's latest exploits was always a winner, as Beatrice loved to brag about her son ad nauseam.

"Pillsbury just flew home for a visit today. He's doing very well at his new job out in L.A. You know he recently graduated with high honors from Stanford Business School. He got half a dozen job offers, but there was one investment firm in Southern California that was especially keen to hire him and managed to outbid the rest of them. It sounds like everything is going splendidly. I couldn't be more proud. And you know Pillsbury will do well there because when Pillsbury puts his mind to something he always does—"

"Oh, oh!" Alison suddenly shrieked, as if she had just been shot.

Beatrice followed Alison's eyes across the dance floor to two men dancing together. "What's wrong, dear?"

"That guy," Alison said. "The one in the red tee shirt."

"Someone you know?"

"It's Nick. My boyfriend."

On the dance floor Beatrice could see a tall handsome man in a red tee shirt and jeans, about thirty years old, with wavy black hair and bulging arm muscles, dancing with a thin young man with a crewcut.

"Oh, my God!" Alison said, her eyes fixed on the two men.

Brucilla and Yong returned from the bar, bearing drinks. They immediately noticed the look on Alison's face.

"Red alert—it's her boyfriend," Beatrice explained to Brucilla as he handed her a glass of Chardonnay. "The hunk in the red shirt, dancing with that other guy. What a cad!"

"How can he do this to me?" Alison asked. She walked slowly over toward the dance floor, all the way up to the edge, until she was no more than ten feet from him.

Nick suddenly noticed her. He stopped dancing at once, pulled away from his partner, and dropped his hands to his sides. He stared back at Alison. Then he shuffled across the dance floor toward her.

"What are you doing?" Alison said.

"Hey, babe," Nick said, smiling meekly. "We're just having a little fun, no big deal. When did you get here?"

"A little fun? I catch you dancing with another man in a gay disco, and it's just a little fun? How long has this been going on?"

"With Jerry, just a couple of months."

"You know what I mean. With guys in general, how long have you been doing this?"

"Since I was a teenager. But it's nothing serious. Not like with you and me."

"A few years? And when were you going to tell me you prefer guys?"

"I don't prefer guys. I'm bisexual."

"I'm not enough for you by myself?"

"That's not it. I just like guys too, and they like me. I'm sexually fluid. Is that a problem?"

"Of course it is."

"Why?"

"Because for the past year I've thought we had something."

"We do. But I have this other something too," Nick said.

"This is too weird for me," Alison said, turning away from him. "I can't do this."

"Why? You have a problem with gay guys? Then what are you doing in a gay disco? Why are you judging me for being here?"

"I'm here on business."

"Oh, sure. And what kind of business is that?"

"We're doing research, looking for gay money managers—my colleagues and I, that is."

"In a gay bar. A likely story," Nick said with a smirk. "Well, it looks like you found one. You weren't available tonight so I'm here with Jerry."

"I can see that. Well, I don't feel like sharing my man with…with Jerry. Get lost." She tried to fight back the tears as she walked away but they started streaming down her face anyway.

Nick stood there looking confused for a moment, and then returned to Jerry. They headed for the front door of the disco and left.

"You see the luck I have with men, Beatrice?" Alison sobbed. "All of the good-looking macho hunks I meet wind up being insensitive jerks, just like Nick. It's been the same old story since high school. I want to believe they love me, but it always turns out they were just into my body all along, but not me. Not the real me. I thought for sure men would improve by this point in my life. What am I doing wrong?"

Then she aimed her lamentation at Brucilla. "Men are so shallow! Why aren't there any *real* guys out there, Brucilla? Twenty-eight years old and I can't find a real man, one who cares about me. Not my big boobs—me. Boobs are just big glands. They're a curse, not a thing to love. Why are men so attracted to them? Anybody can have boobs!"

"It's true," Brucilla said. "Anyone can." You could buy them on the Internet in practically any size, he was thinking, for ninety-nine dollars plus shipping and handling, and they would arrive in a box in two days.

Yong was just about to offer her the comfort of his Confucian saying about how big breasts could feed many children when the anguish on her face made him recall the one about the perils of provoking a woman on the brink of a nuclear meltdown.

"What awful luck I have in men," she wailed. "My hedge fund manager boyfriend is a double-dealing switch-hitter. Now I find he's hedged in ways I never could have imagined!"

"Hedge fund manager!" Beatrice said. "You say he's a hedge fund manager?"

"Yes," Alison said with a sniffle, "he runs a relative value long/short fund."

"An institutional quality relative value long/short fund?"

"Yes. He works for Bravado Asset Management in Chevy Chase. That's how we met. We were at a party, he had big biceps, and he told me all about his short positions. I was swept off my feet."

"A bisexual money manager! Where did he go?" Beatrice's head swiveled in all directions, her eyes searching the disco for a red shirt. "Where is he? Maybe we can catch him before he gets away."

"He left with his, his—new boyfriend!" Alison moaned. "Oh, I can hardly say it! He's sexually fluid!"

"Well, let's get him back here, right now!" Beatrice insisted. "We've got to find him! Vain Capital needs him! He qualifies for the MaxiGay Fund!"

"Don't worry, I know where he lives—with me in my condo in Bethesda. Or he has for the past year," Alison blubbered. "But that's all over now."

She contemplated what it would be like to live without a man again. Experience had proved to her beyond any doubt that they were entirely too much trouble. This time she would get a cat, a female one, and have it spayed immediately before it could get any funny ideas.

"Amazing," Beatrice said. "In just ten minutes we've found a bisexual money manager for the MaxiGay portfolio! And to think you were sleeping with him all the time! Alison, I knew you could find one if you just put your mind to it!"

"Well, you can have the bastard, I won't!" Alison declared. "And I don't want him in the MaxiGay Fund either. I'd have to face him in meetings on a regular basis. You want to give him a billion dollars to manage because he's cheated on me with, with—a man? No, no, I won't be a part of it!" She began to bawl. Brucilla handed her another margarita.

"Thank you, Brucilla," she said, gulping it down. "If only I could find a man as sweet and caring as you. Why are guys such insensitive jerks? You were a guy once. What's the answer? Why are they all so worthless, thinking only of themselves? Don't they have any morals?"

Brucilla felt an urge to yank off his wig, sweep up Alison in his arms, and kiss her madly to drive away all her tears forever. But all he could find the courage to do was to pat her gently on the shoulder.

"Oh, don't worry, dear," Beatrice consoled her. "A girl as beautiful as you will never be without a boyfriend long. And not all the good men turn out to be queer. It just seems that way sometimes. But eventually you'll learn that—"

At that moment Beatrice caught sight of a young man who had just walked into the disco. Standing against a wall near the disc jockey's booth, he was about twenty-seven and had red curly hair, a long thin nose, and an intense look about him.

"Oh, my!" Beatrice said with astonishment. "I need to sit down," she said, suddenly feeling faint.

Alison traced Beatrice's eyes to their target. "Someone you know?" she asked.

"It can't be," Beatrice said. She took a chair at an unoccupied table. "What's he doing here? After he flew in from California today, he told me he was going out tonight, but doesn't he know where he is? That's it. He must have wandered in here by mistake."

"Who is it?" Alison asked.

Without answering her, Beatrice got up and walked across the disco to the young man. He nearly jumped at the sight of her.

"Pillsbury?" Beatrice said.

"Mom?" Pillsbury replied.

"What are you doing here?" they both blurted out at the same time.

"You shouldn't be here," she said. "Do you know where you are?"

Pillsbury sighed and looked down at his shoes. "I know where I am. I'm gay, Mom. I go to places like this sometimes."

"You are? You do?"

"Yes, and yes."

Beatrice was thunderstruck. Instinctively, she flashed her sternest look at him, the same one as when he was a little boy and had driven his tricycle into a parked car and then lied to her about it. "How did this happen, Pillsbury?"

"I've always been like this, Mom," Pillsbury said.

"Really? How can that be?"

"I was born this way. You were there when I was born, weren't you?"

Beatrice felt as though she were meeting him for the first time. "I don't know what to say."

"You could say it's okay," Pillsbury suggested. "You could say I'm okay."

But she wondered if it really was okay. She had been raised to think it wasn't. On the other hand, was he not still her son, her darling red-haired son, the one God had given her and she had brought home so many years ago from the hospital, her proudest achievement? Nothing about that had changed. Maybe nothing at all of substance had really changed. He was all the family she had left. It would be far easier to lose an arm or a leg.

"Are you ashamed of me, Mom?" Pillsbury asked.

Was she ashamed? No, that was impossible. She was a Pillsbury. Shame, the stock in trade of Vain Capital, the moral MOM, was for her clients. Could a real mom tell her son, her flesh and blood, that she was ashamed of him?

Beatrice reached out and threw herself around him. "I love you, sweetheart," she said.

Pillsbury felt the weight of a lifelong lie suddenly lifted off him. He kissed his mother on the cheek and hugged her.

"Come on over with me to meet some of my colleagues from work," she said, taking him by the hand. "I want them to meet you."

Beatrice led Pillsbury to where Brucilla, Alison, and Yong were standing and introduced them.

"What do you do in Santa Monica?" Brucilla asked Pillsbury.

"I'm a distressed bond manager," he said. "That is, the bonds are distressed, but I'm happy to manage them."

Alison turned immediately toward Pillsbury. "What's that? Where? What firm? How much do you manage?"

Pillsbury was startled by her keen interest in bonds. "I'm a portfolio manager for a firm called MIP—that's Magic Investment Partners. We run about two billion dollars of distressed debt, buying defaulted bonds of bankrupt companies at bargain prices. We chop up busted companies and trade the used parts, which are usually worth more than the whole. Kind of the way a junkyard works. That's the financial magic that we do."

"Hallelujah!" Alison exclaimed. "That's absolutely fantastic!"

"Actually, it's pretty dull work, just lots of number-crunching, if you want to know the truth," he said matter-of-factly. "Mostly analyzing what the pieces of a broken company are worth. But it pays well for my first job out of business school."

"And you're gay—really, really gay?" Alison asked, as if it were too good to be true.

"Not really, really gay. I'm not a flaming queen by any means," Pillsbury said, looking at Brucilla. "I'm just mildly gay."

"Wonderful! That's plenty gay enough for us."

"By the way, what are all of you doing here at the Far Side Disco?" Pillsbury asked.

"Looking for gay money managers like you," Alison said. "Your mother had a hunch we would find them in a place like this, and we have. She's made it look easy. Well, let me tell you, it's been anything but easy so far. But now we have found you, so our luck must be changing! It must be the famous Pillsbury family luck your mother has always told us about."

A grim look came over Beatrice, who shook her head. "Unfortunately, Pillsbury can't help us. He's not eligible."

"No? Why not?" Alison replied.

"We can't hire our own relatives for the MaxiGay Fund," Beatrice said. "It would be clearly illegal. The state of California would never consent to it. We can't hire Pillsbury, as much as I'd love to."

"And I couldn't stand hiring Nick," Alison said, "as much as we need to."

"So after all this time and effort looking high and low we've finally found two qualifying money managers, but we can't hire either one just because you two already knew them before we started this search," Brucilla said. "And we have a billion dollars to invest with any queer money manager we find, just for being gay. This is insane."

"A billion dollars for being gay! That is insane." Pillsbury agreed. "Most of us do it for nothing."

"Yes, CRAM has a billion dollars to give to each of seven gay managers in the categories LGBTQIA," Alison explained. "But we couldn't find any gay money managers anywhere, until tonight. We've been searching all over, even in San Francisco. But all we could find in any of these places were ordinary people."

"That's because gay people are ordinary people, mostly," Pillsbury said. "But money managers aren't. For a billion dollars in assets, what money manager worth his salt wouldn't be gay? Why the heck are you looking for them in gay bars?"

"Is this the wrong place to find them?" Beatrice asked with a puzzled look.

"Yes, of course," Pillsbury said. "You could go to a stadium-sized bar full of gay people and not run into more than one portfolio manager in a thousand. It would take a hundred years to find one the way you are going about it."

"I see your point, although we did manage to find two of them here tonight in less than an hour," she said.

"Well, this is the wrong place," Pillsbury said firmly.

"But the wrong place is where you find the truth," Beatrice said. "If truth could be found in the right place everyone would have it, wouldn't they?"

"Have you tried advertising in *Pensions Daily*?" Pillsbury asked.

Beatrice looked stumped. "Why, no," she admitted, "we hadn't thought of putting ads in the trade magazines. Would that work?"

"Of course it will work," Pillsbury said. "Money managers are in the business of gathering assets. They're as greedy as anyone. Greedier than most, in fact. For a billion dollars in assets, they will be whatever you want them to be."

"Maybe you're right," Beatrice said. "We've been going about this gay search all wrong. We had no idea they wanted money to come out of the closet."

"Trust me, Mom, you don't need to go to gay bars to find gay money managers. Just advertise for them. They will follow the money."

18 Dodgy Due Diligence

"The Queen Bea promised you guys would help evaluate any gay managers we found," Alison said to Thor Nederbrygge on their way to meet the new prospect. "This one's a hedge fund firm. That's in your bailiwick, not mine." She shot a malicious grin at him.

Thor, the tall Norse god of thunder and hedge funds, gave her a haughty look. "A queer hedge fund manager! Hah! What kind of fruitcake is it?"

"I've saved the surprise just for you."

A stocky man with big jowls rose from his chair to greet them as they entered the conference room to join Brucilla and Yong. He was Hank Higgins, the marketer who had phoned from Pygmalion Capital in New London, Connecticut. Accompanying him was Ernest Doolittle, a short, pudgy fellow in his mid-thirties with a receding blond hairline and a face as round as a pumpkin.

"We think we have a unique fit with your gay program, Alison," Higgins began, turning toward Doolittle. "Ernest here runs the Pygmalion market-neutral hedge fund which, like any fund of its type, has an equal amount of money invested in both long and short positions, leaving us completely hedged against the stock market's moves. We don't care a whit if the market goes up or down, as long as our long and short positions do well. But Ernest is hedged in another special and unusually intimate way."

"What way is that?" Thor asked, arching an eyebrow.

"Both ways, and every which way," said Higgins. "He's a hermaphrodite."

There was a long silence as everyone froze, not knowing what to say next. Doolittle looked down at his lap and shrugged helplessly.

Yong stared at Doolittle. "Hermaphrodite? What is that?"

"Both boy and girl sex parts," Brucilla whispered to him.

"Oh?" Yong said. "Oh!" he repeated. Then he noticed something on Doolittle's cheek. It was some kind of makeup, similar to the talcum powder Brucilla troweled on his face every morning to cover up his beard.

"Yes, a hermaphrodite! Isn't that fabulous? We're so happy to meet you." Alison said. "Oh, you have no idea!"

She watched Thor begin to squirm uncontrollably. Brucilla crossed his legs and twisted in his chair, tugging nervously at his Butt and Hip Builder.

Yong cocked his head sideways in bewilderment, trying to imagine what such a creature looked like naked and how its two sets of reproductive equipment functioned. Could a hermaphrodite have sex with itself? Could it have its own baby? But there were some questions even Yong would hesitate to ask.

Higgins continued his pitch. "I believe your ad in *Pensions Daily* says CRAM needs someone of that type to fill the intersex slot in your fund. I'm willing to bet there's not another like him in the country, maybe in the whole world."

"You may be right. How lucky we are you responded to our ad," Alison replied jubilantly. "Of the seven LGBTQIA dimensions, the intersex category was going to be the toughest nut of all for us to crack, so to speak."

"We knew that would be the case when we saw your ad. Ernest is such a rarity we felt almost obligated to let you know we had him," Higgins declared. "For the sake of California."

Thor and Brucilla sat there exchanging looks, desperately hoping the other would pose the obvious question.

Yong beat them to it. "How we know you are hermaphrodite?" he asked Doolittle.

"How do you know?" Higgins said, seemingly taken aback by the question.

"Yes, how we know you telling truth?"

"Because Ernest says so," Higgins said, looking quite insulted. "Isn't that enough? Is physical inspection of a money manager's genitalia part of your due diligence process? We didn't notice any mention of that requirement in the *Pensions Daily* ad."

"It wasn't in the ad," Alison admitted. "The question of verification has only now come up. We hadn't thought of it before."

"Very well, then, which one of you would like to do the inspection?" Higgins asked.

Thor's face suddenly became flushed. As the head of hedge funds, it would be his job to certify the hermaphrodite's bona fides. He imagined having to take photos of Ernest with his pants down. Would they need to make copies of the pictures for proof to show CRAM? Would the images be considered due diligence or pornography? Could they be construed as sexual harassment? Was this in his job description?

Alison decided to enjoy the deep red glow on Thor's face for a few more seconds before throwing her colleague a lifeline. "Maybe an actual physical inspection of Ernest is unnecessary. CRAM didn't tell us we had to check out a manager's private parts. I think self-identification is the key here. After all, it's good enough to qualify the transgenders. Do you agree, Brucilla?"

"Yes, absolutely," Brucilla said. "What's sauce for us transgenders is sauce for you hermaphrodites. We can't be second-guessing money managers' stated sexual preferences or sniffing at their crotches. If Ernest says he feels like a hermaphrodite, then that's what he is. If a guy's word is good enough to get him into the ladies room in San Francisco, then by golly it ought to be good enough to get him into the CRAM portfolio in Sacramento."

Thor let out a loud sigh. "I couldn't agree more. It's what's between Ernest's ears that really counts, not what's between his legs. Isn't that the very same high standard all our other hedge fund managers have to meet, no more or less? It's only fair to accept Ernest's word for it. It's settled—a hermaphrodite he is. Or intersex, or whatever you people like."

"Speaking of what really counts, Ernest, how has your market-neutral portfolio done?" Alison flipped to the back of the presentation book to look at Pygmalion Capital's performance record.

The performance table showed a nearly unbroken string of annual losses. Doolittle had trailed his benchmark for nine of the past ten years, generating wildly excessive volatility. As the number of Pygmalion's clients had steadily dwindled, the fund's assets had shriveled in five years from five hundred million to seventy-five million dollars.

"I see your performance has struggled a bit," she commented.

"I confess my returns are a few points behind those of Treasury bills," Doolittle conceded. "But then I'm the top-performing hermaphrodite hedge fund manager in the country."

"And you can be very proud of that distinction," Brucilla acknowledged. "Being a sexually unique portfolio manager is a valid accomplishment in its own right. Performance under these circumstances, when you have such special talents to contribute to the vibrancy and diversity of CRAM's portfolio, is really beside the point, isn't it?"

"So we are in the running for the hermaphrodite position?" Higgins asked as Alison showed her guests out.

"Definitely," she said. "At the very top of the list."

Upon returning to her office, Alison noticed that her telephone was blinking furiously with voice mail messages. She pressed a button to listen to them.

"Hello, Ms. Hartswell," a female voice said. "This is Harriet Hammertone calling from Vagus Real Estate Management in Seattle regarding your ad in *Pensions Daily* seeking to allocate a billion dollars to LGBTQIA money managers. We have a hermaphrodite portfolio manager I believe you may be interested in meeting. Please call me back at your earliest convenience." Click.

"Howdy, Ms. Hartswell," the second caller drawled. "This is Kyle Coons, senior vice president of marketing with Hotspur Asset Management in Lubbock, Texas. Hotspur runs five billion in oil and gas partnerships, and we'd be tickled to speak with you about your gay program with CRAM. There's a portfolio manager here by the name of Clem. Well, we cain't tell what CRAM would call Clem, but he says he's an intersex. You'd probably know more about that than we would. I thought we ought to get him on your gaydar and let you be the judge. I'd be much obliged if you could get back to me." Click.

"Good day, Ms. Hartswell," the third caller said. "Gary Butterbunny here, head of marketing with Penobscot Partners in Portland, Maine. We're a private equity firm specializing in buyouts of midsize toxic waste firms. Saw your ad in *Pensions Daily* about allocating a billion dollars to an asexual money manager. We've got a lonely forty-year old portfolio manager who might fit the bill. Call me back if you could." Click.

"Hello, Ms. Hartswell," the fourth caller said. "This is Nancy Hipbite, senior vice president of marketing at Green Mountain Asset Management in Burlington, Vermont. GMAM does three billion in global bond portfolios. We noticed your ad in *Pensions Daily* looking for lesbians to run a billion dollars and we wondered if you'd be able to meet our Ida Bean next week when she's in D.C. Please let me know by tomorrow." Click.

Yong came rushing into her office with a notepad in hand. "Twenty-one on the list now! Three lesbians, eight gays, three bisexuals, two transgenders, two queers, one intersexual, four asexuals. We got enough?"

Alison folded her arms in triumph. "Yes, now we just pick the ones we want." She raised her hand and high-fived him. "We did it, Yong!"

She reflected for a moment on how simple it had been, once you knew the secret.

After receiving Alison's good news, Beatrice closed her office door and phoned the Russky Fund's office in New York.

"Yes, that's right, Yegor," she said. "CRAM will fund our gay money managers with seven billion dollars at the end of July. Please make arrangements to wire your three billion dollars to the fund's prime broker. You can tell your high-ranking Russian official that his very unlikely investment is almost ready."

"*Da, da! Ochen' khorosho*," Yegor Yakov replied. "Thank you. I understand. I will let superiors know. We have money ready for you on time. Gay money managers, *da*. *Vyesyoli, da*. Most unlikely investment."

Yakov settled back in his chair and gazed through his office window at the people scurrying to and fro on the Wall Street sidewalk below. New Yorkers seemed thoroughly unhappy to him. How serious they all looked, how preoccupied with whatever mad things they were busily doing, he imagined. In this part of the city many of them must certainly be money managers. All that brooding about money and always needing to pile up more and more of it without end—that must be why it had taken Vain Capital months to find just seven merry ones. This was just more proof Americans worked much too hard to enjoy life. How could any normal person be merry under such mentally unhealthy conditions as he saw in the beehive below? Russians knew better how to live.

Yakov would show these Americans how to relax properly. He reached into a drawer in his desk, pulled out a flask of vodka, and downed a big swig.

"*Vyesyoli!*" he said with a grin. "With this I am always *vyesyoli!*" Vodka in the morning, vodka in the afternoon, vodka in the evening—that was all it would take to make this Russian merry today.

Beatrice made her next celebratory call to the Butcher. He was glad to hear she had succeeded in landing CRAM and the Russky Fund. But these feats, great as they were, were not enough to satisfy him.

"Weedle will be happy to hear the news," the Butcher said. "But remember, Beatrice, you need to prove to us that you can keep your clients. If your performance lags, CRAM will yank that seven billion dollars right out from under you and Vain Capital will be right back in the soup. Remember, you need to have at least twelve billion by the end of this year."

"How long do you think CRAM will give us to prove ourselves?" she asked.

"No telling, given their shaky financial condition. A year at most, and that's if Pitypander survives the election."

"But a year is nothing, Stanton. All kinds of things beyond our control can ruin a year's returns."

"I understand that, but CRAM doesn't care about your problems, Beatrice," the Butcher said. "Their leadership is under tremendous political pressure, it's constantly turning over, and they are notoriously impatient."

"Well, we'll have their money soon. Be happy for that."

"Getting their money is only half the game, Beatrice. To keep the CRAM account, your MaxiGay Fund will have to outperform right out of the gate."

19 Strategizing in the Kremlin

President Viktor Bludinov hunched over a large table in the middle of his Kremlin office, his narrow blue eyes squinting at the maps General Smiryagin and his aide had spread out before him.

Bludinov reached into his breast pocket for his reading glasses and slipped them on. "Just three thousand soldiers? Will that really be enough to take and hold Narva if it comes to that?"

"There are only about sixty thousand people in Narva, Mr. President, and almost all of them are ethnic Russian," General Smiryagin replied. "Less than four percent of Narva's population is Estonian. Our soldiers can simply waltz across the bridge from Ivangorod into Narva and they will be welcomed by the people with open arms. We won't have to fire a shot."

"And after they waltz across the bridge, how will you hold the town?"

"We will set up defenses around Narva at these locations noted on the map. We will announce a plebiscite to allow the people to vote on whether they would like to be part of Russia or Estonia. That will be no contest. Then we will go to the next town and repeat the process. Taking eastern Estonia will be as easy as our annexation of Crimea in 2014."

"And if we do have to shoot?"

"It won't be the first time," the general said. "Narva was reduced to rubble in World War II. It was an improvement on its previous condition."

"Then they shouldn't mind too much becoming rubble again," Bludinov replied. "Where are our men and materiel?"

"The old fortress of Ivangorod. The men are billeted there and at various other locations around Ivangorod. We can easily bring in many thousands more if necessary."

"Where are NATO's forces?"

"All of Estonia is protected by only six thousand troops, five hundred soldiers from NATO and the rest from the Estonian army, most of them located near the capital, Tallinn, more than two hundred kilometers from Narva. Once a year NATO holds a parade in Tallinn to demonstrate its determination to defend Estonia. After last year's parade, the local rowdies got drunk and beat up the NATO troops for entertainment."

"How long have we been moving our soldiers and supplies into position?"

"About three months. We have everything ready."

"Surely the Americans must have noticed by now. I hope you made things as obvious as possible for them. We wouldn't want their satellites to miss this."

"We painted "Invasion Force" on the roofs of the supply buildings to help them out—in bright red letters in both Russian and English."

"It's odd I haven't heard anything through diplomatic channels. Not a single protest from the American ambassador. Not a peep out of her. Has anyone checked the American Secretary of State's e-mails?"

"Yes, sir. Nothing there either."

"That's odd. Her private e-mail server is usually a goldmine of information. Why don't you increase the size of the letters on the roofs of the supply buildings? Put up a big blinking neon sign if necessary."

"Very good, sir."

"Well, then the trap is set. Eventually the Americans are bound to see what we are doing at Ivangorod. For years they have been reluctant to put more troops into Estonia for fear of provoking us. This buildup will have that obnoxious American president crapping in her pantsuit. I love a good game of chess, especially against an opponent I can't stand! Because I always win at chess, you know."

A woman appeared in the doorway to remind Bludinov of his appointment with the head of the Russky Fund, Yuri Strelnikov. The general and his aide rolled up the maps and took their leave.

Strelnikov, a portly man in a blue striped suit, entered the president's office.

"Yuri Alekseyevich, my old friend, so good to see you," Bludinov said, shaking hands with him. "You have some good news for me, I hope?"

"Yes, Viktor Ivanovich," Strelnikov said. "We have hidden your fifteen billion dollars in all sorts of places where no one will ever think of looking. We've been flying all over the world making arrangements." Strelnikov handed Bludinov his report. "You can see the investments here."

Bludinov read down the list. "Singapore, two billion, very good, Geneva, three billion, very good. Ah, what is this one?" he asked, pointing to an investment in Washington called the MaxiGay Fund.

"Oh, we were referred to that one by an American fellow who has managed money for the Russky Fund. It's run by a firm in Washington called Vain Capital, which specializes in moral investing. This is a commingled fund of merry money managers, who are apparently so rare in America they need a special fund to encourage them."

"Moral investing! That's as absurd as waging a moral war! Survival of the fittest be damned, I suppose!" Bludinov exclaimed. "That sounds like Washington, actually. It's amazing how those self-righteous Western feminists like Phyllis Fibby think they can outlaw nature and common sense. Will they never tire of lecturing me about having my political enemies assassinated? Harangue me at the United Nations for my human rights record, will she? As if I could hold this country of thieves and cutthroats together by serving everyone tea in a samovar. The Americans are ridiculous. They live in a world of political fairy tales and self-delusion. In Russia, we have no choice but to live in the real world."

"Moralists are unbearable, as you say. They are all perfect hypocrites," Strelnikov agreed. "But that's what makes this investment the perfect hiding place to stash your wealth, Viktor Ivanovich. No one will suspect President Bludinov of making moral investments anywhere on the planet, let alone in Washington."

"I agree, Yuri, it's a brilliant plan," Bludinov said, his eyes sparkling with malice. "My money, hidden right in the very capital of moral pretense. What delicious revenge it will be! Think of their reaction—the foul stench of my dirty dollars invested right under their smug little pussy noses. Hah, they won't like that when they find out, will they? We'll see who will win this shame game!"

20 The Fall Client Conference

A lison took her place at the entrance to the grand ballroom of the St. Regis Hotel, greeting the guests arriving at Vain Capital's fall client conference as she nervously awaited the man from CRAM. She was somewhat annoyed at being upstaged by the parrot.

A smash hit at the spring client conference, the parrot had returned for an encore and was alternately squawking and preening itself in its brass cage just outside the ballroom. The multicolored bird was working hard for its dinner, rehearsing the new phrases taught it by the Vain Capital marketing staff, building upon the socially responsible vocabulary it had mastered at the previous conference. "Look at my pretty gay feathers!" it screeched at anyone who happened by. "Make a squawk on the wild side—squawk! MaxiGay makes my day with L-G-B-T-Q-I-A!"

"The MaxiGay Fund, now that we have it up and running, should be the star of our fall show," Beatrice had announced the week before. The conference seemed the perfect venue for unveiling the fund to interested clients like Yule University's Tony Elfuego, who had been talking about allocating three hundred million dollars and seemed to be almost in the bag.

The topics Beatrice had picked for the presentations at this client conference were listed on a placard set outside the ballroom:

> New Frontiers for the Socially Diverse Portfolio
> Putting Your Guilty Portfolio Into Rehab
> Shaming Your Investment Committee Into Action
> The Moral Balance Between Banning and Winning
> Redefining What Outperformance Is
> The ESG Revolution

Beatrice had devised the seating plan with her customary care for matching employees with clients. Brucilla would sit near Morris Morbinders of CRAM and Yegor Yakov of the Russky Fund, enabling both clients to become acquainted with Vain Capital's transgendered money manager. Alison was to help Morbinders bond with Brucilla.

Suddenly, there was the man from CRAM, looking as obdurate as ever. Alison, having abandoned hope of ever penetrating his formidable defenses herself, dutifully introduced him to Brucilla, who bent over to shake the little bald man's hand.

Alison searched Morbinders's face intently for some reaction to Brucilla, a sign, anything at all. Nothing. He sat there as rigid as a cigar store Indian. Did he still have a pulse? Did he notice anything? The acrid smell of Brucilla's smeared makeup, which surely could wake the unconscious, should have produced some response.

"So, Morris," she said, "I'll bet Governor Pitypander was very happy that we were able to deliver the goods for her more than two months ahead of schedule."

"I suppose she might be," Morbinders answered slowly, beginning to wiggle his nose. "Actually, I don't know. I've never met the woman," he admitted, resenting Alison's impertinence, thinking she ought to know he could never know what the governor of California thought about anything unless he heard it thirdhand from his superiors at CRAM. A man of his towering unimportance did not attend meetings of the CRAM board of directors. Nor would he ever condescend to divulge CRAM's office scuttlebutt to a mere money manager. Keeping everyone on pins and needles about how CRAM might be deciding their fate back in Sacramento is what gave him his terrible sway.

"Did she make her speech to the gay community to announce the MaxiGay Fund?" Alison asked.

"I think she is saving that for her rally in San Francisco right after Native Peoples' Day. That is the information I was provided," replied Morbinders.

"Well, I hope the people at CRAM are happy about what we've done."

Happy! Was Pitypander happy? Was CRAM happy? Was anybody happy? Next she would have the effrontery to ask if he was happy. Morbinders would have to put a stop to this insolent probing.

He would give her the dreaded Sphinx. He began to stare like the leonine beast of Giza vacuously into the trackless desert before him.

"We shall discuss how happy CRAM is at our review meeting tomorrow," he said darkly.

Alison trembled and fell silent, bewildered at how CRAM could fail to be satisfied with Vain Capital's efforts—*her* tireless efforts—on its behalf.

Meanwhile Brucilla was having no trouble eliciting responses from other clients. Unlike Morbinders, Yegor Yakov looked on in fascination at the exceptionally tall blond woman with the muscular arms and shoulders. Such vigorous women were the very best at picking potatoes in Pupkina, the tiny village where Yakov had grown up. He fondly recalled how big-boned babushkas like Brucilla were highly prized for their ability to work for hours at such stoop labor without tiring and how all the men of the village swore up and down that they made the sturdiest wives.

Other attendees struggled to conceal their shock. Barton Hinckley, the round-faced man from Mormons on the Mount, seized by the unsettling thought of having several such specimens as his wives, squirmed in his temple undergarments. Sister Lucretia, cloaked in her nun's habit, shook her head disapprovingly, apprehensive that such ambiguous characters might soon be pounding on the door of her convent to demand admission to her order. The woman from United Arab Emirates, draped head to toe in a black niqab, peeked out through her little eye holes to steal astonished glances at the awkward wigged man-woman with the foam-rubber breasts, wondering whether he-she was allowed to leave the house without being escorted by a real male.

Beatrice rang her brass bell to convene the client conference. "We have some new clients here today, so to them I offer a warm welcome to Vain Capital. Please let us help you in any way we can with your righteous investing needs. If you need moral guidance for your portfolios, our staff will be delighted to help you fill out the Moral Objection Menu booklets on the desk outside.

"Today we have a special presentation regarding gay diversity and how it can be achieved in your portfolios with our new MaxiGay Fund. But first I want to introduce an old friend of Vain Capital, our keynote speaker, who will speak on the frightening subject of global warming."

It was Al Gore, of course, breezing into the ballroom from Malibu to deliver his usual lecture on the dire consequences of expelling hot air.

"Recent data from the National Oceanic and Atmospheric Administration conclusively demonstrates the rapid deterioration of climate conditions worldwide," Gore began.

As he droned on, Clarence Clemson of Calhoun University leaned over to Sister Lucretia, pointed at the creature in the pink sequined gown and whispered, "What is that?"

"A transgender, I think, although I'm not altogether sure," she speculated. "Whatever it is, it's mighty tall, isn't it? Must be associated with that MaxiGay Fund that Beatrice mentioned."

"I suppose we'll have to have some of that in the Calhoun University endowment too. The students are certain to want it. They seem to be very keen on embracing illicit lifestyles of every kind."

"I'm not sure how our Mother Superior feels about that sort of thing," Sister Lucretia said. "The church has been accused of a lot of shocking gay hanky-panky in recent years, what with the priests diddling thousands of little boys and all. With all the lawsuits and bad publicity from that I don't imagine the investment committee of Little Sisters of a Baby will want to be seen openly funding sexual perversion anytime soon, especially on the heels of dropping Jesus from our name."

"Oh, so it's just Little Sisters of a Baby now? You really went ahead and did it?" Clemson said, recalling their earlier conversation at the spring client conference.

"Yes, just a month ago we bit the bullet and deleted Jesus. We couldn't see any other way out of our dilemma. His failure to condemn slavery in his own time was causing us constant emotional strain."

"Have you lined up someone else to handle your salvation?" Clemson asked.

"Not yet. We've entered Moses, Mohammed, and Buddha as candidates. We were thinking Moses might do, since he freed the Hebrews, but his laws requiring the slaughter of innocent animals in ritual sacrifice are inconsistent with our commitment to animal rights. And the other two were just as bad on the slavery issue as Jesus was. So we're stuck without a savior. How about you? Where are you on renaming Calhoun?"

Clemson shook his head. "We haven't made a final decision. We're looking for something with staying power. Renaming a big university like Calhoun poses a serious branding challenge, one we don't want to face twice. Our logo is on everything from the stadium to the pencils. We're thinking about picking an ideal instead of another eminent person's name."

"An ideal?"

"Yes, like fortitude, for example," Clemson said. "It meant something completely different to the Romans than it does to us, but even though we don't fall on our swords after losing a battle we still admire fortitude just as much as they did, don't we?"

"Yes, we do. Every bit as much."

"Meanwhile, after the same two thousand years your man Jesus has lost his gig. That's because ideals are flexible. You can always redefine an ideal if it starts to let you down. Can't do that with real folks. People never seem to be able to live up to the notions that caught on after they died, but a well-maintained ideal will shine forever."

"I suppose we would have done better with an ideal," the nun agreed. "Not even Jesus could keep up with the times. I suppose a lack of unimpeachable role models is the price we pay for living in a morally enlightened age."

Sister Lucretia's eyes wandered around the room and soon fell upon the swarthy bearded man from United Arab Emirates, who apparently had grown so weary of Al Gore that he was eager for any diversion to help pass the time. He seemed to be winking at her from across the table. She looked at him more closely. He *was* winking at her, a Muslim man! Or more significantly for her, a man. Sister Lucretia felt the heat begin to steam up inside her habit. She winked back at him. He blinked his eye at her once more. She winked back again, and then again. He returned her winks every time. Soon her eyelids were aflutter in a fit of unrestrained winking. Then, just as her passion had reached a rolling boil and she could flit her eyelids no faster, she saw his eyes being drawn suddenly to the side as he began to wink in a different direction. She traced his roving eye to the transgendered hussy across the table. Ceasing her winking at once, she directed a jealous frown at the tall blond Jezebel.

Unaware of being an interloper, Brucilla noticed the Arab man winking at him. Not wishing to offend a valued client, he tried to return the compliment with his own palpebration, but missed his mark with it and instead shot the draped Arab woman right in the eye holes of her niqab. Although astonished, she guessed it must be an American custom to reciprocate a wink and rather than insult the towering man-woman decided to return it in kind, unleashing yet another exchange of blinking. A ménage à trois of flapping eyelids ensued between Brucilla and the two Arabs. Observing them, Yegor Yakov imagined the strong blond woman had somehow come into play and decided to join the heated competition for her by flashing winks of his own. Heads all around the room began to turn in bewilderment, following the winks ping-ponging back and forth across the table.

Al Gore, distracted by this frenetic activity and thinking that it must reflect a rude disinterest in his presentation on global warming, decided this would be as good a time as any to conclude his declamation and fly back to California on his Gulfstream jet. "And that is the shamefully degraded state of our air quality today, ladies and gentlemen," he said, ending his speech and making a hasty getaway.

Alison was up next with her presentation on new frontiers for the socially diverse portfolio. "At CRAM's request, we designed the MaxiGay Fund to be maximally diversified and gay in all dimensions," she began, her PowerPoint presentation appearing on the screen behind her.

It was just then that Yegor Yakov stepped out of the room to take a call on his mobile phone.

"Eventually we were able to find forty-seven qualified managers who identified themselves as belonging to one of the seven LGBTQIA categories," Alison explained to the audience. "We hired eight managers in all for the MaxiGay Fund: one for each category, plus an extra hermaphrodite as a spare. In the course of our effort, we even sponsored a new firm, Curious Capital, run by our very own transgendered quant, Brucilla Curious."

All eyes turned to Brucilla. He smiled and waved gently like the Queen of England.

Minutes later, Yakov returned to his seat, having missed Alison's presentation.

"During the break we're going to take a photo of everyone meeting the MaxiGay team," Beatrice announced. "Yegor, please join us," she said.

What better time to get to know the strong blond woman with the broad shoulders, Yakov was thinking. The photographer bunched everyone tightly together to get them all into the picture. Yakov made his move, squeezing his arm suggestively around Brucilla's waist and grinning for the camera. With one click the fateful photo was taken.

21   CRAM's Complaint

The man from CRAM arrived at the review meeting and sat at the table wearing his most stolid expression. Alison wondered whether Beatrice was expecting praise from Morbinders for Vain Capital's success in starting the MaxiGay Fund ahead of schedule. It seemed more likely that thunderbolts would shoot out of his little bald head.

Morbinders held a piece of paper. "Beatrice, we have been carefully monitoring your MaxiGay Fund's performance, and it appears from this report that the fund is trailing its benchmark by almost two percentage points. I thought you should know that these returns are entirely unacceptable to CRAM."

Beatrice, Alison, Brucilla, and Yong took turns staring at each other in disbelief.

"But the fund has been in operation only six weeks, Morris," Beatrice said softly. "Surely you wouldn't judge us so soon. Six weeks is only thirty or so trading days. That's just a blip in time. It's nothing."

Morbinders took out his red pencil and circled the offending numbers on his report. "Nothing? Of the eight gay money managers in your fund, seven are already underwater. Your lesbian is lagging by four percentage points, your asexual by three percentage points, your hermaphrodites by four and two, and so on. Not one of your managers has produced a smidgeon of positive alpha. The only one that hasn't fallen behind is Curious Capital, which of course is even with its benchmark because it's a passive index fund."

Alison stewed in silence. How could he lay the shortcomings of the MaxiGay Fund at the feet of Vain Capital? This was CRAM's fund. All the crazy gay requirements were CRAM's ideas, and she had nearly been raped trying to satisfy them.

"As I explained to you when I first came here in the spring," Morbinders continued, "CRAM is critically underfunded. Governor Pitypander has already been forced to slash pension checks for state employees and raise taxes. She is facing re-election in less than two months. To fend off her challenger, she has publicly announced that she has directed CRAM to terminate any firm that trails a benchmark for any substantial period. We don't have time for any more poor returns. She has a gun to her head, and so does CRAM. And therefore—"

"So do we," Beatrice said. "Pitypander's problems are our problems."

"Exactly," Morbinders said, sitting back in his chair and feeling his power. "I thought it was the least I could do to let you know the great danger you are in."

"So how much time do we have to turn the MaxiGay Fund's performance around?"

Morbinders twiddled with his pencil. "I am not at liberty to say at this juncture. CRAM will decide in its own good time. But I can tell you that last week we terminated a firm that underperformed its benchmark by two percentage points after just three months. In a few more weeks you could find yourself in the same situation."

Alison looked like she was about to explode. "But surely CRAM won't fire us before the election," she said, her eyes flaring. "Governor Pitypander needs us at least that long. You said getting the gay vote was why she wanted this investment. She can't be seen dumping all of CRAM's gay money managers before the election when she has just finished touting them in San Francisco to get the gays to vote for her, can she?"

"True, you are safe until the election is over," Morbinders conceded. "But that's a matter of only a few weeks. After that, once she has their votes locked up, all bets are off."

"May we loosen the restrictions on the fund?" Alison asked. "Maybe hire some straight managers?"

"Absolutely not," Morbinders answered. "It must be a gay fund, maximally diversified, sexually fluid, and gay in all dimensions. Nothing can change about that. Being sexually innovative was the whole point of CRAM's investment. The fund is nothing without its gayness."

"Have no fear, Morris. We'll find a way to improve the fund's returns," Beatrice assured him. "With its gayness intact."

Less than an hour after Morbinders had left, Beatrice had already con-
cocted a brilliant idea for boosting the MaxiGay fund's performance.
She reconvened the team to discuss it.

"The fund needs a quick injection of excellent returns from somewhere. Quandary Capital is our best money manager. They could turn
the fund's returns around by themselves, if only they were gay," she declared. "The three of you must go down to Rocket City and see whether
Quandary Capital might be gay."

"Bea, I called them to check on their sexual orientation way back
in April," Alison replied, with some irritation at this facile suggestion.
"They said they weren't."

"How disappointing," Beatrice said. "That's not very good client service. We have hundreds of millions of dollars invested with them. I'm
sure they didn't understand our pressing need for them to be gay. Did
you explain the situation?"

"Regardless of our situation, Dr. Ozturk said that he and Dr. Feiersinger are not gay. They are the founders. I took them at their word. Why
would they lie about a thing like that?"

"Because lots of people do."

"I don't think they were lying."

"Well, whether they were or not, they aren't the only people at Quandary Capital," Beatrice said. "The computers pick the stocks there, but
lots of people there are helping the computers do that. Quandary Capital is a big firm. How many employees do they have?"

"A thousand," Alison answered.

"Goodness! Surely some of them must be gay."

"All right, so suppose we go down to see Quandary Capital," Alison said.
"What will we be able to do in person that we can't do over the phone?"

"Why, you could observe them closely," Beatrice said. "Look for some
limp wrists or fashionable clothing. Or a special talent for design. Maybe a fetish for neatness."

"None of that would have worked in Nick's case. He's a total slob,"
Alison said. "Would it have worked with Pillsbury?"

"No," Beatrice admitted. "Pillsbury has no fashion sense at all. He
can't even match his socks. I still have to buy him clothes, even at his
age. But he doesn't care for football. Looking back on it, I suppose that
was the dead giveaway."

"Wait, I know," Brucilla said. "We could do the global tit test on them. It was working pretty well as a sexual preference indicator before we discovered the power of advertising."

"You want me to flash my rack at a thousand employees?" Alison asked. "How will we arrange that?"

"No, not all the employees, just the researchers," Brucilla proposed. "If we find a single gay researcher, we could claim his gayness touches upon the whole portfolio and renders all of it gay."

"But that's ridiculous," Alison said. "One gay quant researcher doesn't make the whole firm gay."

"What matters is what CRAM thinks, regardless of whether it's ridiculous," Brucilla said. "It's the prerogative of every client to be ridiculous. It's what they pay for. Wouldn't CRAM consider a money manager with one drop of African-American blood to be African-American?"

"Yes, it would," Alison admitted.

"Would it consider a firm fifty-one percent owned by a single black person to be black, even though all of the investment staff was white?"

"Yes. There actually are firms like that, and they get hired for being black."

"So if there's no such thing as diluting blackness, how can there be such a thing as diluting gayness? From a socially responsible point of view, what's the difference between being a little bit black and a little bit gay? No one ever bars the door to an oppressed group. There are no admission standards for being a victim, other than not being a straight white male."

"I guess that makes sense. A little gay goes a long way," Alison conceded. "So we just need to ask to meet Quandary Capital's researchers?"

"Just long enough to perform the tit test on them," Brucilla explained. "You ask to do a walk-through of the research floors for the benefit of Vain Capital's new equity person—that's me. A few minutes with each researcher should do the trick. Just let each of them take a gander at the two of us standing side by side. If anybody down there tests gay-positive, just one person, then we have bingo: Quandary Capital is gay and it qualifies for the MaxiGay Fund."

"What if CRAM wants proof?" Alison asked.

"CRAM didn't need proof for the other managers in the MaxiGay Fund, the hermaphrodites and others," Brucilla said. "They took our word for it, didn't they? They already have minority managers in other programs, so they can't say that the admission standards for gays should be more restrictive than they are for blacks. That would be discrimination against gays. If we find just one gay person, they'll have to accept that Quandary Capital is gay."

"And with Quandary Capital's extraordinary performance, the fund will be saved," Beatrice said. "A brilliant plan! I like the way you think, Brucilla. Very logical. Now you two get down there to Rocket City and flash 'em!"

"You think this will work?" Yong asked Brucilla after the meeting.

"Not a chance," Brucilla said flatly. "I worked with those Quandary Capital researchers. You won't get any gay readings from them."

"Then why did you tell Beatrice we should do it?"

"Because I have a much better idea, and to make it work I need an excuse to visit Quandary Capital. I couldn't tell Beatrice or Alison about it without revealing my secret identity to them."

"What is your idea?"

"I am going to steal the HONEY BOO-BOO anomaly."

Yong looked horrified. "But why? Then they come after you again. Man can stick head in lion's mouth only once."

"If we have the anomaly, we won't need Quandary Capital. I can save the MaxiGay Fund myself by using the anomaly to generate alpha at Curious Capital. I already had part of it figured out when the Quandary Capital founders kicked me out."

"Part is not good enough?"

"No, I need the whole thing or it won't work. I have to duplicate the HONEY BOO-BOO portfolio exactly. If I can just get into Quandary Capital's supercomputers, I can get the rest of what I need. My old password has been canceled, of course. To get a working password, I have to go down there in person and borrow one from somebody."

"How will you find one?"

"I don't know. Every inch of Quandary Capital is covered with cameras, so I'll have to swipe one right in front of them, without Alison or anyone else noticing. But having you two along will help distract them."

22 Return to Rocket City

With Alison and Yong at his side, Brucilla charged into the lions' den wearing a modest turquoise gown, black pumps, and an anxious smile. His eyes turned upward to scan the walls and ceiling of Quandary Capital's offices in search of the tiny cameras he knew were watching him from every angle.

In preparation he had devoted extra time to his makeup that morning, shaving his face to the smoothness of a baby's bottom and caking on an extra layer of face powder and eye shadow for good measure. He had tightened his breast forms until his ribs squeaked and taped them securely to his chest as extra insurance for the failing Velcro straps. Worn after months of daily use, they had been coming undone with alarming frequency.

Dr. Ozturk breezed into the conference room to greet his three visitors. Brucilla, trying not to offer his handshake too forcefully, cranked up his voice several octaves. "So pleased to meet you, Dr. Ozturk. How do you do?" he warbled daintily.

Ozturk's bushy eyebrows shot upward. In all his years in investment management, the Turk had encountered only a few real female quants. The artificial one standing before him seemed to be just more proof, if any were needed, of nature's final overthrow in this wayward country. A sour expression darkened his face as the suffocating smell of Brucilla's perfume began to fill his nostrils. "Mustafa Ozturk," he said to Brucilla in a flat tone of voice, shaking the strange creature's hand.

Ozturk's deep-set eyes quickly turned toward Alison, where they locked onto her semi-sheer white chiffon blouse. Below it lay her pretty pair of heaving breasts, tanned, rounded, and luscious, like buttered dinner rolls. They beckoned to him.

"Ah, Miss Hartswell," he said. "So nice to see you again."

Alison explained that the purpose of their visit was for Brucilla to get an introduction to the Quandary Capital investment process and meet the research staff.

"By all means," Ozturk consented, his eyes transfixed. "I'm sure they will be as delighted to see you as I am. They don't get much recreation, you know. We keep them so busy developing new quant models for your portfolio."

Ozturk led his guests to the researcher cubicles, stopping at the first door.

In the cubicle was Ping Tao Chin, a tall man from the Szechuan province of China.

"Chin's research specialty is big data," Ozturk explained. "He has two doctorates, one in physics and the other in computer science, from Shanghai Jiao Tong University, China's equivalent to MIT, where we found him teaching two years ago. Here at Quandary he mines data from the Internet to figure out how investors feel about stocks and how stock prices might be trending as a result."

"How do they feel, Chin?" Alison asked. "More importantly, how do you feel?"

"Uh, just fine, in both cases," said Chin with a fawning grin.

Alison leaned back against the side of the cubicle, pressing her chest out and leaning her head back. "Do you get much of a chance here to use your physics, Chin?"

Chin's eyes slid immediately from Alison's face down to her breasts. "Ah, um, no, not so much," he said.

"I imagine there's a lot a guy like you could teach me about physics," Alison said, breathing deeply. "I never took it in school. I'm afraid I was too busy fighting off boys to take such a hard subject. All those reactions and opposite reactions, and gravity, and space and time. Too much for a girl to absorb."

Looking moon-eyed, Chin began to hyperventilate. He felt light-headed.

Yong was holding a small notepad. Next to the researcher's name, he drew a straight line and an X, then shook his head, indicating a negative reading for Chin.

In the same fashion they continued down the corridor, dropping in on one researcher after another. Ozturk introduced Alison to quants from Russia, Kazakhstan, India, Bangladesh, China, Romania, Syria, Nigeria, and Egypt. Not all could speak English well but, as Yong diligently noted, they all read the language of big hooters with perfect fluency.

After two and a half hours of such impromptu meetings the visitors from Vain Capital had taken about as much of Ozturk's time as they dared. Brucilla glanced over at Yong's notepad. It showed nothing but X's.

"Perhaps we could meet just one more," Brucilla said. He looked anxiously across the floor for a researcher whose computer screen was turned off. Suddenly he spotted one.

Venkatraman Sivasankaranipetanaran, a heavy-set man with unruly black hair and big ears, swiveled his desk chair around and peered up at them.

"Hello, Venka," Ozturk said. "Some nice people from our client Vain Capital have dropped by to see what it is you do for a living."

"Ah, so good of you to ask. I can never find anyone normal who really wants to know," Venka replied in a lilting Indian accent, showing his toothy grin.

"Venka has PhDs in astrophysics, molecular biology, and materials engineering," Ozturk informed them. "We lured him away from his assistant professorship at Oxford about three years ago. Tell them what you are working on, Venka."

"I am trying to develop an algorithm that ties the lagged serial correlation of baseball scores to free cash flow patterns of U.S. stocks. Did you know that whenever the New York Mets are on a winning streak of at least five games there is a pronounced upward bias in the reported free cash flow of the Russell 1000 Growth Index several weeks later? You should see the information coefficients I'm getting for this factor!"

"Oh, I'd love to," said Alison, squeezing around Ozturk and into the doorway of the cubicle in front of Venka. Brucilla towered over the cubicle wall and maneuvered to where he could get a clear view of the researcher's computer.

Upon seeing Brucilla, Venka rolled back in his desk chair a few inches. His eyes shifted quickly toward Alison and lingered there.

"Information coefficients. That's fascinating, Venka," she said. "I love baseball."

Venka eyes remained locked on her, momentarily unable to turn away. "What's that? Baseball, oh, yes, yes."

Alison looked nervously at Yong, who shook his head and drew another straight line and an X by Venka's name. Her heart began to sink.

"Don't you have any questions for him?" Ozturk asked Alison.

"I have a few questions, Venka," Brucilla said.

"Oh, please, ask away," the researcher replied.

"Have you established Granger causality for your Mets winning streak factor?"

"No. I thought that would be getting entirely too fussy for baseball," Venka said.

"Did you set the number of lags with the Akaike or Schwartz criterion?"

"Akaike."

"Why?" Brucilla asked. "Schwartz's method favors lower order models and is therefore less inclined to lead to overfitting of the data."

"Yes, of course," Venka admitted, "but I prefer complex models over parsimonious ones. I just love factors. Can't get enough of them."

"Do your results survive in vector autoregression?"

"Actually, I'm very fond of my results and didn't want to risk their survival, so I didn't put them through that."

"Does the effect you found work for other U.S. benchmarks besides the Russell 1000 Growth Index? Does it work for certain sectors better than others? Maybe you could show us a little of your data."

"I'll be happy to. My, my, I've never met a client so well versed in quantitative analysis. Oh, I turned my computer off a while ago to update some software on it. Just a minute."

Venka restarted the machine and typed in his username and password. Suddenly a wry smile appeared on Brucilla's face.

As they waited for his computer to boot up, Venka began to notice something vaguely familiar about Brucilla's voice. "Is this your first time here?"

"Oh, yes," said Brucilla, just then feeling the tape helping to secure his breast forms give way. "Although I've read all about Quandary Capital and wanted to visit for a very long time."

"Somehow I feel like I've met you before," Venka said, scrutinizing Brucilla's face. "But of course that's impossible." Then he turned back to his computer and pulled up scatterplots of linear regressions and columns of output data. "You see there," he said, pointing to the bottom of one of his screens. "The statistically significant t-stats are coming from the technology sector."

"Brilliant work, Venka," Brucilla said. Suddenly he felt the worn Velcro strap lose its grip. His left breast began to droop a couple of inches toward his armpit. He broke its fall in the nick of time with the edge of the Quandary Capital presentation book.

Upstairs in the security office Freddie Disposo and Dr. Feiersinger watched the three visitors as they were bidding Ozturk farewell.

"Something about Vain Capital seems fishy to me," Disposo said. "There's that very tall transgendered woman again. Do you see her? She's standing next to the tall real one."

Feiersinger leaned forward to get a better look at the monitor. "You're right. Very peculiar, isn't she? Did you get anything more on her?"

Disposo opened a notebook and found his scribblings about Vain Capital. "Yes, she manages a little firm that Vain Capital helped her set up. Her only client is that fund for queer managers they created for CRAM."

"What is her name?"

"Brucilla Curious."

"What are you thinking?" Feiersinger asked.

"There's just something about her that reminds me of Benson," Disposo said. "See the high cheekbones?"

Feiersinger burst out laughing. "Nonsense, it's just your imagination. That cannot be Benson. For one thing, no one in the world is straighter than Benson, and for another he's not nearly fashionable enough to be a transgender. I worked with him myself. Our people are the world's top quant researchers. We would never have hired such a preposterous fellow. What sort of circus act do you think we are running here, Mr. Disposo?"

Disposo ran his hand through his greasy black hair. "Maybe I'm seeing things. But I've looked all over Washington. Your cowboy has disappeared. I've completely lost his trail."

"You are clutching at straws, Mr. Disposo," Feiersinger said. "How do you know he is still in Washington? Benson could easily have left there without your knowing it. Maybe you should look elsewhere. In any case,

I'm quite sure that woman is not your man. Bruce Benson in a dress— ha, now that would be a sight to see!"

It was a long trip back to Washington for the MaxiGay trio.

"Not a single gay person out of twenty. We failed," Alison moaned as they waited to board the plane. "What will we say to Bea?"

"Fail? You didn't fail. Your boobs were a hit," Brucilla said. "My boobs were the ones that failed. They didn't score once. It was a shutout."

"But our mission failed," Alison said. "Bea will be crushed. We just ran out of time, that's all. They have so many more researchers we could have tested! Bea was right. One of them has to be gay, I just know it."

"Stop beating yourself up. More tit tests wouldn't have helped," Brucilla said. "Those guys are all uber-geeks, with multiple PhDs in very technical subjects. It's a matter of self-selection."

"What about you? You're a quant, but you're not straight at all."

"Um, well, I'm the exception that proves the rule."

"But what do we do now?"

"Keep the faith. Have courage," Brucilla said with resolution. "We're not done for yet. You never know, our performance might turn around."

"What if it doesn't? CRAM will pull out of the MaxiGay Fund. Then Butcher and Weedle will sell us out for sure, and then I'll probably have to leave Washington to find another MOM to work for—maybe even go back to California." Alison looked fiercely at Yong. "Are you absolutely sure they were all perfectly straight? Not even one was just a little bent?"

"Not one," Yong answered firmly. "Nature not easily fooled. Sex most powerful force of nature. More powerful than magnet. More powerful than particle physics. Atomic explosion nothing compared to sex."

Brucilla began to laugh, but the grim look on their faces stopped him. "Don't worry." he whispered to Yong. "I got Venka's password."

23 Cracking the Code

Vain Capital's office looked like a ghost town when Brucilla finally returned from the long day trip to Rocket City at eleven that night. He walked down the dimly lit hall, flipped on the lights in his office, and fired up his computer. Then he typed Quandary Capital's domain name into the Internet browser. Quandary Capital's familiar blue login screen with the big white letters "QC" popped up. He entered "vsivasankara-nipetanaran" for the username and "VenkaMax1212" for the password, and then held his breath.

By working late at night, Brucilla could be sure Venka would not be using his computer in Rocket City. But at any moment the password might be changed.

Suddenly Brucilla was inside the computer network. Now he had total access to Quandary Capital's mighty supercomputers, with all of Venka's icons and files wide open before him on the screen. He plugged a thumb drive into his computer, transferred his decoding program into the network, and clicked "RUN."

It would take hours for the program to do its job. No matter, he would stay until dawn if necessary, watching as it crunched away using Quandary Capital's computer system, seeking all words that could be formed from the twelve letters OOOOIESSDDGT and then comparing them against the English dictionaries and grammar rulebooks in the system's memory banks. After a few minutes, the program reached the same point it had five months earlier when Feiersinger and Ozturk had caught him trying to crack the HONEY BOO-BOO code at Quandary Capital. Words extracted from the twelve-letter string flashed on his screen: IS, GOT, GET, GETS, GOES, DIE, DIES, DOES, DIED, TIED, TIES, SAG, SAGS, SIDE, SIDES, SIT, SITS, SITE, SITES,...

The program then started to match words with each other, juggling them according to rules of English syntax to make sensible answers that would use up all the letters. Single words were listed on the left side of the screen and possible word clusters on the right.

By midnight Brucilla's eyes grew heavy. Soon his elbows were splayed across his desk and his head was resting on his forearms, fast asleep.

At five o'clock in the morning he woke up. Bleary-eyed, he slowly remembered where he was as the fog lifted from his brain. He looked at the screen. There, a list of word combinations appeared with probabilities calculated alongside them. A sentence at the top of the list was blinking at him in red type:

HONEY BOO-BOO DOES IT SO GOOD: 85%

Brucilla stared at the line of text. HONEY BOO-BOO DOES IT SO GOOD had an eighty-five percent probability of being the correct code.

"HONEY BOO-BOO DOES IT SO GOOD," he repeated to himself, over and over, like a magic incantation. He felt the energy of the words throbbing in his brain and coursing throughout his body. The power of this strange mantra was primitive, but real.

Just as I guessed, he was thinking, *the HONEY BOO-BOO anomaly really is all about sex—the very act itself.* This was as it ought to be, he imagined, for what in the world was more anomalous than sex? It seemed only logical that the anomaly should be illogical, something irrational and undiscoverable by standard data analysis. He had stumbled onto it by accident, as apparently so had Dr. Feiersinger. Wasn't that how love worked, by chance encounters? A brainiac's scream of sexual satisfaction held the keys to billions of dollars in investment riches: HONEY BOO-BOO DOES IT SO GOOD! Here were the enchanted words that moved the market.

Brucilla trembled with excitement. The anomaly's very absurdity had been its best protection against discovery. Who in the investment world would believe the HONEY BOO-BOO anomaly could exist? It was like a nuclear bomb of intellectual impossibility, set to blow all investment theory to smithereens. What self-respecting finance professor who had made his reputation by authoring impenetrable articles festooned with Greek math symbols in *The Financial Analysts Journal* could countenance the idea that orgasms could have such alpha-generating power? Could academics bring themselves to acknowledge that it was only rational that the last unexploited market inefficiency must be irrational, since reason could never detect or explain it? No, he realized, they would be the last people on earth to understand.

Would the HONEY BOO-BOO anomaly spur academic research into the efficacy of sexually directed investing? Perhaps this anomaly was only the visible bit of gold ore atop a mother lode of prurient anomalies just waiting to be unearthed. Never mind academics, would real-life investors pursue them? Of course they would, in a stampede! Brucilla pondered the implications of the gold rush these seven words might unleash. Surely sexual investing would be a lot more fun than socially responsible investing, though oddly enough both investment approaches had led Brucilla to exactly the same place, the MaxiGay Fund, where perhaps they could serve the same purpose in saving Vain Capital.

His eyelids drooping again, Brucilla felt his wig weighing like an anvil upon his head. He forced his eyes open, peering at the other possible word combination on the screen:

IT DOES HONEY BOO-BOO SO GOOD: 15%

The computer program had concluded that although this alternative was also feasible, it was completely out of character for Feiersinger. Brucilla agreed. His Austrian boss was venal and murderous, but like almost all quants he was an innately modest man, a technician at heart. He lacked the grandiosity expressed by IT DOES HONEY BOO-BOO SO GOOD. Feiersinger was no Donald Trump.

Brucilla closed the program, erased it from Venka's computer to remove the evidence of his intrusion, and logged off the Quandary Capital computer system. He had a lot more work to do, but his energy was spent. He dragged himself home to get some real sleep.

By early afternoon Brucilla was back in his office, cleaned up and refreshed after a nap, ready to research how the HONEY BOO-BOO portfolio was managed on a day-to-day basis.

He needed more than just the code words. The Quandary Capital portfolio always contained stocks with exactly the same initial letters, but they were not always exactly the same twenty-three stocks. There

was routine turnover in the portfolio, once per month on a regular cy-
cle. How and when did Feiersinger decide which stocks to replace each
month?

Brucilla considered the timing question first. It seemed logical to start
from the premise that the trading of the Quandary Capital portfolio
had something to do with HONEY BOO-BOO herself, something that
occurred once a month with regularity.

"Her period!" he exclaimed. "That's when she doesn't do it so good.
Feiersinger buys and sells when she's on the rag. What better time for
him to trade?"

But what about Feiersinger's stock selection? Did it fit a pattern?

Brucilla would need to borrow Quandary Capital's massive computer
system again. Late that night, after Venka surely would have left the office, he burgled the system again and copied another program into the
network. It downloaded all the stocks of all Quandary Capital portfolios
ever created, along with their trading histories. Then it began to search
for a repeating pattern in the stock picking.

An economically sensible basis for choosing stocks, like buying companies with the strongest earnings or cash flow, would be convention-
al and prudent—and therefore wholly inappropriate for the HONEY
BOO-BOO portfolio. Feiersinger's stock picking must be as simple and
frivolous as the code itself.

Brucilla directed his program to analyze the numerical positions of
replacement stocks and their predecessors in an alphabetized list and
note the difference. For example, if Hillenbrand had been replaced by
Holiday, eighteen places down the list, his program recorded eighteen
for that trade.

Within seconds the program confirmed Brucilla's suspicion: There
was a magic number, and it was twenty-three. Feiersinger always picked
the twenty-third stock down the alphabetized list as the replacement,
equal-weighting his holdings so that each made up one twenty-third of
the total portfolio.

Which letters of the HONEY BOO-BOO code did Feiersinger choose
for his trades each month, Brucilla wondered. He clicked an option on
the menu of his program to analyze the letter pattern. The months and
letters traded each month were listed in two columns:

January:	HO
February:	NE
March:	YB
April:	OO
May:	BO
June:	OD
July:	OE
August:	SI
September:	TS
October:	OG
November:	OO
December:	DH
January:	ON
February:	EY
March:	BO
April:	OB
May:	OO
June:	DO
July:	ES
August:	IT
September:	SO
October:	GO
November:	OD
December:	HO

Feiersinger was simply rotating continuously through the HONEY BOO-BOO code, two letters per month. Trading just one letter more than twenty-three in a calendar year made his trading pattern appear random even though it was in fact completely predictable.

Brucilla had almost everything he needed, but one question festered: When would HONEY BOO-BOO be having her periods? She could get out of synch anytime without his knowing it, wreaking havoc with his portfolio's performance. God forbid she should get pregnant!

Brucilla was certain that the head trader at Quandary Capital, Sami Harami, knew when the portfolio was trading, and that Harami's trades were directed by Feiersinger. Brucilla needed notification of Feiersinger's monthly e-mail to Harami.

To get it, Brucilla inserted code into the Quandary Capital e-mail system to detect Feiersinger's e-mail and instantly post a time-dated message on the Rocket City police department's Facebook page, thanking the cops for their faithful service to the community, signed "HBB OTR." From the safety of the policemen's Facebook page, Brucilla would watch for the signal that HONEY BOO-BOO was "OTR"—on the rag. Now he could synchronize his trades with Feiersinger's, buying and selling at the same prices.

Armed with all necessary details of Quandary Capital's investment method, Brucilla was finally ready to replicate it, converting Curious Capital's index portfolio into a market-dominating marvel that would rescue the sagging performance of the MaxiGay Fund. The new HONEY BOO-BOO portfolio would launch tomorrow, not from Rocket City, but from downtown Washington.

24 The President's Options

"Madam President, this is a map of Estonia," General Barker said, directing his electronic pointer at the screen in the West Wing of the White House. "You can see how vulnerable the whole country is to Russian invasion. The town of Narva is here, straight across this narrow river from Ivangorod on the Russian side of the border, little more than the length of a football field away. Narva is the logical place for the Russians to attack. It is completely exposed and utterly defenseless, like a pocket just waiting to be picked."

"What has changed since our meeting last month?" President Fibby asked.

"Only that the Russians have completed their preparations," General Barker replied. "The gun pointed at Estonia is now fully loaded and cocked. The Russians are ready to invade the country at Bludinov's command."

President Fibby leaned back in her leather chair, unsure which man she was more annoyed at today, Bludinov for creating the crisis or General Barker for forcing her to confront it. "Do the Joint Chiefs of Staff have any better idea of what the Russians are actually planning to do?"

"No, Madam President. We only know they are poised to roll their tanks across that short bridge and take Narva and maybe all of Estonia. The terrain is flat as a tabletop, with hardly any natural barriers—perfect for tanks."

Barker clicked on his remote control. An aerial photograph of Ivangorod Fortress appeared, with red labels indicating rows of buildings, tanks, and troop transports.

"The Russians have stored enough supplies in this old castle in Ivangorod across the river from Narva to support an assault by thousands of troops. They've been waiting so long for us to respond that to amuse themselves they've been painting nasty insults on the roofs of the buildings, in English, and have invited the international news media to take pictures."

"What is that hand painted on the roof, up there in the corner?" the President asked.

"It's giving NATO the finger, ma'am."

"And that other drawing?"

"It's mooning us, ma'am. Or you, to be precise."

"Goodness, is that what that is?"

"Yes, and it's now on CNN for the whole world to see."

"I warned Bludinov to curb his shameful human rights abuses in my speech at the United Nations last summer. Now he retaliates with this outrage," Fibby said. "That's just like him. The man's even more spiteful than my ex-husband. Thinks he can push me around because I'm a woman, does he? It's pretty clear he has no interest in peaceful cooperation. He's determined to force my hand. What are our options, General?"

"I think we have three, ma'am. We can pull back some NATO troops in a futile gesture of goodwill. We can try to negotiate a resolution, despite our overwhelmingly weak position. Or we can rush thousands of troops to Estonia, fortify Narva, and risk setting off a cataclysmic thermonuclear war that will leave the earth a burning cinder."

"Oh, my," said Fibby, turning to Secretary of State Hernandez in hopes of more palatable suggestions. "Javonda, what course of action do our NATO allies favor?"

"The French would like us to pull back and let Estonia and the other Baltic republics go, which is the mode of diplomatic non-response I prefer," Hernandez replied. "The Germans would like to negotiate a profitable trade deal. The Brits would like us to stubbornly stand our ground and fortify the country. And the rest of the Europeans don't care as long as they don't have to pay for it."

"General Barker, how many troops have we got in Estonia?" Fibby asked.

"About five hundred from NATO and fifty-five hundred from Estonia itself. That includes the marching band."

"How long could our men hold out against the Russians?"

"About twenty minutes, ma'am, given their current state of readiness.

But not all of our men are men, by the way," the general replied with a deep sigh.

"No, what are they?"

"Some are women, but some of our men are women too. The transgendered ones, I mean, ma'am. They have been fully integrated into our socially responsible armed forces for years now. Some NATO units in Europe are entirely transgendered."

"All in the same direction? I mean, from men to women, or women to men?"

"Depends on the unit, Madam President. Some units go entirely one way, some lean the other, but most are a hodge-podge of sexual confusion."

"Why can't we continue to sit on our hands?" Fibby asked with growing irritation. "Our policy of non-response seems to have worked splendidly so far. As long as the Russians don't actually invade Narva I don't see why we have to give them the satisfaction of noticing them. We can no longer afford these military adventures, and the Baltic states aren't worth it anyway. Why should we fight for them?"

"Inaction has been working for us, Madam President," Hernandez said. "Bludinov must be bluffing. He wouldn't gamble on attacking a NATO country by sending in the little green men."

"You mean, the soldiers in the Ukraine, the ones with the face masks who pretended they were local separatists and not invading Russian troops?" Fibby asked.

"Yes, ma'am," Hernandez said. "Unlike Ukraine, Estonia is a NATO country. He wouldn't dare try to pull that trick in Estonia."

General Barker could contain himself no longer. "But those are the little green men, according to our intelligence," he protested, pointing at the map. "And what the blazes difference does it make who they are? It doesn't matter if the invader is the abominable snowman—any invasion of a NATO country is still an invasion. We have to respond to maintain NATO's credibility. That's always been U.S. policy."

"No, I think we should continue the waiting game first," Fibby said. "Then, if Bludinov does send in his little green men, we still have plenty of non-aggressive options, like slapping more sanctions on the Russians, or trying to negotiate. I'm sure the Baltic states will understand. It's only reasonable."

"Yes," Hernandez said, smirking at General Barker. "Retreating is better than being burnt to a crisp, even for the Estonians."

"Then it's settled. For now we'll continue our policy of watchful waiting," Fibby declared.

"Yes, ma'am," said the general, putting down his pointer and taking his seat.

"What a passel of trouble the Russians have been lately!" Fibby said. "Javonda, do you have an update on that mysterious investment they made here a couple of months ago?"

"Yes, Madam President," Hernandez said. "I have verification here from Treasury, which detected the movement of the money through our banking system. Incredible as it sounds, the Russians have invested three billion dollars in a fund run by gay money managers, set up here in Washington by a firm named Vain Capital. It's called the MaxiGay Fund. Governor Pitypander had it created for the California state employee pension fund and the Russians decided to join in for reasons we don't understand."

"Maybe they are messing around in our elections again," Fibby said. "Are they trying to help Patty Pitypander get re-elected? But why would they want to do that? I would expect Bludinov to despise Pitypander. He's not fond of powerful women."

"We don't know that there's any connection between the Russians and the Pitypander campaign," Hernandez replied. "Except for this MaxiGay Fund."

"Are the Russians going gay?" Fibby asked.

"No, Bludinov hates them. He has them beaten up, arrested, and packed off to Siberia," Hernandez replied.

"Three billion dollars is a lot of money going to people Bludinov loathes. And we have no explanation for why the Russian government has done this?"

"All we know is the money came from the Russian sovereign wealth fund. We can't imagine why."

"Doesn't the Russky Fund have a lot of ties to the Kremlin?"

"Of course, very close ties," said Hernandez. "Like anything Russian, it's riddled with self-dealing, money laundering, and every other form of corruption. It's practically a piggy bank for the Russian oligarchs and kleptocrats. They use it regularly as a vehicle for smuggling their money out of the country."

"If the Kremlin could be involved, we need to get to the bottom of this right away. Maybe there's something here," Fibby declared. She turned to the Director of Homeland Security. "John, put some more agents on the case if necessary. Look into these Vain Capital people. Find out what skullduggery they're up to."

25   An Unsuitable Investment

Ms. von Vain, we're just here to ask you a few questions about your MaxiGay Fund," said Special Agent Maddux, a stocky man with no neck.

Beatrice felt a chill run up and down her spine. This was not a surprise SEC audit. Those were usually arranged well in advance and were no surprise at all. And she had never been visited by an FBI agent, much less one showing up unannounced with an SEC investigator.

"I'm from the FBI's Criminal Investigations Division," Maddux said, flashing his badge at her. "The Bureau received a call from Treasury regarding a large transfer from the Russky Fund to your MaxiGay Fund."

"A large transfer?" Beatrice repeated.

"Three billion dollars," Maddux said.

"I see, and who might you be?" Beatrice said, turning to the bearded man in the wire rim glasses who had accompanied Maddux.

"Hiram Forceps, from the SEC Enforcement Division's Financial Reporting and Audit Group," the other official said.

Beatrice glanced at the credenza. "Would you like some coffee?"

"Oh, no thank you," Maddux said. "We'll just be a few minutes."

"I think I'll have some," Beatrice said, her throat suddenly feeling parched. She got up and strolled over to the credenza. "What can I do for you gentlemen today?"

"The Treasury Department does not see a lot of three-billion-dollar transfers from Russia to the United States, Ms. von Vain. It raised some eyebrows."

"Oh, whose eyebrows?"

"The Director of the FBI's," Maddux replied.

Beatrice fumbled her spoon, which dropped onto the floor with a clink. She bent down and picked it up. "Oh, well, let's see if I can bring the Director's eyebrows back down. It's easy enough to explain. The Russky Fund is a sovereign wealth fund. Lots of oil-rich countries have them—Norway, Saudi Arabia, Kuwait, to name a few. The Russians have to invest their money somewhere, and there simply aren't enough good opportunities in Russia alone. Other sovereign wealth funds are globally diversified as well."

"Yes, we know all that," Forceps said. "That's not what's raising the Director's eyebrows."

"No?" Beatrice replied, spilling a packet of artificial sweetener all over the top of the credenza.

"We understand that the Russky Fund has to invest globally," Forceps conceded. "What we don't understand is why Russians want to invest in a fund run by gay money managers."

"Why shouldn't they invest with gay money managers?"

"You know why. The Russian government is extremely homophobic," Maddux said. "Bludinov hates queers. He sends gay people to the gulag."

Beatrice returned to the table with her coffee, just managing to get it there without incident. "Well, let's just be thankful the money didn't come from Saudi Arabia. I understand they chop the poor homos' heads off there. I suppose a Saudi investment in our MaxiGay Fund would send the eyebrows flying clean off your Director's head."

"Never mind the Saudis, it's odd enough for the FBI that the money came from the Russian government. It seems to be an unsuitable investment for them," Forceps said.

Beatrice took a sip of her coffee. "Gentlemen, did you come here to ask me why the Russians behave oddly? Why don't you ask them? The Russian embassy is just up Wisconsin Avenue. Wouldn't they have a better idea?"

"We wouldn't expect them to tell us," Forceps said. "But we thought you might—since this firm is a registered U.S. investment advisor, subject to SEC regulations."

"I'm sure they would be happy to meet with you."

"We doubt it," Maddux replied.

"Is it illegal for the Russky Fund to invest in a fund of gay money managers?" Beatrice asked.

"No, it's not illegal," Forceps said. "It's just strange as hell."

"Is it illegal for an American investment firm to accept assets from a Russian sovereign wealth fund?"

"No, not if that's where the money is really from."

"Then how does the U.S. government have a problem?"

Forceps leaned forward. "There would be a big problem for you, Ms. von Vain, if the money came from an illegal Russian activity, here or abroad, and Vain Capital were an accomplice in hiding it. Your firm could be shut down and you could be charged with money laundering, which is a felony carrying a penalty of up to twenty years in jail under Title 18 of the U.S. Code. That's why we are asking if you know where the money came from."

Beatrice's cup rattled against its saucer as she put it down. "The official who came to us asking to invest was from the Russky Fund, a fellow named Yegor Yakov, and the money was wired from the Russky Fund's bank account in New York."

"Were there any individual persons mentioned as the source investors?" Forceps asked.

"We were given no names of individual investors."

"You understand our point of view, I hope, Ms. von Vain," Maddux said. "The Russians are always up to something crooked. It's our job to find out what it is and put a stop to it and any crooked people connected to it."

Connected to something crooked? That did it. Beatrice suddenly remembered just whose great-great-great granddaughter she was. She could feel the outraged spirit of her forebear Parker Pillsbury rising up from within her, stiffening her back. "Gentlemen, the Russky Fund came to us on its own and made an investment in our MaxiGay Fund, alongside California's state employee pension fund. In my book, that makes the Russians no guiltier of investing strangely than the Californians. Have you investigated Governor Pitypander for making odd investments?"

"No, we have a different standard of oddness for California," Forceps said.

"A much higher bar, I'm sure," Beatrice said.

"Yes. Otherwise our San Francisco caseload alone would sink us."

"We have a whole menagerie of socially responsible clients here at Vain Capital, gentlemen," Beatrice said, drawing herself up straight in her chair. "They make what other people might consider to be odd requests for investing their money. It's what we're in business for. We don't question other people's morality—we're just happy they have some so we can help them put it into their portfolios—Californians, Russians, academics, environmentalists, conservatives, liberals, nuns, Mormons, Muslims, Jews, people with teeth, people without teeth, all treated with equal respect for their beliefs and special investing preferences, which you call oddness. I've told you what I can. Now, is there anything else I can do for you today?"

Maddux looked at Forceps, who shook his head.

"I hope not," Beatrice said with a stern look. "Don't think you can intimidate me because I'm a woman. I'm a former congressman's ex-wife, and I think you'll find I'm a force to be reckoned with all by myself. You may have the Director of the FBI, but I have my own high-level connections in this town, I'll have you know. I know people. People like Al Gore. Don't make me call Al Gore."

"No! Not Al Gore!" Forceps said, his lip quivering.

With no solid evidence of wrongdoing, the government men were forced to beat a hasty retreat.

That afternoon, FSB agent Alexei Yuganov was working in the Russian embassy on Wisconsin Avenue when his phone rang. It was his boss, Lieutenant Colonel Sergei Laprinsky, calling him up to his office.

Laprinsky was sitting behind his desk, enveloped as usual by a thick cloud of cigarette smoke.

"Major Yuganov, I have an interesting assignment for you," Laprinsky said, taking a puff of his cigarette. "The Kremlin has information that the CIA and FBI have ordered their agents to investigate an investment made by the Russky Fund in the United States."

Yuganov began to cough uncontrollably. "What kind of investment?" he asked.

"I don't have the vaguest idea, Major. I don't know the first thing about investments. I'm just an old communist, you know. We didn't have to know about such things in the KGB," Laprinsky replied, stubbing out his cigarette in an ashtray. "But whatever the damn thing is, it has attracted a lot of attention in Washington—at the highest levels. According to e-mails we downloaded from the U.S. Secretary of State's private e-mail server, a few months ago Russky Fund made a three-billion-dollar investment in something called the MaxiGay Fund. We checked with a fellow named Yakov at the Russky Fund, and he says it's a fund of jolly money managers run by Vain Capital in Washington. The U.S. government seems to think something's amiss. Of course, we can't just call the Americans up and ask them what their problem is. We aren't supposed to know they have one."

"What is my assignment, sir?"

Laprinsky reached into his shirt pocket, pulled out another cigarette, and lit it. "To find out what all the fuss is about. The Russky Fund says that Vain Capital only invests in very moral portfolios as requested by its clients. And the Russky Fund holds exactly the same very moral investment as the state of California does, so no one on our side understands where we could have gone wrong."

"Where should I start, sir?"

Laprinsky tossed some brown folders across his desk at Yuganov. "Here are the dossiers of the CIA and FBI agents who have been assigned to investigate the MaxiGay investment. Follow them around. See if you can find out what the hell those guys are looking for."

Dr. Feiersinger pointed to the computer screen in the security office at Quandary Capital. "See, there it is on the chart, Mustafa. There is the big jump in the trading of our stocks I called you about. It happened just a few days ago. More than a billion dollars of trading, all at once, and then volume dropped back to normal."

The jagged line on the chart looked like a witch's hat. It was horizontal, then went up almost vertically, and then it fell off just as quickly.

Dr. Ozturk nodded. "Yes, that's a huge spike in volume, especially for the small cap stocks in our portfolio. Very suspicious. Those are large block trades too. Can you tell who did the trading?"

"One of our brokers said it was a new firm called Curious Capital. Have you heard of it?"

"Curious Capital!" Ozturk exclaimed. "Yes, I know that firm. It's managed by that transgendered quant who visited here recently with the pretty young woman from Vain Capital and her impertinent little Asian assistant. The quant's name was Brucilla Curious. She wanted to meet our researchers. You don't suppose—"

"*Mein Gott!* A trangendered quant has run off with our HONEY BOO-BOO anomaly?"

Ozturk looked confused. "I don't see how she could have. I was standing there with Curious during the entire visit. He—or she—was never out of my sight. None of them were."

"Let's have a look at the video of your meeting." They watched the monitor as it showed the visitors going from the conference room to the cubicles to interview the researchers.

Several minutes into the video, Feiersinger suddenly jumped up and pointed at the monitor. "There you see, at cubicle 629, while you were looking at that woman, Curious is looking over Venka's shoulder at his screen. Venka is typing his password right in front of everybody! *Ach, dummkopf!* Curious stole his password right there!"

"How can you be sure? When did Curious use it?" Ozturk asked.

Feiersinger scanned the computer system's records of when it had been accessed by Venka's password. A list of dates and times appeared on the screen. "Late that same night! And late the next night also! Look!"

Feiersinger put his head in his hands. "This transgendered quant did not stumble around blindly in our system. She already knew it! We have been penetrated by someone who already knew exactly what she was after. Who can that be?"

"Otto, bring back the video of Brucilla Curious," Ozturk said. "I want to take another look."

Feiersinger returned to the first video.

"It is hard to believe, but there it is," Ozturk said. "If you ignore the breasts and the wig and the dress and whatever that is she has stuffed under it, their bodies are exactly the same height and shape."

"Who?"

"Bruce Benson and Brucilla Curious."

Feiersinger pulled up pictures of both. "You are right, Mustafa! They are both tall and thin as a pencil. And see the bony face there, it is just the same in both pictures. Disposo suggested this once before, but I didn't believe it. Could our American cowboy be wearing a dress? Is it really possible?"

"I am afraid so. I must say, Benson continues to disappoint me," Ozturk said with a tinge of regret in his voice at the image of the transgendered quant. "He is certainly no John Wayne, is he? I thought

American cowboys had more pride than to stoop to this. I suppose they don't make real ones anymore."

"For that matter, he is no Caitlyn Jenner either," Feiersinger agreed. "But despite his shortcomings he has the gall to sneak in here and snatch our secret, right from under our noses!"

"This is my fault. I should never have let them interview the researchers in their cubicles," Ozturk admitted. "That Alison Hartswell must have cast a spell on me. It is hard to refuse such an alluring woman."

"Yes, it is the same with my HONEY BOO-BOO. I can refuse her nothing," Feiersinger said. Then he thought for a moment. "You say Benson is operating his firm from inside Vain Capital? I wonder if the other Vain Capital people know the anomaly too."

"I highly doubt it," Ozturk said. "They are not quants. They don't have the intelligence."

"So we need not concern ourselves with the other two, only Benson?"

"That's correct, but we must stop him now," Ozturk said. "We cannot allow Benson to go around running billion-dollar HONEY BOO-BOO portfolios. What if he decides to trade ten billion dollars? Fifty billion? What if he reveals the anomaly to someone else? Our alpha will evaporate and our fees will shrink to nothing. HONEY BOO-BOO is probably the last of the anomalies. It is irreplaceable. Call Disposo at once."

26 Looking for Lee

Standing on the sidewalk outside Vain Capital's building, Freddie Disposo could tell he was being closely watched by three people. To his left was a man in a grey sport coat, leaning against a post office box, casting glances in Disposo's direction every so often. He had heard the very same man speaking with a Russian accent in a coffee shop just minutes before. To his right a heavy-set fellow in a blue shirt, sitting behind the wheel of a parked white van, was staring at him through the windshield. Across K Street a woman in a purple sweater loitered under a bus shelter but never caught a bus.

Disposo felt inside the breast pocket of his coat for the Mind Melter gun, but knew it would be of no use. With these three stalking him, ambushing the renegade quant here in broad daylight was out of the question.

The Quandary Capital detective dug into his pocket for his notes and found the address for Lee Yong-gi: 391 South Lee Street, Alexandria, Virginia. He fetched his rental car from the parking garage and drove across the Fourteenth Street bridge, then south on the parkway toward Alexandria.

Disposo cursed when he looked up into his rear view mirror. There was the white van. The black car behind it was driven by the Russian in the grey sport coat, followed by a yellow taxicab carrying the woman in the purple sweater.

Disposo studied the GPS screen on his dashboard for a way to shake off his pursuers. He drove a mile down North Washington Street in Alexandria and took a sudden right at King Street. The white van turned with him, its tires squealing, followed by the black car and the yellow taxicab. Then Disposo sped down to the next corner, swung hard left, and then right, and then right again. Several more blocks and turns later he could no longer see anyone chasing him. He looked at his dashboard again to see where he was, but the street signs no longer matched his GPS screen, which seemed to be missing several street names. He was thoroughly lost.

Disposo saw an elderly woman going by, tottering down the sidewalk with a cane. He pulled up alongside her to ask directions. "Excuse me, ma'am, I thought this would be Stuart Street. But the sign there on the corner says Peace Street. Where is Stuart Street?"

"Oh, there is no Stuart Street anymore," the white-haired old lady answered in a singsong voice. "The city changed its name about a month ago, along with a third of the other streets in Alexandria."

"Why did they do that?"

"Oh, Stuart Street was named after J.E.B. Stuart, a Confederate general. The city council decided it ought to be ashamed of Virginia's history. They said a lot of street names had gone bad over the years, so they changed them."

"Did they change Lee Street too?"

"Oh my, yes, Robert E. Lee was the first to go, don't you know," the old lady said. "It's so sad. He was such a fine gentleman, and a local boy too. They even took the historical plaque off his church. Washington will probably have to go next, and Patrick Henry. Slave owners, all of them, so they are done for."

"That is sad," Disposo said. "I'd always heard Lee was a great man."

"Oh, the best. Robert E. Lee would have reached up from his grave and pulled down his street name himself before offending anyone. He tried to heal the nation after the Civil War. He was a devout Christian, kind even to his worst enemies, so I'm sure if he's looking down on us he'll forgive us. It's a pity we can't manage to forgive him. A little more forgiveness for each other and we wouldn't all have to be so goddam moral and thin-skinned. Don't you think so?"

"Yes, ma'am, I suppose. Do you know how I can get to what used to be Lee Street?"

"No, I'm afraid I haven't gotten a copy of the newly inclusive city map yet," the old crone said. She tapped her forehead with her hand to jog her failing memory. "Dear, dear, what do they call it? I think it may be Diversity Street, or is it Sensitivity Street? I get the new names all mixed up. Goodness, there are so many new virtues these days it's a wonder we have enough streets in Alexandria to celebrate them all."

"I afraid I'm in a hurry, ma'am. I just need one street. Lee Street."

"Lee Street? Oh yes. Whatever they call it now, it was down there by the river. Go that way, then past Queen Street, take a left on King Street before you get to Prince Street or Duke Street, although it doesn't really matter which one of those you take, don't you know, because they are all parallel to each other, so then you cross Washington and then Royal and eventually you'll reach the Potomac. The city had no problem with the monarchs and kept them on the signs, you see, but then I suppose the Revolutionary War generation was more forgiving than we are. Now, mind you, you might notice there's a brand-new obelisk in the middle of Washington Street where the old statue of the Confederate soldier used to be. Don't you know it took the city ten years of court cases to remove that old statue and replace it with an obelisk dedicated to virtue. They just unveiled it yesterday with a big ceremony, with the mayor and city council there. Oh my, there was such a fuss over that! Some people wanted a statue of Harriet Tubman, others thought it should be Susan B. Anthony, but there were flaws with all of them so finally everybody just gave up on real people and went for an Obelisk of Virtue. Now which street was it you were looking for?"

"Lee Street, ma'am."

"Anyway, what you're looking for is Lee Street. It used to be right before you get to the Potomac. If you go too far and find yourself drowning in the river, maybe a man half as good as Robert E. Lee will show up to risk everything he has, jump right in, and try to save you like he did Virginia. I'd say there's a fat chance of finding a man like that around here these days, so do be careful."

Disposo, more confused than ever, thanked the befuddled old lady and made his way to King Street, where he turned left. A block farther down, he saw the white van. The man in the blue shirt was talking to a young woman pushing a baby stroller. Suddenly the man turned and caught sight of Disposo, who immediately stepped on the gas to get away.

The man in the blue shirt turned back toward the lady with the stroller. "Ma'am, I'm FBI Special Agent Bert Maddux. I'm looking for Lee Street. I understand the street names of Alexandria have been purged recently. Any idea where Lee Street was?"

The woman with the stroller shook her head. "Lee?"

"As in Robert E. Lee?"

"Who's that?"

Maddux pulled out his cell phone and dialed a number. "No luck here, Miriam," he said into the phone. "I'm on Inclusiveness Street, I think. Not sure how that one maps to the old street grid. Have you got an ID on the guy with the greasy black hair yet? He drove by a minute ago, heading west."

Miriam, the woman in the purple sweater, answered from a few blocks away. "Bert, headquarters says the greaser is a private detective named Freddie Disposo. Works for a firm called Quandary Capital in Florida. We have no idea why he's been hanging around outside the Vain Capital office, but he seems to be monitoring Curious too. No, I'm on a street called Harmony. No one here knows what happened to Lee. So many signs have been changed around here that nobody knows where they are anymore. The Russian guy in the sport coat? Alexei Yuganov of the FSB—works out of the Russian embassy. The agency knows all about him, except why he's here following us. Or Disposo. Or Curious. Or maybe he's looking for Lee too."

Miriam hung up and then suddenly caught sight of Disposo driving slowly down the street peering at street signs. She locked eyes with him, then reached for her cell phone again to call Maddux.

"Bert, I just saw Disposo again! He's headed north on Harmony Street!"

Maddux jumped back into his white van and headed toward Harmony. Within two minutes he saw Disposo and started to tail him.

Disposo immediately noticed the white van in his rear view mirror. He took a hard left, went a few blocks and made another hard left onto Washington Street with the white van following on his rear bumper. There, coming up right in front of him, was the shiny bronze Obelisk of Virtue, set atop a pedestal in the street's narrow median strip. As the traffic light began to change, he gunned his engine, whipped around the obelisk and past it. The white van was not so nimble. Disposo looked into his rear view mirror in time to see the van swerve suddenly, causing the car behind it to drive up onto the median and glance off the monument's pedestal. The impact of the blow toppled the hollow obelisk and sent it rolling like a log across the pavement, where an oncoming tractor-trailer, unable to stop in time, squashed it flat.

Disposo fled the scene. He drove all the way down to the river, frantically looking at one street sign after another. No Lee anywhere. He doubled back toward King Street, then fifty yards farther up he spotted the Russian, looking lost as well.

"Too many of them. I gotta get out of here," Disposo muttered as he stepped on the gas pedal.

It was just then that Yong came cruising by in his car, with Brucilla in the passenger seat. Disposo was too distracted to notice them.

But Brucilla saw him. "Oh my God!" he shouted suddenly, as he pulled down the windshield visor and dove under the dashboard.

"What the hell?" Yong yelled, nearly driving into a parked car. Brucilla was bent over beside him, hiding.

"That was him!" said Brucilla. "The guy who tailed me in Rocket City the day I escaped Quandary Capital. He had that hair—the greasy Elvis Presley hair. It's him."

"You sure?"

"Yes, that's the guy. They've found me and now they're here to kill me!"

"What? What we gonna do?"

"He's still a few blocks from your apartment. I'll bet the city's newly inclusive street names have thrown him off. He can't find Lee Street. Drop me off at your apartment real quick. Park on a different street."

Brucilla clopped up the stairs, entered Yong's apartment, and slammed the door behind him. Soon afterwards Yong burst through the door, out of breath.

"My cover is blown," Brucilla said. He yanked off his wig and held it in his hand, looking at it angrily. "A lot of help this is. I didn't think they would ever find me in this outfit—at least not so soon." He flung the wig on the floor in disgust.

"Too late. They find you. You steal anomaly. They gonna get you now. Maybe kill us both!"

"I couldn't just let CRAM dump us without giving this a shot. We would all lose everything!"

"Is portfolio fixed now?"

"Yes, it's all converted to the HONEY BOO-BOO method."

"Is it working?"

"Oh, yes! My new portfolio is beating the benchmark by five percentage points already. A few weeks of this and everything will be saved—the MaxiGay Fund, Vain Capital, all of our jobs, and Alison." Brucilla smiled and put his hand to his heart. "Especially Alison."

"Except now you gonna die!"

"Yes, so it seems. That may have been the flaw in my plan."

Yong peeked out the window through an opening in the curtains. He saw a man in a sport coat leaning against a street light, watching a woman in a purple sweater at a bus stop. A man in a white van was parked on the street. "Who is after us?"

"A guy with greasy black hair like Elvis. The one who chased me in Rocket City."

"Three people out there, two men and one woman. No Elvis."

Brucilla took a look for himself. "Those same three people were there a while ago. There may be more than one goon chasing us. I'll bet they sent the whole frickin' mob after me."

"So what we gonna do? No more sexes left for you to hide in. They get you here, or they get you at work."

Brucilla sat down on the sofa and thought for a moment. "Only one thing left to do. The reason they want to rub me out is that the HONEY BOO-BOO anomaly is worth billions. So I have to destroy its value. If it's worthless, there won't be any point in killing me anymore."

"Destroy its value? How?"

"Publish it."

"How will that help?"

"Exposure will kill it, like it does all investment anomalies. As soon as the secret gets out, there will be a mad rush to buy HONEY BOO-BOO stocks and they will be bid up far beyond their true value. Every portfolio manager in the world wants to know how Quandary Capital produces so much alpha. This news will travel faster than a bull branded in the ass with a hot poker."

"Do it then," Yong said. "No time to lose. Anomaly must die."

Brucilla paused to reflect on the gravity of taking this last fateful step. The final extinction of investment anomalies would have a devastating effect on all future generations of investors. If HONEY BOO-BOO were truly the last anomaly, no investor would ever have any hope of beating the market again. Active security selection would be pointless, and the mediocrity of passive management would have won its ultimate stultifying victory over man's instinctive urge to be above average. Revealing the last anomaly would be a sort of an investment crime against nature, like killing off the last dodo, shooting the last passenger pigeon, or spearing the last wooly mammoth. Mankind, forevermore investing in vain, would hold him in the same contempt as it did the destroyers of those marvelous creatures, which now lived only as mere footnotes in the annals of natural history.

And HONEY BOO-BOO was not just any anomaly. Being utterly illogical, it was the best damned anomaly there ever was or could be, giving voice to an infatuated quant's unquenchable passion: HONEY BOO-BOO DOES IT SO GOOD! Killing it would be like killing love itself.

No time for sentimentality. Brucilla must murder the anomaly to save himself. Perhaps posterity would understand why he had to do it, and maybe even forgive his selfishness.

He sat down at his computer that night to write an anonymous eight-page article in the online blog section of *The Investment Analysts Journal*, entitled *"The Complete Methodology of Quandary Capital's HONEY BOO-BOO Anomaly."* In it he described exactly how to create and manage a HONEY BOO-BOO portfolio to the last detail, omitting only one: the timing of Minnie Feiersinger's period, which for the sake of propriety hardly seemed a fitting topic. He advised trading every month around the twenty-eighth and left it at that.

He breathed deeply and then clicked the "PUBLISH" button on his screen. In an instant the deed was done. For better or worse, the HONEY BOO-BOO anomaly was out there in the sunlight now, fully exposed to the merciless Darwinian struggle of investment competition. It was as good as dead.

27 Russian Invasions

As soon as Beatrice got off the telephone with the Butcher she rushed to the television in the Vain Capital break room to see the news for herself.

A well-coifed male anchor was delivering the headlines on an all-news cable channel. "Two major stories have broken today, both of them involving Russia," Marty Amigo announced. "The State Department has disclosed that three thousand masked troops in unmarked vehicles have crossed from the Russian city of Ivangorod into the Estonian town of Narva."

Images of camouflaged soldiers wearing black masks and carrying machine guns filled the screen. The gunmen stood guard at a street corner while babushkas loaded down with sacks of groceries shuttled past them as if they were statues that had always been there and nothing unusual had happened. A column of tanks trundled triumphantly down the street.

"The Russian government vehemently denies that these are Russian troops," continued the anchor, "insisting that they are pro-Russian Estonian separatists acting on their own. According to the State Department, the troops have rolled their tanks and armored personnel carriers across the bridge from Russia and taken positions in and around Narva to secure the town, which had been lightly defended by a squad of transgendered Belgians. It is unclear what the masked troops' objective is. For a discussion of this angle of the story, we go to our Pentagon correspondent, Jennifer Rabbits."

The scene shifted to the lobby of the Pentagon, where a blond woman with the doleful face of a basset hound posed in front of the office of the Chairman of the Joint Chiefs of Staff. "Marty, NATO forces in Estonia, six thousand strong, and U.S. forces worldwide have been placed on an alert status of DEFCON 4, the second lowest level, in an effort to demonstrate restraint and peaceful intentions toward Russia. Since Estonia is a NATO country and the alliance is obligated to defend the tiny nation of one point three million people, this understated response is intended to calm any panic that NATO might be forced into an all-out thermonuclear war to prove its credibility for the sake of such a trifling country. President Phyllis Fibby and Secretary of State Javonda Hernandez have informed the Russians that they ought to be ashamed of themselves for the incursion and called for an emergency meeting of the U.N. Security Council to chide them. Back to you, Marty."

The anchor reappeared with a picture of the White House in the background, its water fountain bubbling serenely on the North Lawn. "Threatening to overshadow the apparent Russian invasion of Estonia is our other major Russian story. It comes from *The Washington Post,* which says one of its reporters has received information leaked from the White House staff about a secret investment made by Russia's sovereign wealth fund in a U.S.-based fund of gay money managers. The Kremlin, notorious for its cruel persecution of gays, flatly denies making any such illicit and immoral investment and dismissed the story as fake news. In this country, political reaction from several quarters has been swift and varied. For that we go to Huma Mohammed on Capitol Hill."

A woman in a black hijab stood on the Capitol steps. "Marty, the capital is abuzz with the political fallout from the revelation of the Russian gay investment. The national gay organization Queers Without Fears has hailed Russia's enlightened move, saying through its spokesman that it shows welcome evidence of the Kremlin's newfound open-mindedness and gives the Russian LGBT community hope for more such social breakthroughs in the future. But on another front, the conservative group American Family Council strongly denounced the wickedness of an American gay fund, but said that if it must exist then only Americans should be allowed to invest in it. Here on Capitol Hill conservative Arizona congressman Harold Blimpton, chairman of the House Committee on Foreign Affairs, has likened the Russian investment to an invasion of the U.S. financial system."

A rotund congressman with jowls and a bald spot appeared on the screen, banging his gavel to restore order at a raucous meeting of his committee. "Gentlemen, for the State Department to allow this Russian investment is an outrage, another policy failure stemming from the Fibby administration's flaccid response to Russia's aggression against its neighbors. I call for this committee to hold hearings immediately to assess the foreign security implications of allowing Russians to hijack a sovereign American gay fund."

The screen flashed back to the anchor, who appeared in front of a video of college students carrying placards in front of an administration building. "Demonstrations have erupted on several college campuses in support of Russia's action, with students loudly demanding that their own colleges' endowments follow the Russian example and invest with gay managers to increase sexual diversity. Students at Oberlin were seen throwing rainbow-colored Monopoly money at school officials and carrying signs reading 'More gay dollars to fund our scholars.'"

The video beside Amigo's head morphed into a shot of an office building on K Street as the news anchor explained, "At the center of this explosive controversy is the American fund of gay money managers, which *The Washington Post* says is called the MaxiGay Fund, set up by the Washington investment firm Vain Capital Management for the nation's largest pension organization, California Retirement Asset Management, or CRAM. Public documents obtained from CRAM's website describe the MaxiGay Fund as being 'maximally diversified, sexually fluid, and gay in all dimensions.' This transgendered person was seen walking into the building housing Vain Capital this morning."

The video zoomed in on Brucilla and Yong elbowing their way through a throng of journalists. Microphones were thrust into Brucilla's face from all directions as reporters pelted him with questions.

"Ma'am, can you tell us anything about Vain Capital's ties to Russia?"

"Ma'am, how did you manage to persuade the Russian government to go gay?"

"Ma'am, why are you supporting the Russian invasion of Estonia?"

Brucilla and Yong were seen pressing their way to the entrance, where they disappeared inside the lobby.

Amigo came back on the screen again. "As you see, efforts to contact Vain Capital for comment on the Russian investment were unsuccessful. In other news—"

Beatrice looked through the window down to the sidewalk twelve stories below. The television crews and cameramen were gone. Thanks to her appointment with her hairdresser she had arrived late to work that morning, narrowly escaping the ravenous pack of reporters herself. She staggered back to her office, closed the door, and called the Butcher.

"Zip it, Beatrice! Don't tell them anything!" the Butcher yelled through the phone. "You have a duty of confidentiality to all your clients, including the Russians. The press has absolutely no right to know who is investing with Vain Capital. It is up to the clients to reveal themselves if they choose. Tell the U.S. government if they ask, but nobody else. Stonewall the press. Forbid everyone working at Vain Capital to speak to them."

"That was my plan, Stanton," Beatrice replied. "I will have meetings with the staff this afternoon. I will explain to them that Client Thirty-One is the Russky Fund, but they are not to discuss the investment with anyone."

"So who is the real investor?" the Butcher asked. "You can tell me."

"I don't know who the real investor is."

"Really?"

"Really. I don't know. Yegor Yakov never told me, and I never asked. The Russky Fund is the only name I know."

"Good," the Butcher said. "When the government shows up, that's what you tell them."

That's what I've already told them, Beatrice was thinking, *days ago*. It was the truth, after all. What trouble could come from telling the truth?

28 The Revenge of Ulysses

When Dr. Ozturk got to the Quandary Capital security office, he saw Dr. Feiersinger shaking his head at a bar chart on the computer screen, with anxiety etched into his face.

"It's a buying frenzy, Mustafa! Fifteen times normal daily volume! And that was just the increase yesterday! Already today there is much more!"

Ozturk stared at the chart, its escalating bars showing the trading volume of the HONEY BOO-BOO stocks shooting up. "What's happening to the prices of our stocks?"

"They are rising by huge amounts, all twenty-three of them! The portfolio was up twenty percent yesterday. And today another fifteen percent since the market opened an hour ago."

Feiersinger clicked on the screen to bring up a chart showing the value of the Quandary Capital portfolio. The graph was climbing like the side of a steep mountain. New orders were flooding into the market.

"A move like this is unsustainable. Who can be doing all this buying? Bruce Benson?" Ozturk asked.

"Oh, no, this is much too big to be just Benson," Feiersinger said. "To move our portfolio so much would take tens of billions of dollars. Our brokers say the buyers are everywhere: hedge funds, mutual funds, institutional long-only managers of various kinds, all parts of the market, including overseas investors."

"How is the overall market doing?"

"The rest of the market is flat. Only our HONEY BOO-BOO stocks are rising like this, and that is drawing even more attention to them."

"Our portfolio must be crushing the benchmark then," Ozturk said.

"Yes, it is. But so what? It can't last. That is why I called you."

"Our worst fear may be coming true," Ozturk said. "Information about the anomaly may have gotten out, beyond just Benson himself. What are the news reports saying?"

Feiersinger typed in some ticker symbols to search for news on several of the HONEY BOO-BOO stocks. Up came a Bloomberg story about a new product launch at a consumer products company in the portfolio, then a story about an earnings miss at a technology company. "This is not it," he muttered. "This ordinary sort of news could never move our stocks so much."

Then down the list of links he saw one leading to *The Investment Analysts Journal.* He clicked on it.

The screen filled with an online article entitled *"The Complete Methodology of Quandary Capital's HONEY BOO-BOO Anomaly,"* by I.M. Ulysses, University of Chicago.

"No!" Feiersinger shouted. "It can't be!" He turned to Ozturk in horror. "Look, Mustafa! This article describes every part of our investment process, step by step! There are detailed instructions here for using the anomaly to replicate a Quandary Capital portfolio!"

Ozturk squinted at the screen. This was not your typical academic finance article composed in the arcane style common to such journals, larded with dense prose to separate the financial cognoscenti from the hoi polloi. Written for the masses, this piece was no more challenging than a recipe for making guacamole dip. Ozturk's eye zeroed in on a counter at the bottom of the screen. It registered 2,439 downloads.

"Oh, no!" he cried.

"Who is I.M. Ulysses?" Feiersinger asked. "Sounds like a Greek."

"But we've never hired a Greek. I don't like Greeks," Ozturk said. "There is no one at Quandary Capital by that name."

"Could it be Bruce Benson in yet another cowardly disguise?" Feiersinger suggested.

"Ulysses! Of course!" Ozturk said, his owlish eyes widening. "The cunning Greek hero who outsmarts the Trojans to get into their fortified city and destroy it from within. Troy was in what is now Turkey, and I am the Turk. It is Benson, without a doubt. He is mocking us. This is his revenge."

"But why is everyone so willing to believe this article? Who would be so gullible as to gamble billions of dollars on the basis of an article by a University of Chicago finance professor they have never met?" Feier-singer asked.

"The entire investment world, Otto. They do it every day without a second thought," Ozturk said. "And no one will care who wrote this. Think of all the money managers out there with lousy performance, investing in vain! To save themselves, they will give it a shot, hoping it really is Quandary Capital's secret. And it is working for them, as you see. It is working so well they are shoveling more and more money into it by the minute!"

"Then we must sue to have the article removed from the website im-mediately," Feiersinger said. "This is our proprietary information that has been leaked."

Ozturk began to pace around the room. "Leaked? Bruce Benson was a leak. This is a hemorrhage—the article has been downloaded more than two thousand times! Sue a non-profit investment journal? They don't have any money. Proprietary information, you say? We can't admit that this is our proprietary information! We can't let the world know the smartest guys in the investment industry depend upon the HONEY BOO-BOO anomaly to generate their alpha!"

They heard a knock at the door. It was Ozturk's secretary, handing her boss a scrawled message: "Please return call regarding HONEY BOO-BOO boom. Rob Wyatt, Reporter, *Wall Street Journal*, 202-555-3932."

"*The Wall Street Journal!*" Ozturk's rocket-shaped head was beginning to throb as if it might actually blast off his shoulders. "We can't talk about this to a newspaper with a circulation of two million!"

"*Ach*, it is over for us, Mustafa," Feiersinger groaned. "First the Wall Street Journal, next CNBC will call! Soon every day trader will be run-ning a HONEY BOO-BOO portfolio in his underwear from his moth-er's basement." Feiersinger watched in despair as the prices of the HON-EY BOO-BOO stocks continued to swell.

"Actually, from the looks of your screen it seems the basement-dwell-ers have already found out," Ozturk said. "And it's not surprising—they would be the first fools to believe that your wife's silly anomaly works. But then, of course, it does work, better than anything. For the life of me, I've never understood why."

"What are we to do?"

"What if we just sold?"

"Impossible," said Feiersinger. "Anything we do will tip our hand. We have fifty billion dollars in these twenty-three stocks. Our positions are so large that the Street would see that we're bailing out. That would prove we are using the anomaly. And if we start selling we might set off a tidal wave of selling which would hurt our remaining positions."

"We could hedge."

"Same problem. Someone will notice. All eyes are upon us now. We're trapped."

"Well, we are not talking to *The Wall Street Journal!*" Ozturk said. "But they already know all about the anomaly. They don't really need to talk to us to write their stupid article. Bruce Benson has seen to that. He has outed HONEY BOO-BOO in one masterstroke."

"How embarrassing!" Feiersinger said, considering how humiliated his wife would feel about the worldwide revelation of her prowess in the bedroom. Then it occurred to him that almost no one knew who HONEY BOO-BOO was. "Perhaps we should just deny we have anything to do with the anomaly."

"Oh, that's just the beginning of what we must deny," Ozturk declared. "We can't even acknowledge the anomaly's existence. We must say it's a ludicrous investment idea. Buying stocks simply because they spell HONEY BOO-BOO DOES IT SO GOOD? We will be laughed out of the investment industry! Our reputation will be in tatters. Our clients will chase us with pitchforks and lawyers, and the SEC will clap us in chains for the rest of our lives. We will not comment on our investment process. It is proprietary. That is our answer to the media."

"What about our employees? For sure they will read the press. How can we control them?"

"Oh, that's much easier. We tell them the published stories are false. We order them not to talk to the media."

"But they are PhDs, Nobel laureates, they are geniuses, Mustafa. Surely they will put it all together and know we are lying through our teeth," Feiersinger said.

"No, Otto, it is precisely because our quants are geniuses that they will never believe that such an idiotic anomaly could work," Ozturk insisted. "It would be an insult to their intelligence and their pride if it did. For the sake of their own egos they need to believe the market is rational and intellectually complex like them. That's why they have never found the HONEY BOO-BOO anomaly themselves, why it has remained hidden from their view under a veil of illogic all this time. A fool could find it, but a genius? Never! It takes a special kind of insight to comprehend the power of folly as a force of nature and a mover of markets—it is a versatile, imaginative, and creatively absurd intelligence that ordinary linear-thinking geniuses lack. Only a few quants like Benson have it."

"How did it come to this? How have we been brought to such a pass?" Feiersinger asked. "What about Disposo? He was supposed to eliminate Benson to stop this sort of catastrophe ever happening."

"Call him at once. Perhaps it's not too late."

Disposo answered his cell phone on the first ring.

"Fellas, I have been running all over Washington chasing your escaped she-quant with my dart gun," the detective said. "Can't get a clear shot at it without someone seeing me. I'm being tailed wherever I go."

"Who is tailing you?"

"That's just it. I don't know who they are. Government spooks, maybe. There are at least three of them, two men and a woman, maybe more. They follow me everywhere. I can't shake them off."

"It might be something to do with Vain Capital," Ozturk suggested. "They've been all over the news. Their gay fund has a Russian connection. Maybe the people following you are Russians."

"Russians? Wait a minute. Yes, there was a Russian following me." Suddenly Disposo realized what he might be up against. "Have you guys ticked off the Russians now? Forget it! Forget this whole thing. This was supposed to be a simple hit. I didn't sign up to take on the FSB for a lousy million dollars. You can't pay me enough to do that. I'm not risking my life for this."

"The Russians are after our anomaly too? God help us!" Feiersinger exclaimed.

"Calm down, Otto. Never mind the Russians. We have nothing to do with them," Ozturk said to him, wincing as he watched the volume of the HONEY BOO-BOO stocks double again. "It's Benson we're after."

Ozturk turned back to the phone. "Alright, we'll make it well worth your while, Mr. Disposo. We'll pay you five million dollars! Just put a stop to that cowboy!"

29 Election Returns

The election should have been over by nine o'clock, but it was almost midnight when the thin woman with the brown puppy dog eyes entered the grand ballroom of San Francisco's Fairmont Hotel to address her hundreds of supporters. It had been such a long night that not even the young people had the energy left to dance to the 1980s rock music blaring from the loudspeakers. The media had been standing at the ready for hours at the back of the room as news reporters speculated on camera as to whether Governor Pitypander might have won easily if only she had spent more time making empty promises to this group or that. As a big television displayed the dolorous returns overhead, campaign workers and political operatives stood around drinking too much spiked punch, their eyes checking the screen every other minute for any improvement in the prognosis.

The two gubernatorial candidates had been running about even all day, trading first place back and forth. Now, with ninety-nine percent of the vote in, the screen bore the grim statistic: "Fist (R)—3,695,392, Pitypander (D)—3,692,203."

Governor Patty Pitypander sucked in her pride and wore her best campaign smile onto the stage as the room erupted in applause. The background rock music changed to "Don't Stop Thinking About Tomorrow." She lifted the microphone from the podium and thanked her placard-waving supporters for all their hard work on her behalf, and then her billionaire husband for enduring her absence during the long, arduous campaign.

"And I want to give thanks to all the various oppressed communities that stood behind my campaign for social justice—the Hispanics, blacks, Asians, the poor, the undocumented immigrants, the teachers unions, the LGBTQIA community, and all the other victimized people of California. My heart goes out to you, whether you work in a barrio or a bar. We have struggled tirelessly on your behalf and you have responded unfailingly with your support. We'll never stop fighting for you against the corrupt corporate interests, the fraudulent instruments of the rich and powerful, and the shameful gun lobbyists who back my craven opponent. But it does appear Mr. Fist has an insurmountable edge over us tonight—"

"No!" her supporters groaned in unison. "No concession, Patty!"

"And I want to compliment Mr. Fist for running a successful campaign, tawdry and mean as it was. We may not agree with the Republicans on much, or anything for that matter beyond the necessity for humans to inhale oxygen, but we both love the people of California, at least some of them, and that's something perhaps we can build on."

"Don't do it, Patty!" someone shouted from the crowd. "Keep fighting! Resist! Resist!"

"Thanks to the efforts of all of you, we came very close. We'll work with the election officials on pursuing a recount, but tonight seems to belong to Mr. Fist, and we congratulate him provisionally on his apparent narrow and thoroughly unworthy victory."

"Pitypander for President!" a tearful campaign staffer called out.

Governor Pitypander smiled and turned her tear-stained face toward the cameras. Leaving her bereft followers to their electoral distress, she waved a heartfelt goodbye for the last time, embraced her husband, and disappeared with him from the stage to embark on their new life on the ski slopes of Aspen.

At Vain Capital the Butcher had dropped in unannounced just in time to witness Beatrice's unsuccessful attempt to retain her round-faced Mormon client.

"You must understand our investment committee's position, Beatrice," Barton Hinckley said. "The national publicity concerning your gay manager fund has made several of our members very uncomfortable. The committee doesn't feel that our association with your firm casts the Mormons on the Mount in the best light. Surely you can see why. Lesbians, transgendered people, queers? We are Mormons. We can't support this depravity."

"But you aren't invested in the MaxiGay Fund, Barton," Beatrice said.

"That doesn't matter now that Vain Capital is all over the news," said Hinckley. "We could tolerate your other clients as long as we could be separate from them. It was no business of ours what they wanted from their portfolios as long as we got what we wanted from ours. But the national media coverage of the MaxiGay Fund has pointed a spotlight at all your clients, including us, and linked us all to the MaxiGay Fund. It's irrelevant that we aren't actually invested in your shameful fund. In the eyes of the public and our members we are tied to it through Vain Capital."

"Barton, there is nothing at all to be ashamed of," Beatrice said. "If anyone thinks that the Mormons on the Mount have gone gay, just have them call me and I'll be happy to straighten them out. Who could possibly believe such a silly thing—Mormons going gay, that's ridiculous! My goodness, what would your Mormon angels think of that?"

She turned and looked at the Butcher, who was cringing for some reason.

"The committee also considered your underperformance in making its decision," Hinckley continued. "Vain Capital doesn't seem to be able to beat the market. You keep underperforming, year after year."

"It's your portfolio restrictions—your Mormon rules against owning anything to do with coffee, tea, tobacco, and liquor—they have crippled your performance," Beatrice said. "The sad truth, Barton, is that sin has been on a roll. Tobacco stocks have been soaring for the past five years. Starbucks has been another big winner. Anyone who goes there can see why. Their Frappuccinos are yummy. Only a Mormon saint could resist them."

"But when we hired you, you told us our restrictions wouldn't matter and you could outperform regardless of them."

"It's a question of time, Barton. We just need more time. Yes, your restrictions have posed a challenge for your returns lately," Beatrice admitted. "But we always view these performance shortfalls as random, temporary setbacks. Your virtue will eventually be rewarded. Not owning sin stocks shouldn't be disadvantageous over the long term. That wouldn't be moral, would it? God wouldn't let a sinful portfolio thrive indefinitely while a righteous one suffered, would he? God just needs time to work his wonders with your portfolios. Won't you give God time to work his miracles?"

Hinckley shook his head. "It's not up to me. Our committee won't give you any more time to work yours. The members are anxious to cut ties with Vain Capital as soon as possible—this month, at the end of November."

"We could offer you a performance fee if you like. Our services would be free unless we outperformed."

"Too late for that," Hinckley said. "The real problem is, we're ashamed of being involved with Vain Capital. Every day we hear another horror story from our young male missionaries, our nineteen-year-olds who go door to door in pairs to proselytize for the church. People think they're collecting for the MaxiGay Fund. Some are even inviting our boys inside to make indecent proposals to them. We are becoming the laughingstock of Salt Lake City."

Ashamed of Vain Capital? The very idea cut Beatrice like a knife. "What can we do to change your mind?"

"Nothing."

After seeing Hinckley off, Beatrice returned to the conference room with the Butcher, who had come to discuss the shocking results of the California gubernatorial election.

"There will be a recount of course, but Fist will still win," the Butcher said with a sullen look on his face. "Patty Pitypander will be out of office soon. I had a good deal of money invested in her through the Pitypander Foundation, all lost now of course."

"Such a tiny margin in such a huge state. What put Fist over the top?" Beatrice asked.

"Mismanagement at CRAM. The pension cutbacks for state retirees and the skyrocketing income taxes to prop up the pension. Fist promised to fix CRAM and the voters believed him. God knows why—he's such a Nazi."

"After all we did to help her, didn't Pitypander get the gay vote? Didn't San Francisco turn out for her?"

"Yes, she got the gay vote alright. They loved the LGBTQIA diversification thing in San Francisco. But it wasn't enough. The cumulative underperformance caused by years of politically correct meddling with CRAM's portfolios by governor after governor over so many decades did her in. You can't cover up bad math with political gimmickry forever. It takes real dollars to pay off retirees."

"What is Fist planning to do to fix CRAM?" Beatrice asked. "Do you think he'll kill the MaxiGay fund?"

"I do."

"Has he said anything about it yet?"

"No, but he has denounced CRAM as a fiscal mess and a moral cesspool and we know he's committed to fixing it. He's an arch-conservative, a no-nonsense guy. And your MaxiGay Fund is all nonsense."

"It is not nonsense!" Beatrice said, scowling at him. "You should see how much interest it has generated at the university endowments, especially with all the recent publicity. And we still have the Russky Fund's money in it."

"Not for long, Beatrice. The Russians are just keeping their heads down for now. They'll probably pull their money from you as soon as the Estonian crisis blows over."

"So what are you saying, Stanton? Are you saying we're finished?"

"Beatrice, you just lost four hundred million dollars from the Mormons because all this publicity about the MaxiGay Fund has embarrassed them. Your Arabs and Catholics could be next. And who knows what your other conservative clients are saying about Vain Capital in their boardrooms. On top of that, CRAM and the Russians are likely to yank their ten billion dollars. If you lose that much, I won't be able to hold back Mark Weedle any longer. He will demand that the Butcher and Weedle Captivation Fund sell its controlling interest in Vain Capital before your firm implodes completely."

Beatrice folded her hands as if in prayer. "Stanton, you've always understood that helping clients to invest their money morally is Vain Capital's mission—it has to be an act of faith for you and me as well as them. Just like our clients, your private equity fund needs to have some faith. Haven't I always managed to come up with replacement clients somehow?"

"Weedle is a hard man who doesn't believe in magic, Beatrice—not even your Pillsbury magic. I've come here today to give you fair warning. Lose the CRAM account and you will be sold to the highest bidder."

30 The Honey Boo-Boo Bust

In the security office at Quandary Capital the bars on the volume chart had risen to levels Dr. Feiersinger had never thought possible.

"What can I tell the clients, Otto?" Dr. Ozturk asked quietly, hoping that the good example of his composure would calm his partner. "I have to tell them something. We are being bombarded with phone calls. Our clients want answers."

"Tell them their portfolios are in utter ruins, Mustafa," Feiersinger moaned. "A tidal wave of selling, that's what yesterday was. The volume of trading in our stocks was forty times normal. Our portfolio was down thirty-five percent. We've lost all our gains from the run-up. The hedge funds are turning on us like jackals."

"But the hedgies were buying our stocks like mad just last week. Why are they selling now? Have they lost faith in the HONEY BOO-BOO anomaly so soon?"

"After word got out about our anomaly they all jumped in at once and drove our stocks to the sky. Now all they see is huge downside risk. The ones who piled in earliest are just trying to get out of the way of the selling avalanche."

"It looks like the selling has spread to the whole market," Ozturk noted, observing the plunging chart for the S&P 500 Index. On another screen news stories carried the headlines "The Boo-Hoo-Hoo of HONEY BOO-BOO" and "HONEY BOO-BOO Goes Bust."

"Yes, the collapse of our stocks has set off a market panic. We can only imagine what this morning's open will look like. Probably Armageddon!"

"For Armageddon I will need something especially soothing to tell the clients," Ozturk said.

In the first two minutes the market was down ten percent, the worst opening in thirty years. Trillions of dollars of wealth were vanishing into the ether. An amount equal to the GDP of France evaporated in an instant. Feiersinger lay back limply in his chair, gaping at the screen, awed by the economic destruction unfolding before him. "It is a market crash, Mustafa! We are doomed."

"How about it's a short-term market disturbance triggered by adverse technical factors which we are confident will soon be corrected?" Ozturk proposed.

Feiersinger began tearing his hair. "No, Mustafa, really, this is serious! We are finished, smashed upon the rocks, blasted to pieces! Look, see there, in the first minute the market is down fifteen percent and our portfolio has plunged another thirty-five percent."

"That won't do. How about a temporary reaction to aberrant mispricing due to volume imbalances?"

"*Nein*, it is *kaput*! Don't you understand? We are *kaput*! Everything is *kaput*!"

"Alright, then. We can rework the explanation if you feel that strongly about it. Let's admit there's some uncomfortable volatility. How about an usually severe market disturbance giving rise to fresh opportunities to exploit aberrant mispricings caused by volume imbalances? That's very upbeat, don't you think? I'll try that version on them."

Suddenly they heard a knock at the door. It was Ozturk's secretary, her brow knotted with anxiety. She handed Ozturk a note that read "Armed government agents in lobby. Both partners must come immediately."

They rushed to the reception desk, where they saw a bearded man in a business suit and three others in blue jackets marked "FBI" in big gold letters. The man in the suit stepped forward and flashed his badge.

"Hiram Forceps, SEC Enforcement Division's Financial Reporting and Audit Group," the man said. "These fellows are FBI agents Martin, Heingartner, and Bistro. Are you gentlemen Mustafa Ozturk and Otto Feiersinger?"

"We are," Ozturk said.

"Are you the owners of Quandary Capital Management, LLC, an SEC-registered investment advisor located in Rocket City, Florida?"

"Yes."

"You are both under arrest," Forceps said, motioning to the FBI agents to proceed. "Please come with us."

FBI agents Martin and Heingartner pulled out sets of handcuffs.

"What!" Ozturk said. "For doing what? You can't arrest us! What is this about?"

"Securities fraud, market manipulation, deceptive sales practices, just for starters," Forceps said, looking down at the arrest warrants. "Please put your hands behind your back."

"But we haven't done anything!" Ozturk turned around with his hands behind him as the agents cuffed him and Feiersinger. "You're making a big mistake."

"HONEY BOO-BOO. That was your big mistake. Women always are, aren't they?"

"I don't know what you mean," Ozturk said.

"I think you do," Forceps said. "Your HONEY BOO-BOO scheme is all over the news. You're the geniuses who engineered this market crash."

"Is it illegal in America to buy stocks just because they spell something very sexy?" Feiersinger asked.

"No, here it's just silly. Maybe it's different where you come from."

"You're throwing us in jail because we're silly investors?" Ozturk asked. "How much room do you have in your jail?"

Forceps scowled at him. "Quants aren't supposed to be silly. A silly quant has to be a fraud. You fellows thought you'd get away with running billions of dollars in portfolios spelling HONEY BOO-BOO DOES IT SO GOOD? Really?"

"But it does work," Feiersinger insisted. "HONEY BOO-BOO is a true market anomaly. Probably the last one."

"You bureaucratic idiot, you can't win a fraud case against us," Ozturk said. "We have the best performance record in the country. We haven't damaged our clients, we've enriched them, and we have the numbers to prove it. How can you prove our method doesn't work?"

"Prove it? This time the SEC isn't waiting for proof," Forceps said. "Bernie Madoff had great numbers too. Our people couldn't figure out why his strategy worked so well either. Turned out Madoff was running a Ponzi scheme with sixty-five billion dollars. Look where waiting for proof got us—took us a decade to live down the embarrassment. No sir, we won't be burned like that again. With you jokers we don't even need to prove fraud. What federal judge would believe you? HONEY BOO-BOO DOES IT SO GOOD! Ha, I'll bet she does! You con artists always think you have more brains than everybody else, but it's that big organ between your legs that always trips you up, isn't it?"

"We are smarter than everybody else," Ozturk said. "We are quants. We have algorithms."

"Well, you can show your algorithms to the cameras, smarty. Ten reporters are outside waiting to take photos of your little perp walk. You'll be on television in a few minutes. Say goodbye to all this! Quandary Capital is closed by order of the SEC."

Minutes later, from the back of the FBI van, Ozturk sent a text message to Freddie Disposo. It read, "Twenty million dollars to get the cowboy."

Beatrice could hardly believe how quickly the MaxiGay Fund's performance had turned around.

"These numbers are marvelous, Brucilla, but I don't understand them," she said at the MaxiGay team's weekly meeting. "Your portfolio is a passively managed index account. It was to produce the returns of its S&P 500 Fossil Fuel Free benchmark and nothing more. You're supposed to just be buying the stocks in the index at the benchmark weights. We didn't expect you to outperform."

"I took some liberties with the portfolio, Beatrice, just this once," Brucilla said. "Since we are hanging by a thread with CRAM, I didn't think you would mind my scooping up some outperformance if I saw some opportunities that might help save us."

She found it hard to disagree. It would be a shame to sacrifice success upon the altar of principle as her clients did. "You're right," she said. "I don't mind, no matter how irregular it is. And under the circumstances, I don't think CRAM will be complaining either. But you are thirty points ahead of your benchmark, dear. Not even Quandary Capital with its one thousand employees could have pulled this off. How have you managed to do it singlehandedly?"

A humble smile appeared on Brucilla's face. "My quant models detected some unusual volume and pricing abnormalities in the HONEY BOO-BOO stocks—you know, the ones everyone is talking about, the ones from Quandary Capital's secret investment method. Their stocks got very hot and then very cold. I managed to buy them just before they exploded to the upside, and then unload them before they crashed."

"I see from Alison's report that the lesbian, gay, and both hermaphrodite portfolios are still lagging. The queer and asexual are treading water. And my goodness, look there, the bisexual portfolio is gasping for air too. But the overall MaxiGay Fund is now up five points?"

"Thanks to Brucilla," Alison confirmed. "Without Curious Capital, we would still be behind and CRAM would fire us for sure. First you saved us in San Francisco and then you saved us here. If you hadn't come along I don't know what we would have done. You're amazing. You have such courage."

Courage? Her compliment stung him to the core. After all these months of longing for her, the one thing he was sure he did not have was courage. *No, I can't tell her who I really am, not yet,* he decided. He glanced at Yong, who seemed to look back at him with pity in his eyes.

"An extraordinary feat, that's for sure," Beatrice repeated. "Well done, Brucilla. Keep up the good work."

Keep it up? Not possible. He had murdered the HONEY BOO-BOO anomaly. He had flung open the doors to the last great gold mine of outperformance and the world had rushed right in and looted it. There was nothing left in that gold mine. But in this one, in Alison's eyes, there was a better treasure to be had, if only he could grasp it.

The meeting was soon interrupted. A secretary appeared in the doorway to the conference room, making the announcement that five men from the SEC were standing impatiently at the reception desk.

Hiram Forceps was accompanied by four auditors from his department. They had come to do a surprise audit of Vain Capital and the MaxiGay Fund.

"We demand to see everything having anything to do with the Russky Fund," Forceps said. "E-mails. Trading confirms. Investment recommendations. Memos of any kind. Every document in this place. Right now."

Beatrice's face flushed with anger. "Why are you doing this, Mr. Forceps? I told you everything I know when you barged in here last month."

"And as I told you last month, Ms. von Vain, there are laws against money laundering and it's very likely you have broken several of them. The Commission does not tolerate secret money flows from corrupt countries and individuals engaged in illegal activities."

"Vain Capital is not involved in illegal activities," Beatrice snapped. "How dare you imply—"

"Ms. von Vain, I have orders from the Commissioner himself to find out where that three billion in Russky Fund money actually came from, and he's in a huge hurry for some reason. Now I don't like people making my department look bad. We'll turn this place upside down if we have to. I can bring in the FBI if you need persuasion. Are you going to cooperate or not?"

"Yes, of course we will," Beatrice said. "You won't find anything, though. I told you the Russky Fund wired us the money under its own name. We have no documents showing an individual investor. There is nothing more we can give you."

The auditors, armed with a long list of items they wanted to see, were placed in a small meeting room to do their work. Vain Capital employees were directed to round up anything on the list, while the auditors proceeded to read every piece of paper brought to them.

By the end of the day the auditors had gone through every document pertaining to Vain Capital's brief relationship with the Russky Fund. The only name they could find was Yegor Yakov. Forceps confronted Beatrice again.

"I don't believe you," Forceps said flatly. "This Yakov guy seems to be nothing but a flunky for somebody else. I think the Russky Fund was just a conduit for laundering this money. Who is the real person behind this investment? Who is Yakov working for?"

"Yegor Yakov is a perfectly nice man who drinks entirely too much at our client conferences," Beatrice said, eyeing one of the items on the table. It was the photograph of Yakov with his arm curled suggestively around Brucilla's waist. "He's our only contact with the Russky Fund, and has been from the start. As I told you, no individual's name was disclosed to us."

Forceps slammed his fist on the table. "Have it your way, Ms. von Vain. The Commissioner has sent me here personally to squeeze it out of you one way or another. Federal law requires you to know who the real investor is and to have proper documentation. I'm going right now to get a court order to get Vain Capital shut down and have you arrested for conspiracy to engage in international money laundering. I'll see you again soon. And you can bet I will have proper documentation."

Beatrice ran to her office and closed the door. It was time to pull some powerful strings. Just as she was reaching for the phone to call the Butcher, it suddenly rang.

"It's the White House," said the receptionist. "President Fibby on line one."

31   The Confession

"It was on the news. The Feds have shut Quandary Capital down and thrown Ozturk and Feiersinger in jail for fraud," Brucilla said to Yong as they walked out of the parking garage. "That means I'm free to be myself now. I don't need to pretend anymore. I'm sure Beatrice and Alison will understand why I had to go undercover."

They went around the corner toward the entrance of the Vain Capital building. "How you know those guys not after you anymore?" Yong asked.

"Because Quandary Capital is finished and the HONEY BOO-BOO anomaly is worthless. Why would they want to kill me now? There's no profit in it. It would be illogical."

"Ah, very logical. Now they want revenge. You tell secret, wreck firm, put them in jail for life. More reason to kill you now than ever."

"But I don't want to do this anymore," Brucilla said. "I want my life back. I want Alison!"

"Why take risk now? Disguise keep you alive. Get you job. Give you free pass to ladies' rooms everywhere. You learn how to do eye shadow." Yong leaned around to take a closer look at Brucilla's garishly blue eyelids. "Almost learn how to do eye shadow."

"Alison admires Brucilla. Maybe she could like me, even love me. This is my big chance with her. I just need to tell her who I am."

"Alison Hartswell not in your league. She will break your heart."

"But I love her."

"Love?" Yong asked, his eyes full of doubt. "Love only thing more powerful than revenge. Confucius say both are forms of madness. Love make man into crazy bastard. Now you talking like crazy bastard."

That's right, I am a crazy bastard, Brucilla was thinking.

As they walked by an alley on K Street, he cast his eyes to the left. A dark figure seemed to be lurking behind the corner of a building, only a few steps away. Brucilla suddenly recognized him, and then he froze. It was the man with the greasy black hair.

"It's Elvis!" Brucilla yelled. "Run!"

Just then Freddie Disposo leapt out of the alley at him, raised a pistol, and fired a single shot at point-blank range.

Brucilla could feel the impact of something hitting him below the waist. Disposo bolted down the alley and disappeared.

"Elvis shot me! I'm hit!" Brucilla yelled, searching all over for the wound. But he felt no pain anywhere. He turned to look behind him. A black object was sticking out of the lower backside of his pink pantsuit. "It's a dart!"

"Are you bleeding?" Yong said.

"I don't think so. I don't feel anything."

Yong reached around Brucilla's rear end, pulled out the dart, and inspected it. "A needle. Stuck in butt."

It was the kind of flying syringe used to anesthetize escaped zoo animals. The inch-long needle had landed harmlessly in the two-inch foam padding of the Butt and Hip Builder.

"It's a syringe! Drop it!" Brucilla shouted. "It's full of poison!"

Yong tossed the dart into the alley. They rushed through the revolving doors of the Vain Capital building.

As the elevator doors closed over them, Brucilla pressed the button to the twelfth floor ten times. He gasped for breath. "I can't do this anymore! What good is a disguise if they know who I am?"

"Disguise save butt once more."

"I won't be so lucky next time," Brucilla said. "And then they'll find me dead, dressed like this. I don't want to leave this world in drag. This is so humiliating. I want to die with my boots on." He looked down at his pink pumps. A tsunami of self-loathing washed over him. "A fine cowboy I turned out to be! What would they think of me in Lonely Butte? You see what too much education does to a man? Made me a big pink poof, that's what! That's it! I've had it!"

Brucilla clopped out of the elevator. He marched straight to Alison's office and thrust his head inside.

"Alison, can we talk?" he asked.

She looked up from the manager reports she was reading, took one look at his anguished face, and sat upright in her chair. "Sure, what's wrong?"

He closed the door gently, trying to slow down his breathing, to appear calm. "Alison, I have a confession to make. I'm your secret admirer, the one who's been sending you those flowers and cards and boxes of chocolate."

There was a long silence. "Oh," she said quietly, her eyelids opening wide. She smiled sweetly at him. "Thank you. They were very nice. I really appreciated them."

"Did you? Do I stand a chance with you? Any chance at all?"

Alison looked at him, then averted her gaze, her mind rummaging through the frequently used stockpile of kind let-downs she kept for such occasions. But as much experience as she had spurning her many suitors, she had none for a man in pink, sporting a blond bouffant wig.

"Oh, Brucilla, I'm straight. I know it's not fashionable these days, but I'm into regular guys. It's not your fault, I think you're wonderful, kind, thoughtful, and brave, like I said yesterday. It's just that I couldn't be interested in a transgendered person, or any kind of non-standard male. Not that way."

"Well, that's the great news. You don't need to be."

"What?"

"I'm not really transgendered. It's all been a big act, to save my life. I'm a guy, a regular, lonely, straight guy," he said. "I came to Vain Capital to hide from a couple of angry quants trying to murder me. They've tracked me down anyway, and they've just tried to kill me out on K Street, so there's no use for me to pretend anymore. They might get me next time, or the time after that. But before I die, I just want you to know —"

He stopped to hold himself back, then decided to let himself go. "That I'm in love with you. I'm insanely in love with you."

He pulled off his wig and threw it on the floor. He kicked off his pink pumps.

"I'm Bruce Benson, from Quandary Capital. And I've loved you since the day I first met you down in Rocket City. You once said you wanted someone to love the real you. Here he is—the real me. Well, almost real, that is, without the wig and these fake breasts and hips, and these lady's clothes and all. I can assure you, there's a real straight man in here somewhere, trying desperately to come out of the closet and admit the truth about himself—which is that I'm straight. There, I've said it. I'm straight! Can you forgive me?"

Through the blue eye shadow and layers of makeup, Alison was just able to recognize Bruce's angular face. She thought back to their meetings at Quandary Capital and recalled her image of him as a homely and awkward man, a condition which she could see his feminine ensemble had only aggravated.

"Oh, Bruce, I, um, uh—"

"It's okay. I know this is a little sudden. I don't expect you to say anything now."

"It's just that I don't really know you, Bruce. Even when you were in Rocket City we barely knew each other, except that we met every few months across a conference table to review the Quandary Capital portfolio together."

"Yes, that's right. And I sure enjoyed those meetings. But how could you know me back then? And since I've been here I've been running around in a dress pretending to be a man who thinks he's a woman. Brucilla is who you know, or who you think you know. But I'm not Brucilla, I'm Bruce. Inside all this, I've been Bruce the whole time. You liked the man in the dress. Could you like the man without the dress, as a normal guy, I mean, in pants?"

Silence.

He looked down at his costume. "My God, what do I expect? I've confused you. I might be a little confused too. Look at me with all this stuff on! I can't stand myself. Oh God, what have I done? I'm so embarrassed. I'm so sorry to have bothered you. My God, Yong was right, I *am* a crazy bastard."

He turned and walked out of her office, then ran down the hall, wigless, shoeless, and distraught.

Beatrice, arriving at work, was startled to behold a tall, frantic man in a pink pantsuit flying past her on his escape to the elevator. "What on earth was that?" she asked Alison.

"It was Brucilla. Or who we all thought was Brucilla. Oh, Bea, it's all my fault again," Alison said, holding her face in her hands. "What is the matter with me? Look what I do to men, even the ones who think they're women. I ought to be locked up. I'm a public menace—I create gender identity problems wherever I go." She pointed to the blond bouffant wig and the pink pumps lying abandoned on her office floor. "You see there? Now I've blown up Brucilla. He's such a sweet guy. And now he's gone all to pieces over me."

"Oh, no, not now, that's impossible!" Beatrice exclaimed. "You'll just have to put him back together, my dear. I've just come from the White House. I've agreed to let them borrow Brucilla. It's a mission of the utmost national importance. And it's probably our only chance to save Vain Capital!"

Alison summoned Yong to seek his advice. He confirmed Brucilla's story about having to flee Quandary Capital and how the whole charade was his own idea.

"He ran out of here so upset, kind of unhinged, like he might hurt himself. Oh, I hope he's okay," she said. "You're his friend. What do you think is wrong with him?"

"Love make him crazy bastard," Yong said. "Too much time pretending to be fake woman, then falling in love with real one. He does not know who he is anymore, cannot tell up from down, completely lost. He is sure of only one thing now. He is in love with you. Nothing else matter."

"We have to find him fast. Where would he go? Home?" she asked.

"Maybe back to apartment. But maybe first to horse statue," Yong said.

"Horse statue?"

"In front of White House."

"You mean Lafayette Square?"

"Yes, on nice days he take lunch to park, to big statue of man riding horse. He was cowboy back in South Dakota. Horses make him think of home."

"Let's go. Maybe we can catch him there. He can't go far without shoes," Alison said.

They walked to Lafayette Square. In the center of the leafy park they saw the bronze equestrian statue of Andrew Jackson, victor of the battle of New Orleans, boldly waving his hat in triumph, his horse rearing up on its hind legs. A pigeon perched on Jackson's head. Tourists strolled by on their way to the White House.

They found Bruce slumped on a park bench nearby, disheveled, lacking his wig and shoes. His eyes were transfixed by the statue.

"Hello there," Alison said, sitting down next to him.

"Hi," Bruce said, barely moving, his eyes locked on Jackson's heroic figure.

"What do you see there?" she asked, looking at the statue.

"A distant ancestor of mine—a man who knew who he was," Bruce said with a long sigh. "A tough man who made no apologies for himself. An America that believed in itself, with no self-doubts. A simpler time. Not like now, with people so confused."

"Did knowing who he was make life easier for him?" Alison asked.

"For Old Hickory? Not at all," Bruce said. "He made a lot of enemies. He was so ornery they couldn't get him any other way so they tried to destroy him by accusing his wife Rachel of adultery and bigamy. But he wasn't ashamed of her. He loved her deeply. He wouldn't give in to them."

"Then what happened?"

"Rachel wasn't as strong as he was. She died of the strain from the publicity just after he was elected president, a short while before he came here to the White House, with his heart full of pain. They could hurt him, but they couldn't break him."

"I hear they want to take down this statue because he was a slave owner," Alison said.

"Yes, it's true Old Hickory was a slave owner, and he was hard on the Indians too, which made him normal for his time. But that's not all he was. To the people back then Old Hickory was a great hero, a guy's guy, the kind it took to build this country out of nothing. I guess they'll pull down all the statues of real guys soon. I came here to remember what one looks like before they're all gone."

"So did I," she said.

"What do you mean?"

"You're a real guy. I came to see you."

"Me? Some real guy. I'm sitting here in a pink dress. It makes a poor impression on women."

"But on the inside you're a real guy," Alison said. "For a real guy to wear a dress like you did and go back to Quandary Capital to save us— that took a lot of courage. I like a guy with courage."

"You do?"

"Good-looking guys, rich guys, smart guys—they're a dime a dozen.

But courage—that's the test of a real man. That's what we have a shortage of these days. Like they say, courage is what makes all the other virtues possible." She looked up at the statue of Jackson. "No one ever gets a statue for cowardice." she said.

"True. But I never thought I was being brave by wearing a dress. I was just hiding."

"Hiding was only choice. Dressing as woman—it was my idea," Yong reminded him. "You hated it."

"It did take a lot of courage at first," Bruce admitted. "Then I sort of got used to it, and after months of pretending I almost forgot who I really was, until just now."

Alison looked at the White House. "The woman who lives there must have some courage too, or she wouldn't have made it there."

"I suppose. It's not easy to get elected president, or be one. What an awful job."

"Would you help the President if she asked?"

"Yes, of course, if my country needed me. Who wouldn't?"

"Well, she's asked for your help."

"Mine?"

"No, not exactly yours. Brucilla's." Alison opened the shopping bag she had brought and pulled out Brucilla's wig and pumps. "The White House called Bea about you. The President needs Brucilla to go on one last mission."

"What's it all about?"

"Bea said it has something to do with national security. Will you do it? I'd be very impressed if you did."

"Oh, yeah?" Bruce said. "How impressed would you be? Do you have the courage to go out on a date with an ugly mutt like me?"

"Absolutely. I've always had a thing for guys in heels."

"It's a deal."

32   The Shaming of Estonia

President Fibby glared at the Russian president across the conference table. Only days before she had reversed her policy of appeasement and warned the West about the perils of the Russian occupation of Narva. Viktor Bludinov had dubbed her speech "the shrill and hysterical rantings of a moody madwoman."

It pained her to admit that the wily little Slav had played her for a fool and outmaneuvered her everywhere. Under the guns of his masked soldiers, the city fathers of Narva were submissively planning a plebiscite on the issue of whether to be annexed by Russia. NATO remained deadlocked in debate, with the French and Germans willing to risk only the two hundred Polish lesbians who had volunteered to man the battlements of the Estonian capital. At the United Nations, American motions for a vote to condemn the stealth Russian invasion were met with vetoes and howls of derision from the Russian delegation. And here at the G20 conference in Berlin, the summit's wary German hosts flatly refused Fibby's demands to put the Estonian crisis on the agenda for fear of incurring Bludinov's wrath.

But as her options for avoiding World War III dwindled, it was the Russian president's sneer that most grated on Fibby. To wipe the smirk off Bludinov's face, President Fibby needed a secret weapon. She had brought one in her purse.

At the end of the day's proceedings, the twenty heads of state were herded together for a photo opportunity in front of the flags of their nations. Fibby then strode across the floor to Bludinov, greeting him with her outstretched hand as the photographers turned their cameras toward the pair.

"President Bludinov," Fibby said, smiling cheerfully through clenched teeth. "How good of you to take time out from your adventures in Estonia to come to Berlin."

"I would not miss this chance, Madam President," replied Bludinov in fluent English. He grinned as he turned his sly face to the cameras. "To keep peace we should meet as often as possible."

"Yes, Viktor, even a hysterical madwoman has an interest in peace," Fibby said.

Bludinov forced a weak laugh. "I hope you are not too concerned about the effect of my remarks on your reputation, Madam President. One does not rise to the presidency of a great country like yours or mine and survive long with a thin skin. There can be no sensitive men or women at this level, as you will learn when you have had more experience."

"Oh, I am not so sure you are as insensitive as you pretend, Viktor. And it is not my reputation but yours that you should be worried about."

"How is that, Madam President? I do not understand. How is my reputation at risk?"

"I'm talking about your fondness for gay investing, Viktor," Fibby said. "I hear you invested three billion dollars in a fund of gay money managers in Washington. What do they call it, the MaxiGay Fund? They say it's gay in all dimensions: lesbians, transsexuals, hermaphrodites, and other degenerates. I didn't know Viktor Bludinov was in favor of promoting sexual perversion. Isn't that a crime in Russia? Wouldn't you go to the gulag for that, after being beaten black and blue?"

He shook his head and laughed again. "You are referring to that ridiculous rumor of an investment by the Russky Fund. It was completely false, a fabrication of the Western press to smear Russia. I have no ties to that investment at all, or to the Russky Fund for that matter. Our sovereign wealth fund is an independent state organization, run solely for the benefit of the Russian people. It is not controlled by any one person."

"Really?" Fibby reached into her purse. She pulled out the photograph of Yegor Yakov with his arm clutched lustily around Brucilla's waist. "Do you recognize this fellow with the tall blond woman in his grasp, Viktor? I think you might. He is your personal agent, Yegor Yakov."

Bludinov's smile vanished, his face turning crimson. "That man is not my personal agent. He works for the Russky Fund. I know nothing else about him."

"Oh? Well, let me tell you more about him then. The CIA informs me that Yegor Yakov is your wife's ne'er-do-well younger brother. He was unemployable and drunk, so to rescue him from the gutter you got him a job at the Russky Fund, where he works strictly on your behalf, secretly squirreling away your stolen billions in places around the world where no one would think to look, most unlikely places, like the MaxiGay Fund. Do you suppose we would have trouble proving who Mr. Yakov is to the world's press? The reporters are right there, standing just fifteen feet away. Would you like me to walk over and show them this photograph to see if they can make this simple connection between you, Yegor Yakov, and your gay investment fund?"

"This is outrageous," Bludinov said as the corners of his mouth tightened. "I have no idea what this photograph is about. Are things so twisted in your decadent country that it is now a crime for a man to embrace a beautiful woman? Who is the lovely lady?"

Fibby waved to a person among the crowd of photographers. A tall transgender wearing a blond wig and a pink pantsuit took a step forward. It was Brucilla. He winked at Bludinov. And winked again.

"I brought her with me for you to see for yourself, Viktor," Fibby said. "She's standing right there, the very same beautiful woman in the photograph, Brucilla Curious. He, or she if you like, is a transgender, one of the managers of your MaxiGay Fund. He's managing your money in a most unlikely place. And if you think that's something, you should see the two hermaphrodites who are working for you."

"Oh, my God!" Bludinov exclaimed, recoiling at the sight of Brucilla.

"Would you like to meet him now, to be photographed alongside him as your brother-in-law Yegor was? I'm sure the reporters would love to get some video of the two of you together—the mighty Viktor Bludinov with one of his queer investment managers. What interesting headlines do you suppose they will think up to go along with the pictures? Come, Viktor, let me introduce you to Brucilla."

"No! No!" he protested. "Absolutely not! Keep that monster away from me!"

Fibby slipped the photograph back into her purse. "I didn't think so. What a scandal a video like that would be in Russia for a he-man like Viktor Bludinov! It would be all over the Internet in minutes. Your carefully cultivated persona, the bare-chested macho man riding a horse through the Siberian wilderness, flying a fighter plane, playing ice hockey, doing karate thrusts, the whole tough guy illusion would be replaced in an instant by a picture of you with your transgendered money manager. Not the right image for you, is it? It's all the fault of this ugly business you started in Narva, of course. You wouldn't do a private summit meeting about Narva when I asked, and you thought we Americans wouldn't have the courage to use our weapons, but you overlooked our most powerful one: our unmatched talent for weaponizing shame. I may be a moody madwoman as you say, but I know where to kick a man, where it really counts—in the nuts. Are you feeling more sensitive down there now, Viktor?"

"Okay! Enough!" Bludinov cried. "What do you want from me?"

"Tomorrow night, after this conference ends, your masked soldiers will be driven out of Narva in a surprise nighttime counterattack by a band of brave Estonian patriots led by a corps of Polish lesbian shock troops. No one will see much of the battle because of the darkness. There will be no casualties because the NATO soldiers will be extraordinarily bad shots. Russia will suffer no embarrassment since you insist the little green men are not Russians but Estonian separatists. It will be the shame of Estonia, not the shame of Russia, or of Bludinov."

"Shame on Estonia?"

"Yes, if you like."

"Very well. The shaming of Estonia will be arranged for tomorrow night," Bludinov promised. "But there must be absolutely no photographs!"

"That's fine, Viktor," Fibby agreed. "No photographs. And one other thing: Your three billion dollars stays in the MaxiGay Fund forever. Now that I have you on the hook, I'm not letting you off. You've invested in vain."

Bludinov wore the humiliated look of a little boy who had just been spanked by his mother for stealing candy. But that was a trivial problem for a man like him. He always knew where to get more.

"Done," he said.

Late the following night, Pavel Demyonovich was standing at a checkpoint on the streets of Narva with three of his comrades when he was startled to hear gunfire. It sounded as if it must be coming from the outskirts of town.

Earlier that day his unit had been ordered to get ready to move out. The men had just been issued a fresh supply of ammunition. Finally, after two boring months languishing in Narva, he assumed this meant they would be moving deeper into Estonia to take the rest of the country. Surely this must be the long-awaited escalation of the invasion.

"Sergei," Demyonovich said, "do you hear that? Gunfire! We are attacking at last!"

Sergei Petrovsky nodded. "It's coming from the main highway out of town, over there." He pointed to the west. "Now we will get some action. It's about time too. I'm sick of this little burg and its tight-assed women."

Suddenly out of the darkness they saw the flash of gunfire, just a hundred meters away, and knew the battle had come much closer to them. Someone was shooting in their direction! Petrovsky looked through his night vision goggles to see if he could make out how many attackers there were. Demyonovich ducked behind a barricade, raised his AK-47, and prepared to fire.

Just then a troop transport rumbled up the street and screeched to a halt. Their sergeant jumped out and waved at them to come over.

"Get in, on the double!" the sergeant yelled. "We are under assault from the west side of town. We have orders to evacuate to Ivangorod at once."

Demyonovich and his comrades clambered onto the back of the truck. It began to head east, toward the border and the bridge to Ivangorod. "Evacuate? I don't understand," he said, catching his breath. "I thought we would be on the attack. We are retreating. Who is attacking us, NATO? Why don't we fight the sonofabitches?"

"I can't believe it," Petrovsky said, looking through his night vision goggles at the shadowy figures swarming toward their abandoned checkpoint.

"Who are they?"

"Women," Petrovsky said. "We are running away from short, ugly women. Look at their hips and how they run like ducks."

Demyonovich took a look through his own goggles. He saw the name tag "Nowakowski" on one of the soldiers. "And look at their uniforms. Those are not only short, ugly women, they are Polish."

Petrovsky pulled the clip of ammunition out of his AK-47 and inspected it. "Oh, my God, what is this?" He put the clip back into his gun and fired off five rounds at a street sign only ten feet away from the truck. Nothing hit the sign. "These are blanks!"

"What?"

"They have taken away our bullets and given us blanks," Petrovsky said. "Can this really be the mighty Red Army? We are Russian men shooting blanks, fleeing from little Polish women who run like ducks?"

Demyonovich fell back against the walls of the truck, his head spinning in a tornado of confusion. "I don't understand. What is Bludinov's grand scheme this time? What is the future of our brave country when little Polish women take up arms and beat Russian men into submission? What have we come to?"

Petrovsky tore the blanks out of his AK-47 and flung them over the side of the bridge into the Narva River. "I think we may be done for, Pavel," he said with disgust. "If Bludinov has given in, there are no real men anymore."

33 The Guns of Victory

The Butcher was delighted to find that Beatrice, far from worrying herself into a frenzy, was bursting with good news in advance of the crucial meeting with CRAM later that day. She explained that although Vain Capital was still in mortal danger, the rest of the world had been saved, thanks to Brucilla's great mission to Berlin.

"President Fibby called to thank me herself," Beatrice said with a huge smile. "The compromising photograph of Yegor Yakov that we gave her and the sight of Brucilla in person did the trick. Bludinov was so embarrassed he nearly ran out of the G20 meeting screaming."

"Were you able to cut a deal with the Feds about the SEC problem, as I suggested?" the Butcher asked.

"No deal was necessary. Fibby has ordered the SEC to shut down its investigation of Vain Capital on the grounds of national security. The government can't allow the details of this top-secret affair to get out. An SEC prosecution would publicize the Russky Fund investment, betray Fibby's delicate understanding with Bludinov, and free him from her clutches. You must never breathe a word about this to anyone."

"Not a word," the Butcher promised.

"The FBI has thrown Brucilla's attacker in jail. The two mad quants who hired him are already there. I never did understand how those Quandary Capital people could outperform all other portfolio managers in the world by such a wide margin, but Brucilla says it was all because they were spelling something naughty with their stocks—naughty but marvelously effective, that is. Discovering their little secret got him into hot water. That's why he came here hiding in drag."

"Brucilla is actually normal? I would never have guessed."

"Stanton, I've learned this year that no one is normal, not even my own son. But Brucilla is straight, if that's what you mean. His real name is Bruce Benson."

"What will happen to him now?"

"I've offered Bruce a job here. He can help us talk to our other quant managers—a kind of 'quant whisperer' if you will. He's very logical and mathy, you know, and completely fluent in the secret language all quants speak—factor models, algorithms, statistics, that sort of thing. Also, this way we can tell the White House we will be happy to change him back into Brucilla anytime he's needed to bring Bludinov to heel again. And having something the White House wants is always a good thing. As you of all people know, when you're in a pinch there's no such thing as having too much access to power. Al Gore isn't always available."

"But can you spare Brucilla? Don't you still need a transgendered money manager in the MaxiGay Fund?"

"Brucilla, or Bruce, has fallen in love with Alison and doesn't care to be a woman anymore since he's no longer on the lam. We'll advertise to recruit a new transgender now that we've discovered they respond so readily to money. And if that doesn't work, we'll just convert our spare hermaphrodite into one. Who would know the difference?"

"What about the Russky Fund's investment in the MaxiGay Fund? Won't Bludinov just take his money back?"

"Oh, he can't have it, that was part of his deal with Fibby! His Max-iGay money can never be moved. Fibby was quite clear—she needs Bludinov's money to stay gay. As long as it's trapped in the MaxiGay Fund and we have Brucilla, Europe is safe from Bludinov. Brucilla has become America's most potent super hero, a kind of Captain America in heels. He'll save the country billions in defense spending. I tell you, they'll never make a bomb as powerful as shame. We Pillsburys have always known that."

"So that's three billion you get to keep at Vain Capital?"

"Yes, and we are adding to it! Tony Elfuego said he is rushing to put three hundred million into the MaxiGay Fund as soon as possible to defuse the explosive situation at Yule. The football team has been terror-izing the new university president unmercifully since they heard about the MaxiGay Fund. They won't play unless the endowment goes gay. And without football Yule's alumni won't give a penny to the school. So it's no gay, no play, no pay."

"Any more client defections because of the MaxiGay Fund?"

"No. The Mormons were the only ones to run off in a huff. Our Jews, Catholics, and Muslims seem to have survived the shock somehow. But I'll never make the mistake of parading a transgender in front of them again."

The Butcher sat back in his chair and smiled. "I'm impressed, Beatrice. Maybe there is something to your Pillsbury magic after all. You've solved almost all your problems."

"Except for one—how to keep the CRAM account and its seven billion," Beatrice said. "I know it looks terrible for us, Stanton. The MaxiGay Fund probably doesn't figure in Governor Fist's plans to fix CRAM. Have you heard anything?"

"No, that's what I'm here to find out," the Butcher said, his face growing taut. "You know, I do care about you, Beatrice. I really do. Despite what you may think, I'm not all business."

"I know," she said with a smile, patting him on the arm. "Deep down, even you private equity guys have a heart."

As Morris Morbinders looked around the conference room at the meeting's attendees, his nose began to twitch. Someone was missing. "Where is your transgendered money manager?" he asked.

"Oh, the poor dear is under the weather," Beatrice said quickly, looking at Bruce. "We have Bruce here filling in for her today."

"Too bad. Our new chief investment officer asked me to congratulate her personally for Curious Capital's remarkable results," Morbinders said. "He thought it was quite unusual, even alarming, for a passive index fund to beat its benchmark substantially, much less by thirty percentage points, but given our desperate financial circumstances he finds it hard to object."

"We will certainly send your compliments," Beatrice said.

Morbinders got down to business. "I would imagine that with the well-publicized change in our senior leadership you must all be wondering about CRAM's plans for Vain Capital and the MaxiGay Fund."

"We've heard your new governor has replaced some key people on the CRAM investment committee, starting with the firing of your chief investment officer," Beatrice acknowledged. "We have braced ourselves for some important changes."

"Well, as you know, overhauling CRAM was one of Governor Fist's key campaign pledges. Our underfunded pension is a huge burden on California's taxpayers, which is why they revolted and elected him. The governor has announced that he fully intends to keep his promise to clean house."

"Oh, dear, I hope this doesn't pose a career problem for you personally, Morris," Beatrice said. "I'm sure CRAM's leadership recognizes the critical contribution that the loyal service of Morris Morbinders has made not only to CRAM but also to the grateful residents of California."

"Yes, well, thank you for your concern," said Morbinders, nearly choking. "The state's civil service regulations do offer employees at my level certain protections from these political upheavals. We will survive this storm as always, by bending with the wind."

"Oh, that will give us such great comfort, Morris—to know you're safe," Beatrice said.

"But as to the matter of CRAM's investment in the MaxiGay Fund, I am afraid I have bad news for you."

Beatrice held her breath. She looked across the table at the Butcher's little green eyes. Even he seemed frozen with apprehension.

"Governor Fist is a lifelong social conservative who deplores America's continuing moral decline," Morbinders began. "He ran on a platform of restoring traditional morality and putting a stop to such hedonistic liberal projects as the MaxiGay Fund. So I'm afraid our gay investment is beyond the pale. Governor Fist has decided that we must go straight."

"Oh, dear, just as we feared, CRAM is going back into the closet," Beatrice said, looking at Alison. "And all that hard work we put in to make them gay in all dimensions—all down the drain."

Morbinders paused a moment to observe the devastation caused by his news. Alison's beautiful face grew longer by the second, until she seemed to be on the verge of tears. Beatrice and Yong hung their heads down. Bruce just sighed.

As Morbinders looked upon the four of them, an unaccustomed feeling came over him, something akin to remorse. For some reason this group's despondency seemed strangely unfulfilling. His usual schadenfreude quickly melted into pity, and for once he felt his own face beginning to sag. He began to feel almost human.

"Fortunately," he announced, "our new chief investment officer was so impressed with the remarkable turnaround of the MaxiGay Fund that he wondered if Vain Capital might be useful to CRAM in another initiative Governor Fist has in mind."

Beatrice suddenly sprang back to life. "What? Well, of course we would be useful. Vain Capital is always useful, to anyone!"

"Governor Fist has pledged to rescue the taxpayers of California from CRAM's past investing practices. But he recognizes that California, as a state teeming with social activism, has a permanent need for socially responsible investing. It's a simple matter of getting the definition of morality right and putting the shame on the right people. And of course, that's Vain Capital's specialty—developing moral portfolios to suit client requests in the name of righteousness."

"It is indeed," Beatrice said. "No moral imperative is too onerous for us! We stand ready to meet any organization's ethical challenge!"

"Being a staunch defender of the Second Amendment and gun rights, Governor Fist has pointed out that government regulations have driven profit margins for gun manufacturers to extraordinary heights, especially for makers of assault rifles. He has proposed to our investment committee that with his statewide pro-gun initiative creating massive new demand for weapons, those already high profit margins can only increase. He believes our portfolios would benefit from guns."

"Guns?"

"Yes, the governor is wondering whether you could liquidate our holdings in your MaxiGay Fund and reinvest the seven billion dollars in proceeds in a MaxiGun Fund. And while we're at it, he would like to add five billion to the pot. More buck for the bang, you might say, ha ha."

Beatrice noticed that the Butcher was nodding furiously at her to take it. "Oh, twelve billion? Why, of course we can do that," she said. "But how could guns possibly help boost your returns?"

Then the Butcher began to stare daggers at her.

Morbinders reached into his briefcase and pulled out some papers. "Governor Fist asked CRAM's consulting firm to study this very question. Our consultant's report, which I have here, explains what we—I mean, what Governor Fist, is thinking." The report was entitled, *Profiting from Freedom: How to Defend the Efficient Frontier With a Gun-Toting Portfolio.*

Morbinders began to read from the executive summary. "The report says 'CRAM could significantly improve its returns by exploiting the market inefficiency artificially created by ill-advised restrictions against gun manufacturers imposed on portfolio managers by misguided state and local governments responding to left-wing social pressures. By emphasizing gun manufacturers in its portfolios, CRAM could expand the efficient frontier by investing more heavily in the conservative dimension of personal responsibility.'"

"Gun manufacturers," Beatrice said. "Of course. That's the answer."

"The report recommends investing heavily in every major category of gun product there is: bullets, assault rifles, shotguns, hand guns, and hunting rifles. We're thinking you could call it BASHH."

"I don't see any reason why we couldn't do that," Beatrice said. "Tilting a portfolio toward gun makers should be easy enough. We could equally weight the BASHH categories, so as not to offend anyone." She looked at Alison for confirmation.

"Sure easier than finding hermaphrodites," Alison said. "Do the money managers we hire need to be gun nuts themselves?"

"No," Morbinders said, "although that would be a nice touch."

"Well, there are plenty of those around," Bruce chimed in. "I'm a gun expert myself. I was whacking prairie dogs on our ranch at Lonely Butte at the age of six."

A gun fund, Beatrice was thinking, her imagination set in motion by the vast marketing potential of this novel idea. "So I assume CRAM will not object to our creating a commingled fund our other clients could join?"

"Not at all," Morbinders said. "Governor Fist wants to promote enthusiasm for firearms any way he can."

"We already have two clients who would be naturals for this fund—the National Handgun Association and the National Federation of Cemeteries. Maybe we could even tempt the Mormons to come back."

It did occur to her that the Little Sisters of a Baby would object rather strenuously to this new initiative. But she would leave that moral issue for another day.

A few minutes after Morbinders left, Alison and Yong ran into Bruce in the hallway.

"A new client will be here in just a few minutes. Want to join us?" she asked.

"Sure, who are they?" Bruce asked.

"Lawyers With Scruples," Alison replied. "It's a foundation on K Street that Bea just landed. Their account is starting next month, so we need to discuss how we propose to set up their portfolio of money managers."

"What are they into?"

"They are ultra-sensitive lawyers with fine-tuned ethical principles," Alison explained. "They want our money managers to screen out paper manufacturers."

"What have they got against paper?"

"Oh, they feel guilty about the legal profession's long history of using too much of it. They recognize the central role they've played in the killing of billions of trees and the wholesale destruction of forests, and they want to make amends to the environment. Now that paper is large-ly obsolete and legal documents are generated and stored in electronic format, they feel they can afford to admit their legacy of shame and promote a paper-free world."

"Sounds like an assignment tailor-made for Vain Capital."

"It would be if they would just stop arguing with each other at our meetings with them," Alison said. "Typical lawyers."

"Speaking of meetings, are we still on for dinner at six tonight?" Bruce asked.

"Yes," she said with a coy smile.

"Lawyers talk too much," Yong said, shaking his head. "Yak, yak, all the time, but say nothing, make problems everywhere. Too many law-yers here. In South Korea, not so many. In North Korea, no lawyers period. Bullet through head solve many problems."

"I thought you liked this country," Bruce said. "Have you changed your mind about America?"

"Yes and no," Yong said. "I think more like American every day. Un-derstanding country much better. I have learned many new things."

"How so?"

"Everything not perfect. Crazy people all over. Freedom make much waste. Colleges here teach many wrong ideas. I must relearn everything they teach me."

"Like what?"

"Like man is rational, investing capital for highest and best use," Yong said. "Very wrong. At Vain Capital, I have found truth is exact opposite.

Man is irrational, he is crazy bastard. He never learn from his mistakes. Most of time he invest in vain."

Bruce smiled, reached out for Alison's hand, and squeezed it. And she let him.

With the proof of man's irrationality standing right in front of him, Yong decided to say nothing and just to look away. He recalled a Confucian saying, his favorite one of all: *Silence is a true friend who never betrays.*

About the Author

WILLIAM WORSLEY learned about what goes on inside money management firms by hiring, firing, and monitoring them on behalf of large pensions, endowments, and foundations. Over three decades he met with hundreds of U.S. and international investment firms specializing in public and private equity, fixed income, and currency hedging. A chartered financial analyst, he has been investing in the stock market since he was 13. In 2016 he retired as managing director of a firm that oversees money managers.

In an earlier career he was a senior text editor at Time-Life Books, where he wrote and edited articles on a wide variety of popular topics. He holds three degrees from the University of Virginia, including a BA and MA in English, and an MBA from the Darden School. He lives in the Washington, D.C., area, where he was born and raised.

CPSIA information can be obtained
at www.ICGtesting.com
Printed in the USA
LVOW03s0714231017
553426LV00002B/162/P